LORD OF THE DEAD

The mummy-case did not appear to be sealed as is the usual custom, and Gordon opened it without difficulty. A hideous reptilian shape, swathed in moldering wrapping, met our eyes. Gordon parted the wrappings and revealed an inch of withered, leathery arm; he shuddered when he touched it, as at the touch of some inhumanly cold thing. Then he rapped on the shrunken breast, which gave out a solid thump, like some ghastly sort of wood.

"Dead for a thousand years." He shrugged and closed the case. The thing we were after was alive.

I stood stock-still in the center of the floor. Through the wrappings of the mummy's face great eyes had burned into mine: eyes like pools of yellow fire that seared my soul and froze me where I stood, speechless with terror . . .

Skull-Face

by Robert E. Howard

"Santiago pitched headlong from the teocalli."

SKULL-FACE

ROBERT E. HOWARD

with an introduction by Richard A. Lupoff

A BERKLEY MEDALLION BOOK

published by

BERKLEY PUBLISHING CORPORATION

BERKLEY MEDALLION BOOKS are published by
Berkley Publishing Corporation
200 Madison Avenue
New York, N. Y. 10016

BERKLEY MEDALLION BOOK ® TM 757,375

Printed in the United States of America

Berkley Medallion Edition, FEBRUARY, 1978

ACKNOWLEDGMENTS

Skull-Face, copyright 1929 by Popular Fiction Publishing Company for *Weird Tales*, October, November, December 1929.

Names in the Black Book, copyright 1934 by Super Magazines for *Super-Detective Stories*, May 1934.

CONTENTS

Pictures in the Flames—An Introduction,
    by Richard A. Lupoff   1

Skull-Face   13

Lord of the Dead   115

Names in the Black Book   153

Taverel Manor   189

PICTURES IN THE FLAMES—
AN INTRODUCTION

Richard A. Lupoff

"Skull-Face" slipped into the pages of *Weird Tales* so quietly, and received so little emphasis from the editor of that magazine, that one is almost inclined to think that Farnsworth Wright was ashamed to publish the story. He was very wrong, if that was indeed his feeling. But it is an occasion for puzzlement; for double puzzlement, in fact. If Wright didn't really care for the story, why did he buy it in the first place? And what did he have against it, anyhow?

The latter question is easily answered—or, more accurately, a reasonably plausible answer is easily devised. Truth, now—truth is something obtained with greater difficulty, if at all.

Arthur Conan Doyle begat Sherlock Holmes, patterning him on Doyle's old med school prof, Dr. Bell. Holmes was a superb hero but he needed a sidekick to act as amanuensis and foil. Hence, Dr. Watson, a fairly accurate representation of Doyle himself. But that did not complete the picture—there had to be a foe. And thus the sinister, fascinating Moriarty.

And in the wake of Doyle's success with Holmes and company there followed a squadron of imitators, one of the more interesting being one Arthur Sarsfield Ward, who wrote as "Sax Rohmer." But where most of Doyle's imitators concentrated their efforts on producing pseudo-Holmeses (as they do to this day), Rohmer soft-pedaled his Holmes-and-Watson analogues and created a marvelously melodramatic pseudo-Moriarty...

The Insidious Dr. Fu Manchu.

And in due course, admirers of Rohmer's sinister superman created imitations of *him*. Dr. Yen-Sin, by Donald E. Keyhoe. Wu Fang, by Robert J. Hogan. And countless others down through the decades.

But before there was a Yen-Sin or a Wu Fang, there was Robert E. Howard's Kathulos of Egypt.

One infers that Farnsworth Wright was a trifle diffident about running such openly derivative material in *Weird Tales*. But as for his motive in taking the novel at all—well, Howard was already a regular contributor to the magazine, with a growing following of readers. And besides, derivative or not, "Skull-Face" was a humdinger of a yarn!

Howard had first appeared in *Weird Tales* with a little story, "Spear and Fang," in July, 1925. He'd returned over and over; got the cover illustration for the first time in April, 1926, for "Wolfshead." He'd introduced Solomon Kane in August, 1928, and Kull in August of '29. (Conan was yet to come.)

So "Skull-Face" was accepted and used, but it was not emphasized. The first issue containing an installment of the story was that of October, 1929. The cover was devoted to a story by Gaston Leroux, he of *Phantom of the Opera* fame. "Skull-Face" had received no mention in the advance-notices page of earlier issues; now that it appeared, there was no ballyhoo in "The Eyrie" and no blurb at all on the story. There was a crude illustration with the story, by Hugh Rankin, showing Skull-Face as a distorted monster, and a little quotation from the text, describing the scene.

There were no accompanying cover paintings with the later two installments, nor blurbs. The illustrations were rather poor; John Gordon is portrayed as a moustached Watson, and Stephen Costigan as a super-muscular Holmes. This in itself is somewhat odd, for by the time the Doyle characters had filtered through Rohmer to Howard, they were hardly Holmes and Watson at all. Rather, Stephen Costigan is a fairly typical Robert E. Howard hero: muscular, courageous, hot tempered. And John Gordon resembles Nayland Smith of the Rohmer version, but certainly not Dr. Watson!

However editor Wright soft-pedaled Skull-Face, the *Weird Tales* readers were not to be steered from their regular bards to the imported M. Leroux. "Skull-Face," part I, was voted the readers' favorite over the Frenchman's "The Woman with the

Velvet Collar." The following month, the latest story in Seabury Quinn's perennially popular Jules de Grandin series popped to first place. And in December, the concluding installment of "Skull-Face" was on top again, despite another cover-featured story from Leroux.

Letters to "The Eyrie" were wildly enthusiastic over the serial, and several of them raised intriguing questions. A reader named Norman O'Brien wrote the following:

"Having finished 'Skull-Face,' don't you think it natural I should voice a wish for you to engage Mr. Howard to write us a serial about Kathulos at the time that person was a sorcerer in Atlantis? I am sure many *Weird Tales* readers feel the same way."

Another reader, W. J. O'Neail, wrote this:

"I was very much interested in tracing the apparent connection between the character Kathulos, in Robert E. Howard's 'Skull-Face,' and that of Cthulhu in Mr. Lovecraft's 'The Call of Cthulhu.' Could you inform me whether there is any legend or tradition surrounding that character?"

Finally, Conrad Ruppert wrote:

"I need hardly say that the story I enjoyed the most was 'Skull-Face' by Robert E. Howard. I thought at first that it was Sax Rohmer writing under a new name."

Regarding the Kathulos-Cthulhu connection, it surely appears that some such tiein was intended. Bob Howard and H. P. Lovecraft were pen-pals and were thoroughly familiar with each other's works. Yet the connection was never explicated by either.

The mention of Rohmer needs no further comment.

But as for the suggestion of another Kathulos story—ah, therein lies a long and hopelessly tangled yarn!

Bob Howard never did write that story of Kathulos in Atlantis—it would have been a beauty, if he had! But he wrote a number of stories more or less connected with "Skull-Face" (might we dub them, collectively, the Kathulos Mythos?), and like Hercules fighting the hydra, he managed to create two new problems for each one he solved. What follows, then, is by no means a complete explication of the Mythos—but more of a tentative sketch that may lead to an eventual complete study.

First of all, note that in the years following "Skull-Face," Howard wrote all or part of *four* stories related to it. Two of these, "Lord of the Dead" and "Names in the Black Book," feature a hero almost identical to Stephen Costigan, called Steve Harrison. There is a figure resembling Kathulos—Erlik Khan, Lord of the Dead. And of course there are other characters, most notably the beautiful Eurasian, Joan La Tour.

"Lord of the Dead" was sold to *Strange Detective* magazine, but that periodical suspended publication before using the story, and it was not published until now. Its sequel was published in *Super-Detective Stories* in 1934. Imagine the puzzlement of readers upon encountering a story that was apparently a sequel to—nothing!

There was a third story in the group, called "Teeth of Doom." But for some unexplained reason, Howard himself changed the hero to Brock Rollins and the by-line to Patrick Ervin. Although the story appeared (as "The Tomb's Secret") in *Strange Detective*, it seems by now *too* remote from the Kathulos group for inclusion here.

But then there was "Taverel Manor." This was a more direct sequel to "Skull-Face." Kathulos, Gordon, and Costigan are back—and using their right names!

But while Howard had the story in his typewriter, *Weird Tales* underwent one of its recurring financial fevers and nearly ceased publication. It was saved, but frequency of publication had to be cut from monthly to bi-monthly, and editor Wright let it be known that he preferred to run no serials in the less frequently appearing magazine. So Howard set the partial manuscript aside (we have this sequence from copies of letters he wrote to his friend Lovecraft)—and never did resume work on it!

The story was completed in 1977 by the undersigned, Richard A. Lupoff. Every attempt was made to keep to the spirit and style of Howard's fragment, and no major characters were created by the latter collaborator. One ambiguity is subject to debate. Howard introduced a character named Joan. No last name was given. Did he have Joan La Tour in mind? There is no way to be certain, but for the sake of the completion, the problem was resolved in favor of making the connection to the Lord of the Dead stories, and Joan was identified as Joan La Tour.

The exact place where Howard's prose ends and Lupoff's begins will be revealed in due course. But for the time being, it might be more fun to withhold that information. The only hint to be given just here is that "Taverel Manor" is not one of those "collaborations" in which the later writer inflates a tiny fragment into a giant structure. Howard's section of the story is very substantial—maybe considerably longer than Lupoff's, and certainly not much shorter. More than that, let the reader deduce for himself.

But the connections between the Kathulos cycle and Howard's other works do not end here. Consider the following:

While Stephen Costigan, the hero of "Skull-Face" and "Taverel Manor," is clearly interchangeable with Steve Harrison of the Erlik Khan stories, *this* Stephen Costigan is *not* interchangeable with "Sailor Steve Costigan" who *is* identical with fighting Dennis Dorgan!

And Erlik Khan, who may or may not be another identity of Kathulos of Egypt—or a minion of Kathulos—pops up in the adventures of Howard's hero Francis X. Gordon, in *Top-Notch* magazine and elsewhere. Or maybe that's just somebody else who happens to be *named* Erlik Khan.

And Taverel Manor, the setting of the story of that name, is of course the family seat of the Taverels. We learn of at least four Taverels: Sir Haldred (an analogue of Sir Haldred Fenton from "Skull-Face"?), Sir Rupert, the black sheep Joseph Taverel living in self-imposed exile in America, and old Captain Hilton Taverel who returned from Thibet in 1849.

Robert E. Howard used the name John Taverel as a by-line for three minor stories!

And when Howard wrote his autobiographical novel, *Post Oaks and Sand Roughs* (as yet unpublished), he chose for his protagonist the name—no, not John Taverel but—Stephen Costigan!

Howard equals Stephen Costigan but not Steve Costigan. But Stephen Costigan equals Brock Rollins when Robert E. Howard equals Patrick Ervin. And Kathulos equals Erlik Khan—or does he? And is connected, somehow, with Lovecraft's Cthulhu—or is he? And Steve Harrison does equal both Brock Rollins and Stephen Costigan (but not Sailor Steve Costigan, who is really Dennis Dorgan).

And...

But...

Unless...

The field is open for innumerable exercises in the higher criticism, and the game is hereby declared begun!

All of the foregoing serious (or semi-serious) logic-bashing should not be permitted to get in the way of the reader's enjoyment. In our attempts to determine the exact literary value and the deep sociological significance of these stories, we should not lose sight of the fact that they were pulp fiction cast in the classic mold. The touchstones of pulp were color, verve, fast pace, dynamic action, and characters who may have been less than deep and subtle, but who were never less than howlingly vivid.

The stories were intended for fun.

Even after forty-odd years, they still work. There is a creak here and a rusty spot there, abandoned social conventions and attitudes stick out, and the cynical reader can see the whole cycle as pure camp. But the stories can be read in the spirit of fun, and that is really the right way to read them. The suggested reading sequence is "Skull-Face," "Lord of the Dead," "Names in the Black Book," and finally "Taverel Manor."

And even if Bob Howard never did write the story of Kathulos in Atlantis, down there in Cross Plains, Texas ... today's reader is perfectly free, sitting before a glowing fireplace late some dreary night, to conjure up pictures in the flames. There—there is the Scorpion, the Master, Skull-Face himself. What kind of setting do we see? Is Kathulos's Atlantis a city of graceful towers and unimaginable science? Is it a land of flashing blades, flames, and gore? A bucolic countryside crossed by knights and monstrous beings of remote, exotic origin?

Whatever it is, the vision flickers and sways in the blazing logs. Relaxed, almost hypnotized, one is drawn into the strange landscape. The sound of a brazen gong is heard, the swish of silken raiment, we see the glitter of jewels—and of razor-honed metal.

The author now is—you.

Richard A. Lupoff
California
March, 1977

SKULL—

BY ROBERT·E· HOWARD

"Kathulos leaped into frenzied activity, hissing orders like a cat."

SKULL-FACE

1. The Face in the Mist

"We are no other than a moving row
Of Magic Shadow-shapes that come and go."
                                        —OMAR KHAYYAM

The horror first took concrete form amid that most unconcrete
of all things—a hashish dream. I was off on a timeless, spaceless
journey through the strange lands that belong to this state of
being, a million miles away from earth and all things earthly; yet
I became cognizant that something was reaching across the
unknown voids—something that tore ruthlessly at the separat-
ing curtains of my illusions and intruded itself into my visions.

I did not exactly return to ordinary waking life, yet I was
conscious of a seeing and a recognizing that was unpleasant and
seemed out of keeping with the dream I was at that time
enjoying. To one who has never known the delights of hashish,
my explanation must seem chaotic and impossible. Still, I was
aware of a rending of mists and then the Face intruded itself into
my sight. I thought at first it was merely a skull; then I saw that it
was a hideous yellow instead of white, and was endowed with
some horrid form of life. Eyes glimmered deep in the sockets and
the jaws moved as if in speech. The body, except for the high,
thin shoulders, was vague and indistinct, but the hands, which
floated in the mists before and below the skull, were horribly
vivid and filled me with crawling fears. They were like the hands
of a mummy, long, lean and yellow, with knobby joints and
cruel curving talons.

Then, to complete the vague horror which was swiftly taking
possession of me, a voice spoke—imagine a man so long dead

13

that his vocal organs had grown rusty and unaccustomed to speech. This was the thought which struck me and made my flesh crawl as I listened.

"A strong brute and one who might be useful somehow. See that he is given all the hashish he requires."

Then the face began to recede, even as I sensed that I was the subject of conversation, and the mists billowed and began to close again. Yet for a single instant a scene stood out with startling clarity. I gasped—or sought to. For over the high, strange shoulder of the apparition another face stood out clearly for an instant, as if the owner peered at me. Red lips, half parted, long dark eyelashes, shading vivid eyes, a shimmery cloud of hair. Over the shoulder of Horror, breathtaking beauty for an instant looked at me.

2. The Hashish Slave

"Up from Earth's center through the Seventh Gate
I rose, and on the Throne of Saturn sate."
—OMAR KHAYYAM

My dream of the skull-face was borne over that usually uncrossable gap that lies between hashish enchantment and humdrum reality. I sat cross-legged on a mat in Yun Shatu's Temple of Dreams and gathered the fading forces of my decaying brain to the task of remembering events and faces.

This last dream was so entirely different from any I had ever had before, that my waning interest was roused to the point of inquiring as to its origin. When I first began to experiment with hashish, I sought to find a physical or psychic basis for the wild flights of illusion pertaining thereto, but of late I had been content to enjoy without seeking cause and effect.

Whence this unaccountable sensation of familiarity in regard to that vision? I took my throbbing head between my hands and laboriously sought a clue. A living dead man and a girl of rare beauty who had looked over his shoulder. Then I remembered.

Back in the fog of days and nights which veils a hashish addict's memory, my money had given out. It seemed years or possibly centuries, but my stagnant reason told me that it had probably been only a few days. At any rate, I had presented myself at Yun Shatu's sordid dive as usual and had been thrown out by the great Negro Hassim when it was learned I had no more money.

My universe crashing to pieces about me, and my nerves humming like taut piano wires for the vital need that was mine, I

15

crouched in the gutter and gibbered bestially, till Hassim swaggered out and stilled my yammerings with a blow that felled me, half stunned.

Then as I presently rose, staggeringly and with no thought save of the river which flowed with cool murmur so near me—as I rose, a light hand was laid like the touch of a rose on my arm. I turned with a frightened start, and stood spellbound before the vision of loveliness which met my gaze. Dark eyes limpid with pity surveyed me and the little hand on my ragged sleeve drew me toward the door of the Dream Temple. I shrank back, but a low voice, soft and musical, urged me, and filled with a trust that was strange, I shambled along with my beautiful guide.

At the door Hassim met us, cruel hands lifted and a dark scowl on his ape-like brow, but as I cowered there, expecting a blow, he halted before the girl's upraised hand and her word of command which had taken on an imperious note.

I did not understand what she said, but I saw dimly, as in a fog, that she gave the black man money, and she led me to a couch where she had me recline and arranged the cushions as if I were king of Egypt instead of a ragged, dirty renegade who lived only for hashish. Her slim hand was cool on my brow for a moment, and then she was gone and Yussef Ali came bearing the stuff for which my very soul shrieked—and soon I was wandering again through those strange and exotic countries that only a hashish slave knows.

Now as I sat on the mat and pondered the dream of the skull-face I wondered more. Since the unknown girl had led me back into the dive, I had come and gone as before, when I had plenty of money to pay Yun Shatu. Someone certainly was paying him for me, and while my subconscious mind had told me it was the girl, my rusty brain had failed to grasp the fact entirely, or to wonder why. What need of wondering? So someone paid and the vivid-hued dreams continued, what cared I? But now I wondered. For the girl who had protected me from Hassim and had brought the hashish for me was the same girl I had seen in the skull-face dream.

Through the soddenness of my degradation the lure of her struck like a knife piercing my heart and strangely revived the memories of the days when I was a man like other men—not yet a sullen, cringing slave of dreams. Far and dim they were, shimmery islands in the mist of years—and what a dark sea lay between!

I looked at my ragged sleeve and the dirty, claw-like hand protruding from it; I gazed through the hanging smoke which fogged the sordid room, at the low bunks along the wall whereon lay the blankly staring dreamers—slaves, like me, of hashish or of opium. I gazed at the slippered Chinamen gliding softly to and fro bearing pipes or roasting balls of concentrated purgatory over tiny flickering fires. I gazed at Hassim standing, arms folded, beside the door like a great statue of black basalt.

And I shuddered and hid my face in my hands because with the faint dawning of returning manhood, I knew that this last and most cruel dream was futile—I had crossed an ocean over which I could never return, had cut myself off from the world of normal men or women. Naught remained now but to drown this dream as I had drowned all my others—swiftly and with hope that I should soon attain that Ultimate Ocean which lies beyond all dreams.

So these fleeting moments of lucidity, of longing, that tear aside the veils of all dope slaves—unexplainable, without hope of attainment.

So I went back to my empty dreams, to my fantasmagoria of illusions; but sometimes, like a sword cleaving a mist, through the high lands and the low lands and seas of my visions floated, like half-forgotten music, the sheen of dark eyes and shimmery hair.

You ask how I, Stephen Costigan, American and a man of some attainments and culture, came to lie in a filthy dive of London's Limehouse? The answer is simple—no jaded debauchee, I, seeking new sensations in the mysteries of the Orient. I answer—Argonne! Heavens, what deeps and heights of horror lurk in that one word alone! Shell-shocked—shell-torn. Endless days and nights without end and roaring red hell over No Man's Land where I lay shot and bayoneted to shreds of gory flesh. My body recovered, how I know not; my mind never did.

And the leaping fires and shifting shadows in my tortured brain drove me down and down, along the stairs of degradation, uncaring until at last I found surcease in Yun Shatu's Temple of Dreams, where I slew my red dreams in other dreams—the dreams of hashish whereby a man may descend to the lower pits of the reddest hells or soar into those unnamable heights where the stars are diamond pinpoints beneath his feet.

Not the visions of the sot, the beast, were mine. I attained the unattainable, stood face to face with the unknown and in cosmic calmness knew the unguessable. And was content after a fashion, until the sight of burnished hair and scarlet lips swept away my dream-built universe and left me shuddering among its ruins.

3. The Master of Doom

"And He that toss'd you down into the Field,
He knows about it all—He knows! He knows!"
—OMAR KHAYYAM

A hand shook me roughly as I emerged languidly from my latest debauch.

"The Master wishes you! Up swine!"

Hassim it was who shook me and who spoke.

"To hell with the Master!" I answered, for I hated Hassim—and feared him.

"Up with you or you get no more hashish," was the brutal response, and I rose in trembling haste.

I followed the huge black man and he led the way to the rear of the building, stepping in and out among the wretched dreamers on the floor.

"Muster all hands on deck!" droned a sailor in a bunk. "All hands!"

Hassim flung open the door at the rear and motioned me to enter. I had never before passed through that door and had supposed it led into Yun Shatu's private quarters. But it was furnished only with a cot, a bronze idol of some sort before which incense burned, and a heavy table.

Hassim gave me a sinister glance and seized the table as if to spin it about. It turned as if it stood on a revolving platform and a section of the floor turned with it, revealing a hidden doorway in the floor. Steps led downward in the darkness.

Hassim lighted a candle and with a brusque gesture invited me to descend. I did so, with the sluggish obedience of the dope

19

addict, and he followed, closing the door above us by means of
an iron lever fastened to the under side of the floor. In the semi-
darkness we went down the rickety steps, some nine or ten I
should say, and then came upon a narrow corridor.

Here Hassim again took the lead, holding the candle high in
front of him. I could scarcely see the sides of this cave-like
passageway but knew that it was not wide. The flickering light
showed it to be bare of any sort of furnishings save for a number
of strange-looking chests which lined the walls—receptacles
containing opium and other dope, I thought.

A continuous scurrying and the occasional glint of small red
eyes haunted the shadows, betraying the presence of vast
numbers of the great rats which infest the Thames waterfront of
that section.

Then more steps loomed out of the dark in front of us as the
corridor came to an abrupt end. Hassim led the way up and at
the top knocked four times against what seemed the underside of
a floor. A hidden door opened and a flood of soft, illusive light
streamed through.

Hassim hustled me up roughly and I stood blinking in such a
setting as I had never seen in my wildest flights of vision. I stood
in a jungle of palm-trees through which wriggled a million vivid-
hued dragons! Then, as my startled eyes became accustomed to
the light, I saw that I had not been suddenly transferred to some
other planet, as I had at first thought. The palm-trees were there,
and the dragons, but the trees were artificial and stood in great
pots and the dragons writhed across heavy tapestries which hid
the walls.

The room itself was a monstrous affair—inhumanly large, it
seemed to me. A thick smoke, yellowish and tropical in
suggestion, seemed to hang over all, veiling the ceiling and
baffling upward glances. This smoke, I saw, emanated from an
altar in front of the wall to my left. I started. Through the
saffron, billowing fog two eyes, hideously large and vivid,
glittered at me. The vague outlines of some bestial idol took
indistinct shape. I flung an uneasy glance about, marking the
Oriental divans and couches and the bizarre furnishings, and
then my eyes halted and rested on a lacquer screen just in front of
me.

I could not pierce it and no sound came from beyond it, yet I
felt eyes searing into my consciousness through it, eyes that
burned through my very soul. A strange aura of evil flowed from

that strange screen with its weird carvings and unholy decorations.

Hassim salaamed profoundly before it and then, without speaking, stepped back and folded his arms, statue-like.

A voice suddenly broke the heavy and oppressive silence.

"You who are a swine, would you like to be a man again?"

I started. The tone was inhuman, cold—more, there was a suggestion of long disuse of the vocal organs—the voice I had heard in my dream!

"Yes," I replied, trance-like, "I would like to be a man again."

Silence ensued for a space; then the voice came again with a sinister whispering undertone at the back of its sound like bats flying through a cavern.

"I shall make you a man again because I am a friend to all broken men. Not for a price shall I do it, nor for gratitude. And I give you a sign to seal my promise and my vow. Thrust your hand through the screen."

At these strange and almost unintelligible words I stood perplexed, and then, as the unseen voice repeated the last command, I stepped forward and thrust my hand through a slit which opened silently in the screen. I felt my wrist seized in an iron grip and something seven times colder than ice touched the inside of my hand. Then my wrist was released, and drawing forth my hand I saw a strange symbol traced in blue close to the base of my thumb—a thing like a scorpion.

The voice spoke again in a sibilant language I did not understand, and Hassim stepped forward deferentially. He reached about the screen and then turned to me, holding a goblet of some amber-colored liquid which he proffered me with an ironical bow. I took it hesitatingly.

"Drink and fear not," said the unseen voice. "It is only an Egyptian wine with life-giving qualities."

So I raised the goblet and emptied it; the taste was not unpleasant, and even as I handed the beaker to Hassim again, I seemed to feel new life and vigor whip along my jaded veins.

"Remain at Yun Shatu's house," said the voice. "You will be given food and a bed until you are strong enough to work for yourself. You will use no hashish nor will you require any. Go!"

As in a daze, I followed Hassim back through the hidden door, down the steps, along the dark corridor and up through the other door that led us into the Temple of Dreams.

As we stepped from the rear chamber into the main room of

the dreamers, I turned to the Negro wonderingly.

"Master? Master of what? Of Life?"

Hassim laughed, fiercely and sardonically.

"Master of Doom!"

4. The Spider and the Fly

"There was the Door to which I found no Key;
There was the Veil through which I might not see."
                                    —OMAR KHAYYAM

I sat on Yun Shatu's cushions and pondered with a clearness of
mind new and strange to me. As for that, all my sensations were
new and strange. I felt as if I had wakened from a monstrously
long sleep, and though my thoughts were sluggish, I felt as
though the cobwebs which had clogged them for so long had
been partly brushed away.

I drew my hand across my brow, noting how it trembled. I
was weak and shaky and felt the stirrings of hunger—not for
dope but for food. What had been in the draft I had quenched in
the chamber of mystery? And why had the 'Master' chosen me,
out of all the other wretches of Yun Shatu's, for regeneration?

And who was this Master? Somehow the word sounded
vaguely familiar—I sought laboriously to remember. Yes—I had
heard it, lying half-waking in the bunks or on the floor—
whispered sibilantly by Yun Shatu or by Hassim or by Yussef
Ali, the Moor, muttered in their low-voiced conversations and
mingled always with words I could not understand. Was not
Yun Shatu, then, master of the Temple of Dreams? I had
thought and the other addicts thought that the withered
Chinaman held undisputed sway over this drab kingdom and
that Hassim and Yussef Ali were his servants. And the four
China boys who roasted opium with Yun Shatu and Yar Khan
the Afghan, and Santiago the Haitian and Ganra Singh, the

23

renegade Sikh—all in the pay of Yun Shatu, we supposed—bound to the opium lord by bonds of gold or fear.

For Yun Shatu was a power in London's Chinatown and I had heard that his tentacles reached across the seas into high places of mighty and mysterious tongues. Was that Yun Shatu behind the lacquer screen? No; I knew the Chinaman's voice and besides I had seen him puttering about in the front of the Temple just as I went through the back door.

Another thought came to me. Often, lying half torpid, in the late hours of night or in the early grayness of dawn, I had seen men and women steal into the Temple, whose dress and bearing were strangely out of place and incongruous. Tall, erect men, often in evening dress, with their hats drawn low about their brows, and fine ladies, veiled, in silks and furs. Never two of them came together, but always they came separately and, hiding their features, hurried to the rear door, where they entered and presently came forth again, hours later sometimes. Knowing that the lust for dope finds resting-place in high positions sometimes, I had never wondered overmuch, supposing that these were wealthy men and women of society who had fallen victims to the craving, and that somewhere in the back of the building there was a private chamber for such. Yet now I wondered—sometimes these persons had remained only a few moments—was it always opium for which they came, or did they, too, traverse that strange corridor and converse with the One behind the screen?

My mind dallied with the idea of a great specialist to whom came all classes of people to find surcease from the dope habit. Yet it was strange that such a one should select a dope-joint from which to work—strange, too, that the owner of that house should apparently look on him with so much reverence.

I gave it up as my head began to hurt with the unwonted effort of thinking, and shouted for food. Yussef Ali brought it to me on a tray, with a promptness which was surprising. More, he salaamed as he departed, leaving me to ruminate on the strange shift of my status in the Temple of Dreams.

I ate, wondering what the One of the screen wanted with me. Not for an instant did I suppose that his actions had been prompted by the reasons he pretended; the life of the underworld had taught me that none of its denizens leaned toward philanthropy. And underworld the chamber of mystery had been, in spite of its elaborate and bizarre nature. And where could it be located? How far had I walked along the corridor? I shrugged my shoulders, wondering if it were not all a hashish-induced dream; then my eye fell upon my hand—and the scorpion traced thereon.

"Muster all hands!" droned the sailor in the bunk. "All hands!"

To tell in detail of the next few days would be boresome to any who have not tasted the dire slavery of dope. I waited for the craving to strike again—waited with sure sardonic hopelessness. All day, all night—another day—then the miracle was forced upon my doubting brain. Contrary to all theories and supposed facts of science and common sense the craving had left me as suddenly and completely as a bad dream! At first I could not credit my senses but believed myself to be still in the grip of a dope nightmare. But it was true. From the time I quaffed the goblet in the room of mystery, I felt not the slightest desire for the stuff which had been life itself for me. This, I felt vaguely, was somehow unholy and certainly opposed to all rules of nature. If the dread being behind the screen had discovered the secret of breaking hashish's terrible power, what other monstrous secrets had he discovered and what unthinkable dominance was his? The suggestion of evil crawled serpent-like through my mind.

I remained at Yun Shatu's house, lounging in a bunk or on cushions spread upon the floor, eating and drinking at will, but now that I was becoming a normal man again, the atmosphere became most revolting to me and the sight of the wretches writhing in their dreams reminded me unpleasantly of what I myself had been, and it repelled, nauseated me.

So one day, when no one was watching me, I rose and went out on the street and walked along the waterfront. The air, burdened though it was with smoke and foul scents, filled my lungs with strange freshness and aroused new vigor in what had once been a powerful frame. I took new interest in the sounds of men living and working, and the sight of a vessel being unloaded at one of the wharfs actually thrilled me. The force of longshoremen was short, and presently I found myself heaving and lifting and carrying, and though the sweat coursed down my brow and my limbs trembled at the effort, I exulted in the thought that at last I was able to labor for myself again, no matter how low or drab the work might be.

As I returned to the door of Yun Shatu's that evening—

hideously weary but with the renewed feeling of manhood that comes of honest toil—Hassim met me at the door.

"You been where?" he demanded roughly.

"I've been working on the docks," I answered shortly.

"You don't need to work on docks," he snarled. "The Master got work for you."

He led the way, and again I traversed the dark stairs and the corridor under the earth. This time my faculties were alert and I decided that the passageway could not be over thirty or forty feet in length. Again I stood before the lacquer screen and again I heard the inhuman voice of living death.

"I can give you work," said the voice. "Are you willing to work for me?"

I quickly assented. After all, in spite of the fear which the voice inspired, I was deeply indebted to the owner.

"Good. Take these."

As I started toward the screen a sharp command halted me and Hassim stepped forward and reaching behind took what was offered. This was a bundle of pictures and papers, apparently.

"Study these," said the One behind the screen, "and learn all you can about the man portrayed thereby. Yun Shatu will give you money; buy yourself such clothes as seamen wear and take a room at the front of the Temple. At the end of two days, Hassim will bring you to me again. Go!"

The last impression I had, as the hidden door closed above me, was that the eyes of the idol, blinking through the everlasting smoke, leered mockingly at me.

The front of the Temple of Dreams consisted of rooms for rent, masking the true purpose of the building under the guise of a waterfront boarding-house. The police had made several visits to Yun Shatu but had never got any incriminating evidence against him.

So in one of these rooms I took up my abode and set to work studying the material given me.

The pictures were all of one man, a large man, not unlike me in build and general facial outline, except that he wore a heavy beard and was inclined to blondness whereas I am dark. The name, as written on the accompanying papers, was Major Fairlan Morley, special commissioner to Natal and the Transvaal. This office and title were new to me and I wondered at the connection between an African commissioner and an opium house on the Thames waterfront.

The papers consisted of extensive data evidently copied from authentic sources and all dealing with Major Morley, and a number of private documents considerably illuminating on the major's private life.

An exhaustive description was given of the man's personal appearance and habits, some of which seemed very trivial to me. I wondered what the purpose could be, and how the One behind the screen had come in possession of papers of such intimate nature.

I could find no clue in answer to this question but bent all my energies to the task set out for me. I owed a deep debt of gratitude to the unknown man who required this of me and I was determined to repay him to the best of my ability. Nothing, at this time, suggested a snare to me.

5. The Man on the Couch

"What dam of lances sent thee forth to jest at dawn with
Death?"

—KIPLING

At the expiration of two days, Hassim beckoned me as I stood in
the opium room. I advanced with a springy, resilient tread,
secure in the confidence that I had culled the Morley papers of
all their worth. I was a new man; my mental swiftness and
physical readiness surprised me—sometimes it seemed unnatural.

Hassim eyed me through narrowed lids and motioned me to
follow, as usual. As we crossed the room, my gaze fell upon a
man who lay on a couch close to the wall, smoking opium. There
was nothing at all suspicious about his ragged, unkempt clothes,
his dirty, bearded face or the blank stare, but my eyes, sharpened
to an abnormal point, seemed to sense a certain incongruity in
the clean-cut limbs which not even the slouchy garments could
efface.

Hassim spoke impatiently and I turned away. We entered the
rear room, and as he shut the door and turned to the table, it
moved of itself and a figure bulked up through the hidden
doorway. The Sikh, Ganra Singh, a lean sinister-eyed giant,
emerged and proceeded to the door opening into the opium
room, where he halted until we should have descended and
closed the secret doorway.

Again I stood amid the billowing yellow smoke and listened
to the hidden voice.

"Do you think you know enough about Major Morley to impersonate him successfully?"

Startled, I answered, "No doubt I could, unless I met someone who was intimate with him."

"I will take care of that. Follow me closely. Tomorrow you sail on the first boat for Calais. There you will meet an agent of mine who will accost you the instant you step upon the wharfs, and give you further instructions. You will sail second class and avoid all conversation with strangers or anyone. Take the papers with you. The agent will aid you in making up and your masquerade will start in Calais. That is all. Go!"

I departed, my wonder growing. All this rigmarole evidently had a meaning, but one which I could not fathom. Back in the opium room Hassim bade me be seated on some cushions to await his return. To my question he snarled that he was going forth as he had been ordered, to buy me a ticket on the Channel boat. He departed and I sat down, leaning my back against the wall. As I ruminated, it seemed suddenly that eyes were fixed on me so intensely as to disturb my sub-mind. I glanced up quickly but no one seemed to be looking at me. The smoke drifted through the hot atmosphere as usual; Yussef Ali and the Chinese glided back and forth tending to the wants of the sleepers.

Suddenly the door to the rear room opened and a strange and hideous figure came haltingly out. Not all of those who found entrance to Yun Shatu's back room were aristocrats and society members. This was one of the exceptions, and one whom I remembered as having often entered and emerged therefrom—a tall, gaunt figure, shapeless and ragged wrappings and nondescript garments, face entirely hidden. Better that the face be hidden, I thought, for without doubt the wrapping concealed a grisly sight. The man was a leper, who had somehow managed to escape the attention of the public guardians and who was occasionally seen haunting the lower and more mysterious regions of the East End—a mystery even to the lowest denizens of Limehouse.

Suddenly my supersensitive mind was aware of a swift tension in the air. The leper hobbled out the door, closed it behind him. My eyes instinctively sought the couch whereon lay the man who had aroused my suspicions earlier in the day. I could have sworn that cold steely eyes gleamed menacingly before they flickered shut. I crossed to the couch in one stride and bent over the prostrate man. Something about his face seemed unnatural—a healthy bronze seemed to underlie the pallor of complexion.

"Yun Shatu!" I shouted. "A spy is in the house!"

Things happened then with bewildering speed. The man on the couch with one tigerish movement leaped erect and a revolver gleamed in his hand. One sinewy arm flung me aside as I sought to grapple with him and a sharp decisive voice sounded over the babble which broke forth:

"You there! Halt! Halt!"

The pistol in the stranger's hand was leveled at the leper, who was making for the door in long strides!

All about was confusion; Yun Shatu was shrieking volubly in Chinese and the four China boys and Yussef Ali were rushing in from all sides, knives glittering in their hands.

All this I saw with unnatural clearness even as I marked the stranger's face. As the flying leper gave no evidence of halting, I saw the eyes harden to steely points of determination, sighting along the pistol barrel—the features set with the grim purpose of the slayer. The leper was almost to the outer door, but death would strike him down ere he could reach it.

And then, just as the finger of the stranger tightened on the trigger, I hurled myself forward and my right fist crashed against his chin. He went down as though struck by a trip-hammer, the revolver exploding harmlessly in the air.

In that instant, with the blinding flare of light that sometimes comes to one, I knew that the leper was none other than the Man Behind the Screen!

I bent over the fallen man, who though not entirely senseless had been rendered temporarily helpless by that terrific blow. He was struggling dazedly to rise but I shoved him roughly down again and seizing the false beard he wore, tore it away. A lean bronzed face was revealed, the strong lines of which not even the artificial dirt and grease paint could alter.

Yussef Ali leaned above him now, dagger in hand, eyes slits of murder. The brown sinewy hand went up—I caught the wrist.

"Not so fast, you black devil! What are you about to do?"

"This is John Gordon," he hissed, "the Master's greatest foe! He must die, curse you!"

John Gordon! The name was familiar somehow, and yet I did not seem to connect it with the London police nor account for the man's presence in Yun Shatu's dope-joint. However, on one point I was determined.

"You don't kill him, at any rate. Up with you!" This last to Gordon, who with my aid staggered up, still very dizzy.

"That punch would have dropped a bull," I said in wonderment; "I didn't know I had it in me."

The false leper had vanished. Yun Shatu stood gazing at me as immobile as an idol, hands in his wide sleeves, and Yussef Ali stood back, muttering murderously and thumbing his dagger edge, as I led Gordon out of the opium room and through the innocent-appearing bar which lay between that room and the street.

Out in the street I said to him: "I have no idea as to who you are or what you are doing here, but you see what an unhealthful place it is for you. Hereafter be advised by me and stay away."

His only answer was a searching glance, and then he turned and walked swiftly though somewhat unsteadily up the street.

6. The Dream Girl

"I have reached these lands but newly
From an ultimate dim Thule."

—Poe

Outside my room sounded a light footstep. The doorknob
turned cautiously and slowly; the door opened. I sprang erect
with a gasp. Red lips, half parted, dark eyes like limpid seas of
wonder, a mass of shimmering hair—framed in my drab
doorway stood the girl of my dreams!

She entered, and half turning with a sinuous motion, closed
the door. I sprang forward, my hands outstretched, then halted
as she put a finger to her lips.

"You must not talk loudly," she almost whispered; "*He* did
not say I could not come; yet—"

Her voice was soft and musical, with just a touch of foreign
accent which I found delightful. As for the girl herself, every
intonation, every movement proclaimed the Orient. She was a
fragrant breath from the East. From her night-black hair, piled
high above her alabaster forehead, to her little feet, encased in
high-heeled pointed slippers, she portrayed the highest ideal of
Asiatic loveliness—an effect which was heightened rather than
lessened by the English blouse and skirt which she wore.

"You are beautiful!" I said dazedly. "Who are you?"

"I am Zuleika," she answered with a shy smile. "I—I am glad
you like me. I am glad you no longer dream hashish dreams."

Strange that so small a thing should set my heart to leaping
wildly!

"I owe it all to you, Zuleika," I said huskily. "Had not I

32

dreamed of you every hour since you first lifted me from the gutter, I had lacked the power of even hoping to be freed from my curse."

She blushed prettily and intertwined her white fingers as if in nervousness.

"You leave England tomorrow?" she said suddenly.

"Yes. Hassim has not returned with my ticket—" I hesitated suddenly, remembering the command of silence.

"Yes, I know, I know!" she whispered swiftly, her eyes widening. "And John Gordon has been here! He saw you!"

"Yes!"

She came close to me with a quick lithe movement.

"You are to impersonate some man! Listen, while you are doing this, you must not ever let Gordon see you! He would know you, no matter what your disguise! He is a terrible man!"

"I don't understand," I said, completely bewildered. "How did the Master break me of my hashish craving? Who is this Gordon and why did he come here? Why does the Master go disguised as a leper—and who is he? Above all, why am I to impersonate a man I never saw or heard of?"

"I can not—I dare not tell you!" she whispered, her face paling. "I—"

Somewhere in the house sounded the faint tones of a Chinese gong. The girl started like a frightened gazelle.

"I must go! *He* summons me!"

She opened the door, darted through, halted a moment to electrify me with her passionate exclamation: "Oh, be careful, be very careful, sahib!"

Then she was gone.

7. The Man of the Skull

> "What the hammer? what the chain?
> In what furnace was thy brain?
> What the anvil? what dread grasp
> Dare its deadly terrors clasp?"
>
> —BLAKE

Awhile after my beautiful and mysterious visitor had left, I sat in meditation. I believed that I had at last stumbled on to an explanation of a part of the enigma, at any rate. This was the conclusion I had reached: Yun Shatu, the opium lord, was simply the agent or servant of some organization or individual whose work was on a far larger scale than merely supplying dope addicts in the Temple of Dreams. This man or these men needed co-workers among all classes of people; in other words, I was being let in with a group of opium smugglers on a gigantic scale. Gordon no doubt had been investigating the case, and his presence alone showed that it was no ordinary one, for I knew that he held a high position with the English government, though just what, I did not know.

Opium or not, I determined to carry out my obligation to the Master. My moral sense had been blunted by the dark ways I had traveled, and the thought of despicable crime did not enter my head. I was indeed hardened. More, the mere debt of gratitude was increased a thousandfold by the thought of the girl. To the Master I owed it that I was able to stand up on my feet and look into her clear eyes as a man should. So if he wished my services as a smuggler of dope, he should have them. No doubt I was to impersonate some man so high in governmental esteem that the usual actions of the customs officers would be deemed unnecessary; was I to bring some rare dream-producer into England?

These thoughts were in my mind as I went downstairs, but ever back of them hovered other and more alluring suppositions—what was the reason for the girl, here in this vile dive—a rose in a garbage-heap—and who was she?

As I entered the outer bar, Hassim came in, his brows set in a dark scowl of anger, and, I believed, fear. He carried a newspaper in his hand, folded.

"I told you to wait in opium room," he snarled.

"You were gone so long that I went up to my room. Have you the ticket?"

He merely grunted and pushed on past me into the opium room, and standing at the door I saw him cross the floor and disappear into the rear room. I stood there, my bewilderment increasing. For as Hassim had brushed past me, I had noted an item on the face of the paper, against which his black thumb was tightly pressed as if to mark that special column of news.

And with the unnatural celerity of action and judgment which seemed to be mine those days, I had in that fleeting instant read:

African Special Commissioner Found Murdered!
The body of Major Fairlan Morley was yesterday discovered in a rotting ship's hold at Bordeaux...

No more I saw of the details, but that alone was enough to make me think! The affair seemed to be taking on an ugly aspect. Yet—

Another day passed. To my inquiries, Hassim snarled that the plans had been changed and I was not to go to France. Then, late in the evening, he came to bid me once more to the room of mystery.

I stood before the lacquer screen, the yellow smoke acrid in my nostrils, the woven dragons writhing along the tapestries, the palm-trees rearing thick and oppressive.

"A change has come in our plans," said the hidden voice. "You will not sail as was decided before. But I have other work that you may do. Mayhap this will be more to your type of usefulness, for I admit you have somewhat disappointed me in regard to subtlety. You interfered the other day in such manner as will no doubt cause me great inconvenience in the future."

I said nothing, but a feeling of resentment began to stir in me.

"Even after the assurance of one of my most trusted servants," the toneless voice continued, with no mark of any emotion save a slightly rising note, "you insisted on releasing my most deadly enemy. Be more circumspect in the future."

"I saved your life!" I said angrily.

"And for that reason alone I overlook your mistake—this time!"

A slow fury suddenly surged up in me.

"This time! Make the best of it this time, for I assure you there will be no next time. I owe you a greater debt than I can ever hope to pay, but that does not make me your slave. I have saved your life—the debt is as near paid as a man can pay it. Go your way and I go mine!"

A low, hideous laugh answered me, like a reptilian hiss.

"You fool! You will pay with your whole life's toil! You say you are not my slave? I say you are—just as black Hassim there beside you is my slave—just as the girl Zuleika is my slave, who had bewitched you with her beauty."

These words sent a wave of hot blood to my brain and I was conscious of a flood of fury which completely engulfed my reason for a second. Just as all my moods and senses seemed sharpened and exaggerated those days, so now this burst of rage transcended every moment of anger I had ever had before.

"Hell's fiends!" I shrieked. "You devil—who are you and what is your hold on me? I'll see you or die!"

Hassim sprang at me, but I hurled him backward and with one stride reached the screen and flung it aside with an incredible effort of strength. Then I shrank back, hands outflung, shrieking. A tall, gaunt figure stood before me, a figure arrayed grotesquely in a silk brocaded gown which fell to the floor.

From the sleeves of this gown protruded hands which filled me with crawling horror—long, predatory hands, with thin bony fingers and curved talons—withered skin of a parchment brownish-yellow, like the hands of a man long dead.

The hands—but, oh God, the face! A skull to which no vestige of flesh seemed to remain but on which taut brownish-yellow skin grew fast, etching out every detail of that terrible death's-head. The forehead was high and in a way magnificent, but the head was curiously narrow through the temples, and from under penthouse brows great eyes glimmered like pools of yellow fire. The nose was high-bridged and very thin; the mouth was a mere colorless gash between thin, cruel lips. A long, bony neck supported this frightful vision and completed the effect of a reptilian demon from some mediaeval hell.

I was face to face with the skull-faced man of my dreams!

8. Black Wisdom

The terrible spectacle drove for the instant all thoughts of rebellion from my mind. My very blood froze in my veins and I stood motionless. I heard Hassim laugh grimly behind me. The eyes in the cadaverous face blazed fiendishly at me and I blanched from the concentrated Satanic fury in them.

Then the horror laughed sibilantly.

"I do you a great honor, Mr. Costigan; among a very few, even of my own servants, you may say that you saw my face and lived. I think you will be more useful to me living than dead."

I was silent, completely unnerved. It was difficult to believe that this man lived, for his appearance certainly belied the thought. He seemed horribly like a mummy. Yet his lips moved when he spoke and his eyes flamed with hideous life.

"You will do as I say," he said abruptly, and his voice had taken on a note of command. "You doubtless know, or know of, Sir Haldred Frenton?"

"Yes."

Every man of culture in Europe and America was familiar with the travel books of Sir Haldred Frenton, author and soldier of fortune.

"You will go to Sir Haldred's estate tonight—"

"Yes?"

"*And kill him!*"

I staggered, literally. This order was incredible—unspeakable! I had sunk low, low enough to smuggle opium, but to deliberately murder a man I had never seen, a man noted for his kindly deeds! That was too monstrous even to contemplate.

"You do not refuse?"

The tone was as loathly and as mocking as the hiss of a serpent.

"Refuse?" I screamed, finding my voice at last. "Refuse? You incarnate devil! Of course I refuse! You—"

Something in the cold assurance of his manner halted me—froze me into apprehensive silence.

"You fool!" he said calmly. "I broke the hashish chains—do you know how? Four minutes from now you will know and curse the day you were born! Have you not thought it strange, the swiftness of brain, the resilience of body—the brain that should be rusty and slow, the body that should be weak and sluggish from years of abuse? That blow that felled John Gordon—have you not wondered at its might? The ease with which you mastered Major Morley's records—have you not wondered at that? You fool, you are bound to me by chains of steel and blood and fire! I have kept you alive and sane—I alone. Each day the life-saving elixir has been given you in your wine. You could not live and keep your reason without it. And I and only I know its secret!"

He glanced at a queer timepiece which stood on a table at his elbow.

"This time I had Yun Shatu leave the elixir out—I anticipated rebellion. The time is near—ha, it strikes!"

Something else he said, but I did not hear. I did not see, nor did I feel in the human sense of the word. I was writhing at his feet, screaming and gibbering in the flames of such hells as men have never dreamed of.

Aye, I knew now! He had simply given me a dope so much stronger that it drowned the hashish. My unnatural ability was explainable now—I had simply been acting under the stimulus of something which combined all the hells in its make-up which stimulated, something like heroin, but whose effect was unnoticed by the victim. What it was, I had no idea, nor did I believe anyone knew save that hellish being who stood watching me with grim amusement. But it had held my brain together, instilling into my system a need for it, and now my frightful craving tore my soul asunder.

Never, in my moments of worst shell-shock or my moments of hashish-craving, have I ever experienced anything like that. I burned with the heat of a thousand hells and froze with an iciness that was colder than any ice, a hundred times. I swept down to the deepest pits of torture and up to the highest crags of torment—a million yelling devils hemmed me in, shrieking and stabbing. Bone by bone, vein by vein, cell by cell I felt my body disintegrate and fly in bloody atoms all over the universe—and each separate cell was an entire system of quivering, screaming nerves. And they gathered from far voids and reunited with a greater torment.

Through the fiery bloody mists I heard my own voice screaming, a monotonous yammering. Then with distended eyes I saw a golden goblet, held by a claw-like hand, swim into view— a goblet filled with an amber liquid.

With a bestial screech I seized it with both hands, being dimly aware that the metal stem gave beneath my fingers, and brought the brim to my lips. I drank in frenzied haste, the liquid slopping down onto my breast.

9. Kathulos of Egypt

"Night shall be thrice night over you,
And Heaven an iron cope."
—CHESTERTON

The Skull-faced One stood watching me critically as I sat panting on a couch, completely exhausted. He held in his hand the goblet and surveyed the golden stem, which was crushed out of all shape. This my maniac fingers had done in the instant of drinking.

"Superhuman strength, even for a man in your condition," he said with a sort of creaky pedantry. "I doubt if even Hassim here could equal it. Are you ready for your instructions now?"

I nodded, wordless. Already the hellish strength of the elixir was flowing through my veins, renewing my burnt-out force. I wondered how long a man could live as I lived being constantly burned out and artificially rebuilt.

"You will be given a disguise and will go alone to the Frenton estate. No one suspects any design against Sir Haldred and your entrance into the estate and the house itself should be a matter of comparative ease. You will not don the disguise—which will be of unique nature—until you are ready to enter the estate. You will then proceed to Sir Haldred's room and kill him, breaking his neck with your bare hands—this is essential—"

The voice droned on, giving its ghastly orders in a frightfully casual and matter-of-fact way. The cold sweat beaded my brow.

"You will then leave the estate, taking care to leave the imprint of your hand somewhere plainly visible, and the automobile, which will be waiting for you at some safe place

41

nearby, will bring you back here, you having first removed the disguise. I have, in case of later complications, any amount of men who will swear that you spent the entire night in the Temple of Dreams and never left it. But there must be no detection! Go warily and perform your task surely, for you know the alternative."

I did not return to the opium house but was taken through winding corridors, hung with heavy tapestries, to a small room containing only an Oriental couch. Hassim gave me to understand that I was to remain there until after nightfall and then left me. The door was closed but I made no effort to discover if it was locked. The Skull-faced Master held me with stronger shackles than locks and bolts.

Seated upon the couch in the bizarre setting of a chamber which might have been a room in an Indian zenana, I faced fact squarely and fought out my battle. There was still in me some trace of manhood left—more than the fiend had reckoned, and added to this were black despair and desperation. I chose and determined on my only course.

Suddenly the door opened softly. Some intuition told me whom to expect, nor was I disappointed. Zuleika stood, a glorious vision before me—a vision which mocked me, made blacker my despair and yet thrilled me with wild yearning and reasonless joy.

She bore a tray of food which she set beside me, and then she seated herself on the couch, her large eyes fixed upon my face. A flower in a serpent den she was, and the beauty of her took hold of my heart.

"Steephen!" she whispered and I thrilled as she spoke my name for the first time.

Her luminous eyes suddenly shone with tears and she laid her little hand on my arm. I seized it in both my rough hands.

"They have set you a task which you fear and hate!" she faltered.

"Aye," I almost laughed, "but I'll fool them yet! Zuleika, tell me—what is the meaning of all this?"

She glanced fearfully around her.

"I do not know all"—she hesitated—"your plight is all my fault but I—I hoped—Steephen, I have watched you every time you came to Yun Shatu's for months. You did not see me but I saw you, and I saw in you, not the broken sot your rags proclaimed, but a wounded soul, a soul bruised terribly on the

ramparts of life. And from my heart I pitied you. Then when
Hassim abused you that day"—again tears started to her eyes—
"I could not bear it and I knew how you suffered for want of
hashish. So I paid Yun Shatu, and going to the Master I—I—oh,
you will hate me for this!" she sobbed.

"No—no—never—"

"I told him that you were a man who might be of use to him
and begged him to have Yun Shatu supply you with what you
needed. He had already noticed you, for his is the eye of the
slaver and all the world is his slave market! So he bade Yun
Shatu do as I asked; and now—better if you had remained as
you were, my friend."

"No! No!" I exclaimed. "I have known a few days of
regeneration, even if it was false! I have stood before you as a
man, and that is worth all else!"

And all that I felt for her must have looked forth from my
eyes, for she dropped hers and flushed. Ask me not how love
comes to a man; but I knew that I loved Zuleika—had loved this
mysterious Oriental girl since first I saw her—and somehow I
felt that she, in a measure, returned my affection. This
realization made blacker and more barren the road I had
chosen; yet—for pure love must ever strengthen a man—it
nerved me to what I must do.

"Zuleika," I said, speaking hurriedly, "time flies and there are
things I must learn; tell me—who are you and why do you
remain in this den of Hades?"

"I am Zuleika—that is all I know. I am Circassian by blood
and birth; when I was very little I was captured in a Turkish raid
and raised in a Stamboul harem; while I was yet too young to
marry, my master gave me as a present to—to *Him*."

"And who is he—this skull-faced man?"

"He is Kathulos of Egypt—that is all I know. My master."

"An Egyptian? Then what is he doing in London—why all
this mystery?"

She intertwined her fingers nervously.

"Steephen, please speak lower; always there is someone
listening everywhere. I do not know who the Master is or why he
is here or why he does these things. I swear by Allah! If I knew I
would tell you. Sometimes distinguished-looking men come
here to the room where the Master receives them—not the room
where you saw him—and he makes me dance before them and
afterward flirt with them a little. And always I must repeat

exactly what they say to me. That is what I must always do—in Turkey, in the Barbary States, in Egypt, in France and in England. The Master taught me French and English and educated me in many ways himself. He is the greatest sorcerer in all the world and knows all ancient magic and everything."

"Zuleika," I said, "my race is soon run, but let me get you out of this—come with me and I swear I'll get you away from this fiend!"

She shuddered and hid her face.

"No, no, I can not!"

"Zuleika," I asked gently, "what hold has he over you, child—dope also?"

"No, no!" she whimpered. "I do not know—I do not know—but I can not—I never can escape him!"

I sat, baffled for a few moments; then I asked, "Zuleika, where are we right now?"

"This building is a deserted storehouse back of the Temple of Silence."

"I thought so. What is in the chests in the tunnel?"

"I do not know."

Then suddenly she began weeping softly. "You too, a slave, like me—you who are so strong and kind—oh Steephen, I can not bear it!"

I smiled. "Lean closer, Zuleika, and I will tell you how I am going to fool this Kathulos."

She glanced apprehensively at the door.

"You will speak low. I will lie in your arms and while you pretend to caress me, whisper your words to me."

She glided into my embrace, and there on the dragon-worked couch in that house of horror I first knew the glory of Zuleika's slender form nestling in my arms—of Zuleika's soft cheek pressing my breast. The fragrance of her was in my nostrils, her hair in my eyes, and my senses reeled; then with my lips hidden by her silky hair I whispered, swiftly:

"I am going first to warn Sir Haldred Frenton—then to find John Gordon and tell him of this den. I will lead the police here and you must watch closely and be ready to hide from *Him*— until we can break through and kill or capture him. Then you will be free."

"But you!" she gasped, paling. "You must have the elixir, and only he—"

"I have a way of outdoing him, child," I answered.

She went pitifully white and her woman's intuition sprang at the right conclusion.

"You are going to kill yourself!"

And much as it hurt me to see her emotion, I yet felt a torturing thrill that she should feel so on my account. Her arms tightened about my neck.

"Don't, Steephen!" she begged. "It is better to live, even—"

"No, not at that price. Better to go out clean while I have the manhood left."

She stared at me wildly for an instant; then, pressing her red lips suddenly to mine, she sprang up and fled from the room. Strange, strange are the ways of love. Two stranded ships on the shores of life, we had drifted inevitably together, and though no word of love had passed between us, we knew each other's heart—through grime and rags, and through accouterments of the slave, we knew each other's heart and from the first loved as naturally and as purely as it was intended from the beginning of Time.

The beginning of life now and the end for me, for as soon as I had completed my task, ere I felt again the torments of my curse, love and life and beauty and torture should be blotted out together in the stark finality of a pistol ball scattering my rotting brain. Better a clean death than—

The door opened again and Yussef Ali entered.

"The hour arrives for departure," he said briefly. "Rise and follow."

I had no idea, of course, as to the time. No window opened from the room I occupied—I had seen no outer window whatever. The rooms were lighted by tapers in censers swinging from the ceiling. As I rose the slim young Moor slanted a sinister glance in my direction.

"This lies between you and me," he said sibilantly. "Servants of the same Master we—but this concerns ourselves alone. Keep your distance from Zuleika—the Master has promised her to me in the days of the empire."

My eyes narrowed to slits as I looked into the frowning, handsome face of the Oriental, and such hate surged up in me as I have seldom known. My fingers involuntarily opened and closed, and the Moor, marking the action, stepped back, hand in his girdle.

"Not now—there is work for us both—later perhaps"; then in a sudden cold gust of hatred, "Swine! ape-man! when the Master is finished with you I shall quench my dagger in your heart!"

I laughed grimly.

"Make it soon, desert-snake, or I'll crush your spine between my hands."

10. The Dark House

"Against all man-made shackles and a man-made Hell—
Alone—at last—unaided—I rebel!"

—MUNDY

I followed Yussef Ali along the winding hallways, down the steps—Kathulos was not in the idol-room—and along the tunnel, then through the rooms of the Temple of Dreams and out into the street, where the street lamps gleamed drearily through the fogs and a slight drizzle. Across the street stood an automobile, curtains closely drawn.

"That is yours," said Hassim, who had joined us. "Saunter across natural-like. Don't act suspicious. The place may be watched. The driver knows what to do."

Then he and Yussef Ali drifted back into the bar and I took a single step toward the curb.

"Steephen!"

A voice that made my heart leap spoke my name! A white hand beckoned from the shadows of a doorway. I stepped quickly there.

"Zuleika!"

"Shhh!"

She clutched my arm, slipped something into my hand; I made out vaguely a small flask of gold.

"Hide this, quick!" came her urgent whisper. "Don't come back, go away and hide. This is full of elixir—I will try to get you some more before that is all gone. You must find a way of communicating with me."

"Yes, but how did you get this?" I asked amazedly.

47

"I stole it from the Master! Now please, I must go before he misses me."

And she sprang back into the doorway and vanished. I stood undecided. I was sure that she had risked nothing less than her life in doing this and I was torn by the fear of what Kathulos might do to her, were the theft discovered. But to return to the house of mystery would certainly invite suspicion, and I might carry out my plan and strike back before the Skull-faced One learned of his slave's duplicity.

So I crossed the street to the waiting automobile. The driver was a Negro whom I had never seen before, a lanky man of medium height. I stared hard at him, wondering how much he had seen. He gave no evidence of having seen anything, and I decided that even if he had noticed me step back into the shadows he could not have seen what passed there nor have been able to recognize the girl.

He merely nodded as I climbed in the back seat, and a moment later we were speeding away down the deserted and fog-haunted streets. A bundle beside me I concluded to be the disguise mentioned by the Egyptian.

To recapture the sensations I experienced as I rode through the rainy, misty night would be impossible. I felt as if I were already dead and the bare and dreary streets about me were the roads of death over which my ghost had been doomed to roam forever. A torturing joy was in my heart, and bleak despair—the despair of a doomed man. Not that death itself was so repellent—a dope victim dies too many deaths to shrink from the last—but it was hard to go out just as love had entered my barren life. And I was still young.

A sardonic smile crossed my lips—they were young, too, the men who died beside me in No Man's Land. I drew back my sleeve and clenched my fists, tensing my muscles. There was no surplus weight on my frame, and much of the firm flesh had wasted away, but the cords of the great biceps still stood out like knots of iron, seeming to indicate massive strength. But I knew my might was false, that in reality I was a broken husk of a man, animated only by the artificial fire of the elixir, without which a frail girl might topple me over.

The automobile came to a halt among some trees. We were on the outskirts of an exclusive suburb and the hour was past midnight. Through the trees I saw a large house looming darkly against the distant flares of night-time London.

"This is where I wait," said the Negro. "No one can see the automobile from the road or from the house."

Holding a match so that its light could not be detected outside the car, I examined the "disguise" and was hard put to restrain an insane laugh. The disguise was the complete hide of a gorilla! Gathering the bundle under my arm I trudged toward the wall which surrounded the Frenton estate. A few steps and the trees where the Negro hid with the car merged into one dark mass. I did not believe he could see me, but for safety's sake I made, not for the high iron gate at the front but for the wall at the side where there was no gate.

No light showed in the house. Sir Haldred was a bachelor and I was sure that the servants were all in bed long ago. I negotiated the wall with ease and stole across the dark lawn to a side door, still carrying the grisly "disguise" under my arm. The door was locked, as I had anticipated, and I did not wish to arouse anyone until I was safely in the house, where the sound of voices would not carry to one who might have followed me. I took hold of the knob with both hands, and, exerting slowly the inhuman strength that was mine, began to twist. The shaft turned in my hands and the lock within shattered suddenly, with a noise that was like the crash of a cannon in the stillness. An instant more and I was inside and had closed the door behind me.

I took a single stride in the darkness in the direction I believed the stair to be, then halted as a beam of light flashed into my face. At the side of the beam I caught the glimmer of a pistol muzzle. Beyond a lean shadowy face floated.

"Stand where you are and put up your hands!"

I lifted my hands, allowing the bundle to slip to the floor. I had heard that voice only once but I recognized it—knew instantly that the man who held that light was John Gordon.

"How many are with you?"

His voice was sharp, commanding.

"I am alone," I answered. "Take me into a room where a light can not be seen from the outside and I'll tell you some things you want to know."

He was silent; then, bidding me take up the bundle I had dropped, he stepped to one side and motioned me to precede him into the next room. There he directed me to a stairway and at the top landing opened a door and switched on lights.

I found myself in a room whose curtains were closely drawn. During this journey Gordon's alertness had not relaxed, and now he stood, still covering me with his revolver. Clad in conventional garments, he stood revealed a tall, leanly but powerfully built man, taller than I but not so heavy—with steel-gray eyes and clean-cut features. Something about the man attracted me, even as I noted a bruise on his jawbone where my fist had struck in our last meeting.

"I can not believe," he said crisply, "that this apparent clumsiness and lack of subtlety is real. Doubtless you have your own reasons for wishing me to be in a secluded room at this time, but Sir Haldred is efficiently protected even now. Stand still."

Muzzle pressed against my chest, he ran his hand over my garments for concealed weapons, seeming slightly surprised when he found none.

"Still," he murmured as if to himself, "a man who can burst an iron lock with his bare hands has scant need of weapons."

"You are wasting valuable time," I said impatiently. "I was sent here tonight to kill Sir Haldred Frenton—"

"By whom?" the question was shot at me.

"By the man who sometimes goes disguised as a leper."

He nodded, a gleam in his scintillant eyes.

"My suspicions were correct, then."

"Doubtless. Listen to me closely—do you desire the death or arrest of that man?"

Gordon laughed grimly.

"To one who wears the mark of the scorpion on his hand, my answer would be superfluous."

"Then follow my directions and your wish shall be granted."

His eyes narrowed suspiciously.

"So that was the meaning of this open entry and non-resistance," he said slowly. "Does the dope which dilates your eyeballs so warp your mind that you think to lead me into ambush?"

I pressed my hands against my temples. Time was racing and every moment was precious—how could I convince this man of my honesty?

"Listen; my name is Stephen Costigan of America. I was a frequenter of Yun Shatu's dive and a hashish addict—as you have guessed, but just now a slave of stronger dope. By virtue of this slavery, the man you know as a false leper, whom Yun Shatu and his friends call 'Master', gained dominance over me and sent me here to murder Sir Haldred—why, God only knows. But I have gained a space of respite by coming into possession of some of this dope which I must have in order to live, and I fear and hate this Master. Listen to me and I swear, by all things holy and unholy, that before the sun rises the false leper shall be in your power!"

I could tell that Gordon was impressed in spite of himself.

"Speak fast!" he rapped.

Still I could sense his disbelief and a wave of futility swept over me.

"If you will not act with me," I said, "let me go and somehow I'll find a way to get to the Master and kill him. My time is short—my hours are numbered and my vengeance is yet to be realized."

"Let me hear your plan, and talk fast," Gordon answered.

"It is simple enough. I will return to the Master's lair and tell him I have accomplished that which he sent me to do. You must follow closely with your men and while I engage the Master in conversation, surround the house. Then, at the signal, break in and kill or seize him."

Gordon frowned. "Where is this house?"

"The warehouse back of Yun Shatu's has been converted into a veritable Oriental palace."

"The warehouse!" he exclaimed. "How can that be? I had thought of that first, but I have carefully examined it from without. The windows are closely barred and spiders have built webs across them. The doors are nailed fast on the outside and the seals that mark the warehouse as deserted have never been broken or disturbed in any way."

"They tunneled up from beneath," I answered. "The Temple of Dreams is directly connected with the warehouse."

"I have traversed the alley between the two buildings," said Gordon, "and the doors of the warehouse opening into that alley are, as I have said, nailed shut from without just as the owners left them. There is apparently no rear exit of any kind from the Temple of Dreams."

"A tunnel connects the buildings, with one door in the rear room of Yun Shatu's and the other in the idol-room of the warehouse."

"I have been in Yun Shatu's back room and found no such door."

"The table rests upon it. You noted the heavy table in the center of the room? Had you turned it around the secret door would have opened in the floor. Now this is my plan: I will go in through the Temple of Dreams and meet the Master in the idol-room. You will have men secretly stationed in front of the warehouse and others upon the other street, in front of the Temple of Dreams. Yun Shatu's building, as you know, faces the waterfront, while the warehouse, fronting the opposite direction, faces a narrow street running parellel with the river. At the signal let the men in this street break open the front of the warehouse and rush in, while simultaneously those in front of Yun Shatu's make an invasion through the Temple of Dreams. Let these make for the rear room, shooting without mercy any who may seek to deter them, and there open the secret door as I have said. There being, to the best of my knowledge, no other exit from the Master's lair, he and his servants will necessarily seek to make their escape through the tunnel. Thus we will have them on both sides."

Gordon ruminated while I studied his face with breathless interest.

"This may be a snare," he muttered, "or an attempt to draw me away from Sir Haldred, but—"

I held my breath.

"I am a gambler by nature," he said slowly. "I am going to follow what you Americans call a hunch—but God help you if you are lying to me!"

I sprang erect.

"Thank God! Now aid me with this suit, for I must be wearing it when I return to the automobile waiting for me."

His eyes narrowed as I shook out the horrible masquerade and prepared to don it.

"This shows, as always, the touch of the master hand. You were doubtless instructed to leave marks of your hands, encased in those hideous gauntlets?"

"Yes—though I have no idea why."

"I think I have—the Master is famed for leaving no real clues to mark his crimes—a great ape escaped from a neighboring zoo earlier in the evening and it seems too obvious for mere chance, in the light of this disguise. The ape would have gotten the blame for Sir Haldred's death."

The thing was easily gotten into and the illusion of reality it created was so perfect as to draw a shudder from me as I viewed myself in a mirror.

"It is now two o'clock," said Gordon. "Allowing for the time it will take you to get back to Limehouse and the time it will take me to get my men stationed, I promise you that at half-past four the house will be closely surrounded. Give me a start—wait here until I have left this house, so I will arrive at least as soon as you."

"Good!" I impulsively grasped his hand. "There will doubtless be a girl there who is in no way implicated with the Master's evil-doings, but only a victim of circumstances such as I have been. Deal gently with her."

"It shall be done. What signal shall I look for?"

"I have no way of signaling for you and I doubt if any sound in the house could be heard on the street. Let your men make their raid on the stroke of five."

I turned to go.

"A man is waiting for you with a car, I take it? Is he likely to suspect anything?"

"I have a way of finding out, and if he does," I replied grimly, "I will return alone to the Temple of Dreams."

11. Four Thirty-Four

"Doubting, dreaming dreams no
mortal ever dared to dream before."

The door closed softly behind me, the great dark house looming up more starkly than ever. Stooping, I crossed the wet lawn at a run, a grotesque and unholy figure, I doubt not, since any man had at a glance sworn me to be not a man but a giant ape. So craftily had the Master devised!

I clambered the wall, dropped to the earth beyond and made my way through the darkness and the drizzle to the group of trees which masked the automobile.

The Negro driver leaned out of the front seat. I was breathing hard and sought in various ways to simulate the actions of a man who has just murdered in cold blood and fled the scene of his crime.

"You heard nothing, no sound, no scream?" I hissed, gripping his arm.

"No noise except a slight crash when you first went in," he answered. "You did a good job—nobody passing along the road could have suspected anything."

"Have you remained in the car all the time?" I asked. And when he replied that he had, I seized his ankle and ran my hand over the soles of his shoe; it was perfectly dry, as was the cuff of his trouser leg. Satisfied, I climbed into the back seat. Had he taken a step on the earth, shoe and garment would have showed it by the telltale dampness.

I ordered him to refrain from starting the engine until I had removed the apeskin, and then we sped through the night and I fell victim to doubts and uncertainties. Why should Gordon put any trust in the word of a stranger and a former ally of the Master's? Would he not put my tale down as the ravings of a dope-crazed addict, or a lie to ensnare or befool him? Still, if he had not believed me, why had he let me go?

I could but trust. At any rate, what Gordon did or did not do would scarcely affect my fortunes ultimately, even though Zuleika had furnished me with that which would merely extend the number of my days. My thought centered on her, and more than my hope of vengeance on Kathulos was the hope that Gordon might be able to save her from the clutches of the fiend. At any rate, I thought grimly, if Gordon failed me, I still had my hands and if I might lay them upon the bony frame of the Skull-faced One—

Abruptly I found myself thinking of Yussef Ali and his strange words, the import of which just occurred to me, "*The Master has promised her to me in the days of the empire!*"

The days of the empire—what could that mean?

The automobile at last drew up in front of the building which hid the Temple of Silence—now dark and still. The ride had seemed interminable and as I dismounted I glanced at the timepiece on the dashboard of the car. My heart leaped—it was four thirty-four, and unless my eyes tricked me I saw a movement in the shadows across the street, out of the flare of the street lamp. At this time of night it could mean only one of two things—some menial of the Master watching for my return or else Gordon had kept his word. The Negro drove away and I opened the door, crossed the deserted bar and entered the opium room. The bunks and the floor were littered with the dreamers, for such places as these know nothing of day or night as normal people know, but all lay deep in sottish slumber.

The lamps glimmered through the smoke and a silence hung mist-like over all.

12. The Stroke of Five

"He saw gigantic tracks of death,
And many a shape of doom."
—CHESTERTON

Two of the China boys squatted among the smudge fires, staring at me unwinkingly as I threaded my way among the recumbent bodies and made my way to the rear door. For the first time I traversed the corridor alone and found time to wonder again as to the contents of the strange chests which lined the walls.

Four raps on the under side of the floor, and a moment later I stood in the idol-room. I gasped in amazement—the fact that across a table from me sat Kathulos in all his horror was not the cause of my exclamation. Except for the table, the chair on which the Skull-face sat and the altar—now bare of incense—the room was perfectly bare! Drab, unlovely walls of the unused warehouse met my gaze instead of the costly tapestries I had become accustomed to. The palms, the idol, the lacquered screen—all were gone.

"Ah, Mr. Costigan, you wonder, no doubt."

The dead voice of the Master broke in on my thoughts. His serpent eyes glittered balefully. The long yellow fingers twined sinuously upon the table.

"You thought me to be a trusting fool, no doubt!" he rapped suddenly. "Did you think I would not have you followed? You fool, Yussef Ali was at your heels every moment!"

An instant I stood speechless, frozen by the crash of these words against my brain; then as their import sank home, I launched myself forward with a roar. At the same instant, before

56

my clutching fingers could close on the mocking horror on the other side of the table, men rushed from every side. I whirled, and with the clarity of hate, from the swirl of savage faces I singled out Yussef Ali, and crashed my right fist against his temple with every ounce of my strength. Even as he dropped, Hassim struck me to my knees and a Chinaman flung a man-net over my shoulders. I heaved erect, bursting the stout cords as if they were strings, and then a blackjack in the hands of Ganra Singh stretched me stunned and bleeding on the floor.

Lean sinewy hands seized and bound me with cords that cut cruelly into my flesh. Emerging from the mists of semi-unconsciousness, I found myself lying on the altar with the masked Kathulos towering over me like a gaunt ivory tower. About in a semicircle stood Ganra Singh, Yar Khan, Yun Shatu and several others whom I knew as frequenters of the Temple of Dreams. Beyond them—and the sight cut me to the heart—I saw Zuleika crouching in a doorway, her face white and her hands pressed against her cheeks, in an attitude of abject terror.

"I did not fully trust you," said Kathulos sibilantly, "so I sent Yussef Ali to follow you. He reached the group of trees before you and following you into the estate heard your very interesting conversation with John Gordon—for he scaled the house-wall like a cat and clung to the windowledge! Your driver delayed purposely so as to give Yussef Ali plenty of time to get back—I have decided to change my abode anyway. My furnishings are already on their way to another house, and as soon as we have disposed of the traitor—you!—we shall depart also, leaving a little surprise for your friend Gordon when he arrives at five-thirty."

My heart gave a sudden leap of hope. Yussef Ali had misunderstood, and Kathulos lingered here in false security while the London detective force had already silently surrounded the house. Over my shoulder I saw Zuleika vanish from the door.

I eyed Kathulos, absolutely unaware of what he was saying. It was not long until five—if he dallied longer—then I froze as the Egyptian spoke a word and Li Kung, a gaunt, cadaverous Chinaman, stepped from the silent semicircle and drew from his sleeve a long thin dagger. My eyes sought the timepiece that still rested on the table and my heart sank. It was still ten minutes until five. My death did not matter so much, since it simply hastened the inevitable, but in my mind's eye I could see

Kathulos and his murderers escaping while the police awaited the stroke of five.

The Skull-face halted in some harangue, and stood in a listening attitude. I believe his uncanny intuition warned him of danger. He spoke a quick staccato command to Li Kung and the Chinaman sprang forward, dagger lifted above my breast.

The air was suddenly supercharged with dynamic tension. The keen dagger-point hovered high above me—loud and clear sounded the skirl of a police whistle and on the heels of the sound there came a terrific crash from the front of the warehouse!

Kathulos leaped into frenzied activity. Hissing orders like a cat spitting, he sprang for the hidden door and the rest followed him. Things happened with the speed of a nightmare. Li Kung had followed the rest, but Kathulos flung a command over his shoulder and the Chinaman turned back and came rushing toward the altar where I lay, dagger high, desperation in his countenance.

A scream broke through the clamor and as I twisted desperately about to avoid the descending dagger, I caught a glimpse of Kathulos dragging Zuleika away. Then with a frenzied wrench I toppled from the altar just as Li Kung's dagger, grazing my breast, sank inches deep into the dark-stained surface and quivered there.

I had fallen on the side next to the wall and what was taking place in the room I could not see, but it seemed as if far away I could hear men screaming faintly and hideously. Then Li Kung wrenched his blade free and sprang, tigerishly, around the end of the altar. Simultaneously a revolver cracked from the doorway—the Chinaman spun clear around, the dagger flying from his hand—he slumped to the floor.

Gordon came running from the doorway where a few moments earlier Zuleika had stood, his pistol still smoking in his hand. At his heels were three rangy, clean-cut men in plain clothes. He cut my bonds and dragged me upright.

"Quick! Where have they gone?"

The room was empty of life save for myself, Gordon and his men, though two dead men lay on the floor.

I found the secret door and after a few seconds' search located the lever which opened it. Revolvers drawn, the men grouped about me and peered nervously into the dark stairway. Not a sound came up from the total darkness.

"This is uncanny!" muttered Gordon. "I suppose the Master and his servants went this way when they left the building—as they are certainly not here now!—and Leary and his men should have stopped them either in the tunnel itself or in the rear room of Yun Shatu's. At any rate, in either event they should have communicated with us by this time."

"Look out, sir!" one of the men exclaimed suddenly, and Gordon, with an ejaculation, struck out with his pistol barrel and crushed the life from a huge snake which had crawled silently up the steps from the blackness beneath.

"Let us see into this matter," said he, straightening.

But before he could step onto the first stair, I halted him; for, flesh crawling, I began dimly to understand the silence in the tunnel, the absence of the detectives, the screams I had heard some minutes previously while I lay on the altar. Examining the lever which opened the door, I found another smaller lever—I began to believe I knew what those mysterious chests in the tunnel contained.

"Gordon," I said hoarsely, "have you an electric torch?"

One of the men produced a large one.

"Direct the light into the tunnel, but as you value your life, do not put a foot upon the steps."

The beam of light struck through the shadows, lighting the tunnel, etching out boldly a scene that will haunt my brain all the rest of my life. On the floor of the tunnel, between the chests which now gaped open, lay two men who were members of London's finest secret service. Limbs twisted and faces horribly distorted they lay, and above and about them writhed, in long glittering scaly shimmerings, scores of hideous reptiles.

The clock struck five.

13. The Blind Beggar Who Rode

"He seemed a beggar such as lags
Looking for crusts and ale."
—CHESTERTON

The cold gray dawn was stealing over the river as we stood in the deserted bar of the Temple of Dreams. Gordon was questioning the two men who had remained on guard outside the building while their unfortunate companions went in to explore the tunnel.

"As soon as we heard the whistle, Leary and Murken rushed the bar and broke into the opium room, while we waited here at the bar door according to orders. Right away several ragged dopers came tumbling out and we grabbed them. But no one else came out and we heard nothing from Leary and Murken; so we just waited until you came, sir."

"You saw nothing of a giant Negro, or of the Chinaman Yun Shatu?"

"No, sir. After a while the patrolmen arrived and we threw a cordon around the house, but no one was seen."

Gordon shrugged his shoulders; a few cursory questions had satisfied him that the captives were harmless addicts and he had them released.

"You are sure no one else came out?"

"Yes sir—no, wait a moment. A wretched old blind beggar did come out, all rags and dirt and with a ragged girl leading him. We stopped him but didn't hold him—a wretch like that couldn't be harmful."

"No?" Gordon jerked out. "Which way did he go?"

"The girl led him down the street to the next block and then an automobile stopped and they got in and drove off, sir."

Gordon glared at him.

"The stupidity of the London detective has rightfully become an international jest," he said acidly. "No doubt it never occurred to you as being strange that a Limehouse beggar should ride about in his own automobile."

Then impatiently waving aside the man, who sought to speak further, he turned to me and I saw the lines of weariness beneath his eyes.

"Mr. Costigan, if you will come to my apartment we may be able to clear up some new things."

14. The Black Empire

"Oh the new spears dipped in life-blood as
    the woman shrieked in vain!
Oh the days before the English! When
    will those days come again?"

—MUNDY

Gordon struck a match and absently allowed it to flicker and go out in his hand. His Turkish cigarette hung unlighted between his fingers.

"This is the most logical conclusion to be reached," he was saying. "The weak link in our chain was lack of men. But curse it, one can not round up an army at two o'clock in the morning, even with the aid of Scotland Yard. I went on to Limehouse, leaving orders for a number of patrolmen to follow me as quickly as they could be got together, and to throw a cordon about the house.

"They arrived too late to prevent the Master's servants slipping out of the side doors and windows, no doubt, as they could easily do with only Finnegan and Hansen on guard at the front of the building. However, they arrived in time to prevent the Master himself from slipping out in that way—no doubt he lingered to effect his disguise and was caught in that manner. He owes his escape to his craft and boldness and to the carelessness of Finnegan and Hansen. The girl who accompanied him—"

"She was Zuleika, without doubt."

I answered listlessly, wondering anew what shackles bound her to the Egyptian sorcerer.

"You owe your life to her," Gordon rapped, lighting another match. "We were standing in the shadows in front of the warehouse, waiting for the hour to strike, and of course ignorant as to what was going on in the house, when a girl appeared at one of the barred windows and begged us for God's sake to do something, that a man was being murdered. So we broke in at once. However, she was not to be seen when we entered."

"She returned to the room, no doubt," I muttered, "and was forced to accompany the Master. God grant he knows nothing of her trickery."

"I do not know," said Gordon, dropping the charred match stem, "whether she guessed at our true identity or whether she just made the appeal in desperation.

"However, the main point is this: evidence points to the fact that, on hearing the whistle, Leary and Murkin invaded Yun Shatu's from the front at the same instant my three men and I made our attack on the warehouse front. As it took us some seconds to batter down the door, it is logical to suppose that they found the secret door and entered the tunnel before we effected an entrance into the warehouse.

"The Master, knowing our plans beforehand, and being aware that an invasion would be made through the tunnel and having long ago made preparations for such an exigency—"

An involuntary shudder shook me.

"—the Master worked the lever that opened the chests—the screams you heard as you lay upon the altar were the death shrieks of Leary and Murken. Then, leaving the Chinaman behind to finish you, the Master and the rest descended into the tunnel—incredible as it seems—and threading their way unharmed among the serpents, entered Yun Shatu's house and escaped therefrom as I have said."

"That seems impossible. Why should not the snakes turn on them?"

Gordon finally ignited his cigarette and puffed a few seconds before replying.

"The reptiles might still have been giving their full and hideous attention to the dying men, or else—I have on previous occasions been confronted with indisputable proof of the Master's dominance over beasts and reptiles of even the lowest or most dangerous orders. How he and his slaves passed unhurt among those scaly fiends must remain, at present, one of the many unsolved mysteries pertaining to that strange man."

I stirred restlessly in my chair. This brought up a point for the purpose of clearing up which I had come to Gordon's neat but bizarre apartments.

"You have not yet told me," I said abruptly, "who this man is and what is his mission."

"As to who he is, I can only say that he is known as you name him—the Master. I have never seen him unmasked, nor do I know his real name nor his nationality."

"I can enlighten you to an extent there," I broke in. "I have seen him unmasked and have heard the name his slaves call him."

Gordon's eyes blazed and he leaned forward.

"His name," I continued, "is Kathulos and he claims to be an Egyptian."

"Kathulos!" Gordon repeated. "You say he claims to be an Egyptian—have you any reason for doubting his claim of that nationality?"

"He may be of Egypt," I answered slowly, "but he is different, somehow, from any human I ever saw or hope to see. Great age might account for some of his peculiarities, but there are certain lineal differences that my anthropological studies tell me have been present since birth—features which would be abnormal to any other man but which are perfectly normal in Kathulos. That sounds paradoxical, I admit, but to appreciate fully the horrid inhumanness of the man, you would have to see him yourself."

Gordon sat all attention while I swiftly sketched the appearance of the Egyptian as I remembered him—and that appearance was indelibly etched on my brain forever.

As I finished he nodded.

"As I have said, I never saw Kathulos except when disguised as a beggar, a leper or some such thing—when he was fairly swathed in rags. Still, I too have been impressed with a strange *difference* about him—something that is not present in other men."

Gordon tapped his knee with his fingers—a habit of his when deeply engrossed by a problem of some sort.

"You have asked as to the mission of this man," he began slowly. "I will tell you all I know.

"My position with the British government is a unique and peculiar one. I hold what might be called a roving commission—an office created solely for the purpose of suiting my special needs. As a secret service official during the war, I convined the powers of a need of such office and of my ability to fill it.

"Somewhat over seventeen months ago I was sent to South Africa to investigate the unrest which has been growing among the natives of the interior ever since the World War and which has of late assumed alarming proportions. There I first got on the track of this man Kathulos. I found, in roundabout ways, that Africa was a seething cauldron of rebellion from Morocco to Cape Town. The old, old vow had been made again—the Negroes and the Mohammedans, banded together, should drive the white men into the sea.

"This pact has been made before but always, hitherto, broken. Now, however, I sensed a giant intellect and a monstrous genius behind the veil, a genius powerful enough to accomplish this union and hold it together. Working entirely on hints and vague whispered clues, I followed the trail up through Central Africa and into Egypt. There, at last, I came upon definite evidence that such a man existed. The whispers hinted of a living dead man—*a skull-faced* man. I learned that this man was the high priest of the mysterious Scorpion society of northern Africa. He was spoken of variously as Skull-face, the Master, and the Scorpion.

"Following a trail of bribed officials and filched state secrets, I at last trailed him to Alexandria, where I had my first sight of him in a dive in the native quarter—disguised as a leper. I heard him distinctly addressed as 'mighty Scorpion' by the natives, but he escaped me.

"All trace vanished then; the trail ran out entirely until rumors of strange happenings in London reached me and I came back to England to investigate an apparent leak in the War Office.

"As I thought, the Scorpion had preceded me. This man, whose education and craft transcend anything I ever met with, is simply the leader and instigator of a world-wide movement such as the world has never seen before. He plots, in a word, the overthrow of the white races!

"His ultimate aim is a black empire, with himself as emperor of the world! And to that end he has banded together in one monstrous conspiracy the black, the brown and the yellow."

"I understand now what Yussef Ali meant when he said 'the days of the empire'," I muttered.

"Exactly," Gordon rapped with suppressed excitement. "Kathulos' power is unlimited and unguessed. Like an octopus his tentacles stretch to the high places of civilization and the far corners of the world. And his main weapon is—dope! He has flooded Europe and no doubt America with opium and hashish, and in spite of all effort it has been impossible to discover the break in the barriers through which the hellish stuff is coming. With this he ensnares and enslaves men and women.

"You have told me of the aristocratic men and women you saw coming to Yun Shatu's dive. Without doubt they were dope addicts—for, as I said, the habit lurks in high places—holders of governmental positions, no doubt, coming to trade for the stuff they craved and giving in return state secrets, inside information and promise of protection for the Master's crimes.

"Oh, he does not work haphazardly! Before ever the black flood breaks, he will be prepared; if he has his way, the governments of the white races will be honeycombs of corruption—the strongest men of the white races will be dead. The white men's secrets of war will be his. When it comes, I look for a simultaneous uprising against white supremacy, of all the colored races—races who, in the last war, learned the white men's way of battle, and who, led by such a man as Kathulos and armed with white men's finest weapons, will be almost invincible.

"A steady stream of rifles and ammunition has been pouring into East Africa and it was not until I discovered the source that it was stopped. I found that a staid and reliable Scotch firm was smuggling these arms among the natives and I found more: the manager of this firm was an opium slave. That was enough. I saw Kathulos' hand in the matter. The manager was arrested and committed suicide in his cell—that is only one of the many situations with which I am called upon to deal.

"Again, the case of Major Fairlan Morley. He, like myself, held a very flexible commission and had been sent to the Transvaal to work upon the same case. He sent to London a number of secret papers for safe-keeping. They arrived some weeks ago and were put in a bank vault. The letter accompanying them gave explicit instructions that they were to be delivered to no one but the Major himself, when he called for them in person, or in event of his death, to myself.

"As soon as I learned that he had sailed from Africa I sent trusted men to Bordeaux, where he intended to make his first landing in Europe. They did not succeed in saving the Major's life, but they certified his death, for they found his body in a deserted ship whose hulk was stranded on the beach. Efforts were made to keep the affair a secret but somehow it leaked into the papers with the result—"

"I begin to understand why I was to impersonate the unfortunate Major," I interrupted.

"Exactly. A false beard furnished you, and your black hair dyed blond, you would have presented yourself at the bank, received the papers from the banker, who knew Major Morley just intimately enough to be deceived by your appearance, and the papers would have then fallen into the hands of the Master.

"I can only guess at the contents of those papers, for events have been taking place too swiftly for me to call for and obtain them. But they must deal with subjects closely connected with the activities of Kathulos. How he learned of them and of the provisions of the letter accompanying them, I have no idea, but as I said, London is honeycombed with his spies.

"In my search for clues, I often frequented Limehouse disguised as you first saw me. I went often to the Temple of Dreams and even once managed to enter the back room, for I suspected some sort of rendezvous in the rear of the building. The absence of any exit baffled me and I had no time to search for secret doors before I was ejected by the giant black man Hassim, who had no suspicion of my true identity. I noticed that very often the leper entered or left Yun Shatu's, and finally it was borne on me that past a shadow of doubt this supposed leper was the Scorpion himself.

"That night you discovered me on the couch in the opium room, I had come there with no especial plan in mind. Seeing Kathulos leaving, I determined to rise and follow him, but you spoiled that."

He fingered his chin and laughed grimly.

"I was an amateur boxing champion in Oxford," said he, "but Tom Cribb himself could not have withstood that blow—or have dealt it."

"I regret it as I regret few things."

"No need to apologize. You saved my life immediately afterward—I was stunned, but not too much to know that that brown devil Yussef Ali was burning to cut out my heart."

"How did you come to be at Sir Haldred Frenton's estate? And how is it that you did not raid Yun Shatu's dive?"

"I did not have the place raided because I knew somehow Kathulos would be warned and our efforts would come to naught. I was at Sir Haldred's that night because I have contrived to spend at least part of each night with him since he returned from the Congo. I anticipated an attempt upon his life when I learned from his own lips that he was preparing, from the studies he made on this trip, a treatise on the secret native societies of West Africa. He hinted that the disclosures he intended to make therein might prove sensational, to say the least. Since it is to Kathulos' advantage to destroy such men as might be able to arouse the Western world to its danger, I knew that Sir Haldred was a marked man. Indeed, two distinct attempts were made upon his life on his journey to the coast from the African interior. So I put two trusted men on guard and they are at their post even now.

"Roaming about the darkened house, I heard the noise of your entry, and, warning my men, I stole down to intercept you. At the time of our conversation, Sir Haldred was sitting in his unlighted study, a Scotland Yard man with drawn pistol on each side of him. Their vigilance no doubt accounts for Yussef Ali's failure to attempt what you were sent to do.

"Something in your manner convinced me in spite of yourself," he meditated. "I will admit I had some bad moments of doubt as I waited in the darkness that precedes dawn, outside the warehouse."

Gordon rose suddenly and going to a strongbox which stood in a corner of the room, drew thence a thick envelope.

"Although Kathulos has checkmated me at almost every move," he said, "I have not been entrely idle. Noting the frequenters of Yun Shatu's, I have compiled a partial list of the Egyptian's right-hand men, and their records. What you have told me has enabled me to complete that list. As we know, his henchmen are scattered all over the world, and there are possibly hundreds of them here in London. However, this is a list of those I believe to be in his closest council, now with him in England. He told you himself that few even of his followers ever saw him unmasked."

We bent together over the list, which contained the following names: "Yun Shatu, Hong Kong Chinese, suspected opium smuggler—keeper of Temple of Dreams—resident of Limehouse seven years. Hassim, ex-Senegalese chief—wanted in French Congo for murder. Santiago, Negro—fled from Haiti under suspicion of voodoo worship atrocities. Yar Khan, Afridi, record unknown. Yussef Ali, Moor, slavedealer in Morocco—suspected of being a German spy in the World War—an instigator of the Fellaheen Rebellion on the upper Nile. Ganra Singh, Lahore, India, Sikh—smuggler of arms into

Afghanistan—took an active part in the Lahore and Delhi riots—suspected of murder on two occasions—a dangerous man. Stephen Costigan, American—resident in England since the war—hashish addict—man of remarkable strength. Li Kung, northern China, opium smuggler."

Lines were drawn significantly through three names—mine, Li Kung's and Yussef Ali's. Nothing was written next to mine, but following Li Kung's name was scrawled briefly in Gordon's rambling characters: "Shot by John Gordon during the raid on Yun Shatu's." And following the name of Yussef Ali: "Killed by Stephen Costigan during the Yun Shatu raid."

I laughed mirthlessly. Black empire or not, Yussef Ali would never hold Zuleika in his arms, for he had never risen from where I felled him.

"I know not," said Gordon somberly as he folded the list and replaced it in the envelope, "what power Kathulos has that draws together black men and yellow men to serve him—that unites world-old foes. Hindoo, Moslem and pagan are among his followers. And back in the mists of the East where mysterious and gigantic forces are at work, this uniting is culminating on a monstrous scale."

He glanced at his watch.

"It is nearly ten. Make yourself at home here, Mr. Costigan, while I visit Scotland Yard and see if any clue has been found as to Kathulos' new quarters. I believe that the webs are closing on him, and with your aid I promise you we will have the gang located within a week at most."

15. The Mark of the Tulwar

"The fed world curls by his drowsy mate
In a tight-trod earth; but the lean wolves wait."
—MUNDY

I sat alone in John Gordon's apartments and laughed mirthlessly. In spite of the elixir's stimulus, the strain of the previous night, with its loss of sleep and its heartrending actions, was telling on me. My mind was a chaotic whirl wherein the faces of Gordon, Kathulos and Zuleika shifted with numbing swiftness. All the mass of information Gordon had given to me seemed jumbled and incoherent.

Through this state of being, one fact stood out boldly. I must find the latest hiding-place of the Egyptian and get Zuleika out of his hands—if indeed she still lived.

A week, Gordon had said—I laughed again—a week and I would be beyond aiding anyone. I had found the proper amount of elixir to use—knew the minimum amount my system required—and knew that I could make the flask last me four days at most. Four days! Four days in which to comb the rat-holes of Limehouse and Chinatown—four days in which to ferret out, somewhere in the mazes of East End, the lair of Kathulos.

I burned with impatience to begin, but nature rebelled, and

staggering to a couch, I fell upon it and was asleep instantly.

Then someone was shaking me.

"Wake up, Mr. Costigan!"

I sat up, blinking. Gordon stood over me, his face haggard.

"There's devil's work done, Costigan! The Scorpion has struck again!"

I sprang up, still half asleep and only partly realizing what he was saying. He helped me into my coat, thrust my hat at me, and then his firm grip on my arm was propelling me out of his door and down the stairs. The street lights were blazing; I had slept an incredible time.

"A logical victim!" I was aware that my companion was saying. "He should have notified me the instant of his arrival!"

"I don't understand—" I began dazedly.

We were at the curb now and Gordon hailed a taxi, giving the address of a small and unassuming hotel in a staid and prim section of the city.

"The Baron Rokoff," he rapped as we whirled along at reckless speed, "a Russian free-lance, connected with the War Office. He returned from Mongolia yesterday and apparently went into hiding. Undoubtedly he had learned something vital in regard to the slow waking of the East. He had not yet communicated with us, and I had no idea that he was in England until just now."

"And you learned—"

"The baron was found in his room, his dead body mutilated in a frightful manner!"

The respectable and conventional hotel which the doomed baron had chosen for his hiding-place was in a state of mild uproar, being suppressed by the police. The management had attempted to keep the matter quiet, but somehow the guests had learned of the atrocity and many were leaving in haste—or preparing to, as the police were planning to hold all for investigation.

The baron's room, which was on the top floor, was in a state to defy description. Not even in the Great War have I seen a more complete shambles. Nothing had been touched; all remained just as the chambermaid had found it a half-hour since. Tables and chairs lay shattered on the floor, and the furniture, floor and walls were spattered with blood. The baron, a tall, muscular man in life, lay in the middle of the room, a fearful spectacle. His skull had been cleft to the brows, a deep gash under his left armpit had shorn through his ribs, and his left arm hung by a shred of flesh. The cold bearded face was set in a look of indescribable horror.

"Some heavy, curved weapon must have been used," said Gordon, "something like a saber, wielded with terrific force. See where a chance blow sank inches deep into the windowsill. And again, the thick back of this heavy chair has been split like a shingle. A saber, surely."

"A tulwar," I muttered, somberly. "Do you not recognize the handiwork of the Central Asian butcher? Yar Khan has been here."

"The Afghan! He came across the roofs, of course, and descended to the window-ledge by means of a knotted rope made fast to something on the edge of the roof. About one-thirty the maid, passing the corridor, heard a terrific commotion in the baron's room—smashing of chairs and a sudden short shriek which died abruptly into a ghastly gurgle and then ceased—to the sound of heavy blows, curiously muffled, such as a sword might make when driven deep into human flesh. Then all noises stopped suddenly.

"She called the manager and they tried the door and, finding it locked, and receiving no answer to their shouts, opened it with the desk key. Only the corpse was there, but the window was open. This is strangely unlike Kathulos' usual procedure. It lacks subtlety. Often his victims have appeared to have died from natural causes. I scarcely understand."

"I see little difference in the outcome," I answered. "There is nothing that can be done to apprehend the murderer as it is."

"True," Gordon scowled. "We know who did it but there is no proof—not even a fingerprint. Even if we knew where the Afghan is hiding and arrested him, we could prove nothing— there would be a score of men to swear alibis for him. The baron returned only yesterday. Kathulos probably did not know of his arrival until tonight. He knew that on the morrow Rokoff would make known his presence to me and impart what he learned in northern Asia. The Egyptian knew he must strike quickly, and lacking time to prepare a safer and more elaborate form of murder, he sent the Afridi with his tulwar. There is nothing we can do, at least not until we discover the Scorpion's hiding-place; what the baron had learned in Mongolia, we shall never know, but that it dealt with the plans and aspirations of Kathulos, we may be sure."

We went down the stairs again and out on the street, accompanied by one of the Scotland Yard men, Hansen. Gordon suggested that we walk back to his apartment and I greeted the opportunity to let the cool night air blow some of the cobwebs out of my mazed brain.

As we walked along the deserted streets, Gordon suddenly cursed savagely.

"This is a veritable labyrinth we are following, leading nowhere! Here, in the very heart of civilization's metropolis, the direct enemy of that civilization commits crimes of the most outrageous nature and goes free! We are children, wandering in the night, struggling with an unseen evil—dealing with an incarnate devil, of whose true identity we know nothing and whose true ambitions we can only guess.

"Never have we managed to arrest one of the Egyptian's direct henchmen, and the few dupes and tools of his we have apprehended have died mysteriously before they could tell us anything. Again I repeat: what strange power has Kathulos that dominates these men of different creeds and races? The men in London with him are, of course, mostly renegades, slaves of dope, but his tentacles stretch all over the East. Some dominance is his: the power that sent the Chinaman, Li Kung, back to kill you, in the face of certain death; that sent Yar Khan the Moslem over the roofs of London to do murder; that holds Zuleika the Circassian in unseen bounds of slavery.

"Of course we know," he continued after a brooding silence, "that the East has secret societies which are behind and above all considerations of creeds. There are cults in Africa and the Orient whose origin dates back to Ophir and the fall of Atlantis. This man must be a power in some or possibly all of these societies. Why, outside the Jews, I know of no Oriental race which is so cordially despised by the other Eastern races, as the Egyptians! Yet here we have a man, an Egyptian by his own word, controlling the lives and destinies of orthodox Moslems, Hindoos, Shintos and devil-worshippers. It's unnatural.

"Have you ever"—he turned to me abruptly—"heard the ocean mentioned in connection with Kathulos?"

"Never."

"There is a widespread superstition in northern Africa, based on a very ancient legend, that the great leader of the colored races would come out of the sea! And I once heard a Berber speak of the Scorpion as 'The Son of the Ocean'."

"That is a term of respect among that tribe, is it not?"

"Yes; still I wonder sometimes."

16. The Mummy Who Laughed

"Laughing as littered skulls that lie
After lost battles turn to the sky
An everlasting laugh."

—CHESTERTON

"A shop open this late," Gordon remarked suddenly.

A fog had descended on London and along the quiet street we were traversing the lights glimmered with the peculiar reddish haze characteristic of such atmospheric conditions. Our footfalls echoed drearily. Even in the heart of a great city there are always sections which seem overlooked and forgotten. Such a street was this. Not even a policeman was in sight.

The shop which had attracted Gordon's attention was just in front of us, on the same side of the street. There was no sign over the door, merely some sort of emblem something like a dragon. Light flowed from the open doorway and the small show windows on each side. As it was neither a café nor the entrance to a hotel we found ourselves idly speculating over its reason for being open. Ordinarily, I suppose, neither of us would have given the matter a thought, but our nerves were so keyed up that we found ourselves instinctively suspicious of anything out of the ordinary. Then something occurred which was distinctly out of the ordinary.

A very tall, very thin man, considerably stooped, suddenly loomed up out of the fog in front of us, and beyond the shop. I had only a glance of him—an impression of incredible gauntness, of worn, wrinkled garments, a high silk hat drawn close over the brows, a face entirely hidden by a muffler; then he turned aside and entered the shop. A cold wind whispered down

the street, twisting the fog into wispy ghosts, but the coldness
that came upon me transcended the wind's.

"Gordon!" I exclaimed in a fierce, low voice; "my senses are
no longer reliable or else Kathulos himself has just gone into that
house!"

Gordon's eyes blazed. We were now close to the shop, and
lengthening his strides into a run he hurled himself into the door,
the detective and I close upon his heels.

A weird assortment of merchandise met our eyes. Antique
weapons covered the walls, and the floor was piled high with
curious things. Maori idols shouldered Chinese josses, and suits
of mediaeval armor bulked darkly against stacks of rare
Oriental rugs and Latin-make shawls. The place was an antique
shop. Of the figure who had aroused our interest we saw
nothing.

An old man clad bizarrely in red fez, brocaded jacket and
Turkish slippers came from the back of the shop; he was a
Levantine of some sort.

"You wish something, sirs?"

"You keep open rather late," Gordon said abruptly, his eyes
traveling swiftly over the shop for some secret hiding place that
might conceal the object of our search.

"Yes, sir. My customers number many eccentric professors
and students who keep very irregular hours. Often the night
boats unload special pieces for me and very often I have
customers later than this. I remain open all night, sir."

"We are merely looking around," Gordon returned, and in an
aside to Hansen: "Go to the back and stop anyone who tries to
leave that way."

Hansen nodded and strolled casually to the rear of the shop.
The back door was clearly visible to our view, through a vista of
antique furniture and tarnished hangings strung up for
exhibition. We had followed the Scorpion—if he it was—so
closely that I did not believe he would have had time to traverse
the full length of the shop and make his exit without our having
seen him as we came in. For our eyes had been on the rear door
ever since we had entered.

Gordon and I browsed around casually among the curios,
handling and discussing some of them but I have no idea as to
their nature. The Levantine had seated himself cross-legged on a
Moorish mat close to the center of the shop and apparently took
only a polite interest in our explorations.

After a time Gordon whispered to me: "There is no advantage in keeping up this pretense. We have looked everywhere the Scorpion might be hiding, in the ordinary manner. I will make known my identity and authority and we will search the entire building openly."

Even as he spoke a truck drew up outside the door and two burly Negroes entered. The Levantine seemed to have expected them, for he merely waved them toward the back of the shop and they responded with a grunt of understanding.

Gordon and I watched them closely as they made their way to a large mummy-case which stood upright against the wall not far from the back. They lowered this to a level position and then started for the door, carrying it carefully between them.

"Halt!" Gordon stepped forward, raising his hand authoritatively.

"I represent Scotland Yard," he said swiftly, "and have sanction for anything I choose to do. Set that mummy down; nothing leaves this shop until we have thoroughly searched it."

The Negroes obeyed without a word and my friend turned to the Levantine, who, apparently not perturbed or even interested, sat smoking a Turkish water-pipe.

"Who was that tall man who entered just before we did, and where did he go?"

"No one entered before you, sir. Or, if anyone did, I was at the back of the shop and did not see him. You are certainly at liberty to search my shop, sir."

And search it we did, with the combined craft of a secret service expert and a denizen of the underworld—while Hansen stood stolidly at his post, the two Negroes standing over the carved mummy-case watched us impassively and the Levantine sitting like a sphinx on his mat, puffing a fog of smoke into the air. The whole thing had a distinct effect of unreality.

At last, baffled, we returned to the mummy-case, which was certainly long enough to conceal even a man of Kathulos' height. The thing did not appear to be sealed as is the usual custom, and Gordon opened it without difficulty. A formless shape, swathed in moldering wrapping, met our eyes. Gordon parted some of the wrappings and revealed an inch or so of withered, brownish, leathery arm. He shuddered involuntarily as he touched it, as a man will do at the touch of a reptile or some inhumanly cold thing. Taking a small metal idol from a stand near by, he rapped on the shrunken breast and the arm. Each gave out a solid thumping, like some sort of wood.

Gordon shrugged his shoulders. "Dead for two thousand years anyway and I don't suppose I should risk destroying a valuable mummy simply to prove what we know to be true."

He closed the case again.

"The mummy may have crumbled some, even for this much exposure, but perhaps it did not."

This last was addressed to the Levantine who replied merely by a courteous gesture of his hand, and the Negroes once more lifted the case and carried it to the truck, where they loaded it on, and a moment later mummy, truck and Negroes had vanished in the fog.

Gordon still nosed about the shop, but I stood stock-still in the center of the floor. To my chaotic and dope-ridden brain I attributed it, but the sensation had been mine, that through the wrappings of the mummy's face, great eyes had burned into mine, eyes like pools of yellow fire, that seared my soul and froze me where I stood. And as the case had been carried through the door, I knew that the lifeless thing in it, dead, God only knows how many centuries, was *laughing*, hideously and silently.

17. The Dead Man from the Sea

Gordon puffed savagely at his Turkish cigarette, staring abstractedly and unseeingly at Hansen, who sat opposite him.

"I suppose we must chalk up another failure against ourselves. That Levantine, Kamonos, is evidently a creature of the Egyptian's and the walls and floors of his shop are probably honeycombed with secret panels and doors which would baffle a magician."

Hansen made some answer but I said nothing. Since our return to Gordon's apartment, I had been conscious of a feeling of intense languor and sluggishness which not even my condition could account for. I knew that my system was full of elixir—but my mind seemed strangely slow and hard of comprehension in direct contrast with the average state of my mentality when stimulated by the hellish dope.

This condition was slowly leaving me, like mist floating from the surface of a lake, and I felt as if I were waking gradually from a long and unnaturally sound sleep.

Gordon was saying: "I would give a good deal to know if Kamonos is really one of Kathulos' slaves or if the Scorpion managed to make his escape through some natural exit as we entered."

"Kamonos is his servant, true enough," I found myself saying slowly, as if searching for the proper words. "As we left, I saw his gaze light upon the scorpion which is traced on my hand. His eyes narrowed, and as we were leaving he contrived to brush close against me—and to whisper in a quick low voice: 'Soho, 48.'"

Gordon came erect like a loosened steel bow.

"Indeed!" he rapped. "Why did you not tell me at the time?"

"I don't know."

My friend eyed me sharply.

"I noticed you seemed like a man intoxicated all the way from the shop," said he. "I attributed it to some aftermath of hashish. But no. Kathulos is undoubtedly a masterful disciple of Mesmer—his power over venomous reptiles shows that, and I am beginning to believe it is the real source of his power over humans.

"Somehow, the Master caught you off your guard in that shop and partly asserted his dominance over your mind. From what hidden nook he sent his thought waves to shatter your brain, I do not know, but Kathulos was somewhere in that shop, I am sure."

"He was. He was in the mummy-case."

"The mummy-case!" Gordon exclaimed rather impatiently. "That is impossible! The mummy quite filled it and not even such a thin being as the Master could have found room there."

I shrugged my shoulders, unable to argue the point but somehow sure of the truth of my statement.

"Kamonos," Gordon continued, "doubtless is not a member of the inner circle and does not know of your change of allegiance. Seeing the mark of the scorpion, he undoubtedly supposed you to be a spy of the Master's. The whole thing may be a plot to ensnare us, but I feel that the man was sincere—Soho 48 can be nothing less than the Scorpion's new rendezvous."

I too felt that Gordon was right, though a suspicion lurked in my mind.

"I secured the papers of Major Morley yesterday," he continued, "and while you slept, I went over them. Mostly they but corroborated what I already knew—touched on the unrest of the natives and repeated the theory that one vast genius was behind all. But there was one matter which interested me greatly and which I think will interest you also."

From his strongbox he took a manuscript written in the close, neat characters of the unfortunate Major, and in a monotonous droning voice which betrayed little of his intense excitement he read the following nightmarish narrative:

"This matter I consider worth jotting down—as to whether it has any bearing on the case at hand, further developments will show. At Alexandria, where I spent some weeks seeking further clues as to the identity of the man known as the Scorpion, I made the acquaintance, through my friend Ahmed Shah, of the noted Egyptologist Professor Ezra Schuyler of New York. He verified the statement made by various laymen, concerning the legend of the 'ocean-man.' This myth, handed down from generation to generation, stretches back into the very mists of antiquity and is, briefly, that some day a man shall come up out of the sea and shall lead the people of Egypt to victory over all others. This legend has spread over the continent so that now all black races consider that it deals with the coming of a universal emperor. Professor Schuyler gave it as his opinion that the myth was somehow connected with the lost Atlantis, which, he maintains, was located between the African and South American continents and to whose inhabitants the ancestors of the Egyptians were tributary. The reasons for his connection are too lengthy and vague to note here, but following the line of his theory he told me a strange and fantastic tale. He said that a close friend of his, Von Lorfmon of Germany, a sort of free-lance scientist, now dead, was sailing off the coast of Senegal some years ago, for the purpose of investigating and classifying the rare specimens of sea life found there. He was using for his purpose a small trading-vessel, manned by a crew of Moors, Greeks and Negroes.

"Some days out of sight of land, something floating was sighted, and this object, being grappled and brought aboard, proved to be a *mummy-case of a most curious kind.* Professor Schuyler explained to me the features whereby it differed from the ordinary Egýptian style, but from his rather technical account I merely got the impression that it was a strangely shaped affair carved with characters neither cuneiform nor hieroglyphic. The case was heavily lacquered, being watertight and airtight, and Von Lorfmon had considerable difficulty in opening it. However, he managed to do so without damaging the case, and a most unusual mummy was revealed. Schuyler said that he never saw either the mummy or the case, but that from descriptions given him by the Greek skipper who was present at the opening of the case, the mummy differed as much from the ordinary man as the case differed from the conventional type.

"Examination proved that the subject had not undergone the

usual procedure of mummification. All parts were intact just as in life, but the whole form was shrunk and hardened to a wood-like consistency. Cloth wrappings swathed the thing and they crumbled to dust and vanished the instant air was let in upon them.

"Von Lorfmon was impressed by the effect on the crew. The Greeks showed no interest beyond that which would ordinarily be shown by any man, but the Moors, and even more the Negroes, seemed to be rendered temporarily insane! As the case was hoisted on board, they all fell prostrate on the deck and raised a sort of worshipful chant, and it was necessary to use force in order to exclude them from the cabin wherein the mummy was exposed. A number of fights broke out between them and the Greek element of the crew, and the skipper and Von Lorfmon thought best to put back to the nearest port in all haste. The skipper attributed it to the natural aversion of seamen toward having a corpse on board, but Von Lorfmon seemed to sense a deeper meaning.

"They made port in Lagos, and that very night Von Lorfmon was murdered in his stateroom and the mummy and its case vanished. All the Moor and Negro sailors deserted ship the same night. Schuyler said—and here the matter took on a most sinister and mysterious aspect—that immediately afterward this widespread unrest among the natives began to smolder and take tangible form; he connected it in some manner with the old legend.

"An aura of mystery, also, hung over Von Lorfmon's death. He had taken the mummy into his stateroom, and anticipating an attack from the fanatical crew, had carefully barred and bolted door and portholes. The skipper, a reliable man, swore that it was virtually impossible to effect an entrance from without. And what signs were present pointed to the fact that the locks had been worked from *within*. The scientist was killed by a dagger which formed part of his collection and which was left in his breast.

"As I have said, immediately afterward the African cauldron began to seethe. Schuyler said that in his opinion the natives considered the ancient prophecy fulfilled. The mummy was *the man from the sea*.

"Schuyler gave as his opinion that the thing was the work of Atlanteans and that the man in the mummy-case was a native of

lost Atlantis. How the case came to float up through the fathoms
of water which cover the forgotten land, he does not venture to
offer a theory. He is sure that somewhere in the ghost-ridden
mazes of the African jungles the mummy has been enthroned as
a god, and, inspired by the dead thing, the black warriors are
gathering for a wholesale massacre. He believes, also, that some
crafty Moslem is the direct moving power of the threatened
rebellion."

Gordon ceased and looked up at me.

"Mummies seem to weave a weird dance through the warp of
the tale," he said. "The German scientist took several pictures of
the mummy with his camera, and it was after seeing these—
which strangely enough were not stolen along with the thing—
that Major Morley began to think himself on the brink of some
monstrous discovery. His diary reflects his state of mind and
becomes incoherent—his condition seems to have bordered on
insanity. What did he learn to unbalance him so? Do you
suppose that the mesmeric spells of Kathulos were used against
him?"

"These pictures—" I began.

"They fell into Schuyler's hands and he gave one to Morley. I
found it among the manuscripts."

He handed the thing to me, watching me narrowly. I stared,
then rose unsteadily and poured myself a tumbler of wine.

"Not a dead idol in a voodoo hut," I said shakily, "but a
monster animated by fearsome life, roaming the world for
victims. Morley had seen the Master—that is why his brain
crumbled. Gordon, as I hope to live again, *that face is the face of
Kathulos!*"

Gordon stared wordlessly at me.

"The Master hand, Gordon," I laughed. A certain grim
enjoyment penetrated the mists of my horror, at the sight of the
steel-nerved Englishman struck speechless, doubtless for the
first time in his life.

He moistened his lips and said in a scarcely recognizable
voice, "Then, in God's name, Costigan, nothing is stable or
certain, and mankind hovers at the brink of untold abysses of
nameless horror. If that dead monster found by Von Lorfmon
be in truth the Scorpion, brought to life in some hideous fashion,
what can mortal effort do against him?"

"The mummy at Kamonos's—" I began.

"Aye, the man whose flesh, hardened by a thousand years of non-existence—that must have been Kathulos himself! He would have just had time to strip, wrap himself in the linens and step into the case before we entered. You remember that the case, leaning upright against the wall, stood partly concealed by a large Burmese idol, which obstructed our view and doubtless gave him time to accomplish his purpose. My God, Costigan, with what horror of the prehistoric world are we dealing?"

"I have heard of Hindoo fakirs who could induce a condition closely resembling death," I began. "Is it not possible that Kathulos, a shrewd and crafty Oriental, could have placed himself in this state and his followers have placed the case in the ocean where it was sure to be found? And might not he have been in this shape tonight at Kamonos's?"

Gordon shook his head.

"No. I have seen these fakirs. None of them ever feigned death to the extent of becoming shriveled and hard—in a word, dried up. Morley, narrating in another place the description of the mummy-case as jotted down by Von Lorfmon and passed on to Schuyler, mentions the fact that large portions of seaweed adhered to it—seaweed of a kind found only at great depths, on the bottom of the ocean. The wood, too, was of a kind which Von Lorfmon failed to recognize or to classify, in spite of the fact that he was one of the greatest living authorities on flora. And his notes again and again emphasize the enormous *age* of the thing. He admitted that there was no way of telling how old the mummy was, but his hints intimate that he believed it to be, not thousands of years old, but millions of years!

"No. We must face the facts. Since you are positive that the picture of the mummy is the picture of Kathulos—and there is little room for fraud—one of two things is practically certain: the Scorpion was never dead but ages ago was placed in that mummy-case and his life preserved in some manner, or else—he was dead and has been brought to life! Either of these theories, viewed in the cold light of reason, is absolutely untenable. Are we all insane?"

"Had you ever walked the road to hashish land," I said somberly, "you could believe anything to be true. Had you ever gazed into the terrible reptilian eyes of Kathulos the sorcerer, you would not doubt that he was both dead and alive."

Gordon gazed out the window, his fine face haggard in the

gray light which had begun to steal through them.

"At any rate," said he, "there are two places which I intend exploring thoroughly before the sun rises again—Kamonos' antique shop and Soho 48."

18. The Grip of the Scorpion

"While from a proud tower in the town
Death looks gigantically down."

—POE

Hansen snored on the bed as I paced the room. Another day had passed over London and again the street lamps glimmered through the fog. Their lights affected me strangely. They seemed to beat, solid waves of energy, against my brain. They twisted the fog into strange sinister shapes. Footlights of the stage that is the streets of London, how many grisly scenes had they lighted? I pressed my hands hard against my throbbing temples, striving to bring my thoughts back from the chaotic labyrinth where they wandered.

Gordon I had not seen since dawn. Following the clue of "Soho 48" he had gone forth to arrange a raid upon the place and he thought it best that I should remain under cover. He anticipated an attempt upon my life, and again he feared that if I went searching among the dives I formerly frequented it would arouse suspicion.

Hansen snored on. I seated myself and began to study the Turkish shoes which clothed my feet. Zuleika had worn Turkish slippers—how she floated through my waking dreams, gilding prosaic things with her witchery! Her face smiled at me from the fog; her eyes shone from the flickering lamps; her phantom footfalls re-echoed through the misty chambers of my skull.

They beat an endless tattoo, luring and haunting till it seemed that these echoes found echoes in the hallway outside the room where I stood, soft and stealthy. A sudden rap at the door and I started.

Hansen slept on as I crossed the room and flung the door swiftly open. A swirling wisp of fog had invaded the corridor, and through it, like a silver veil, I saw her—Zuleika stood before me with her shimmering hair and her red lips parted and her great dark eyes.

Like a speechless fool I stood and she glanced quickly down the hallway and then stepped inside and closed the door.

"Gordon!" she whispered in a thrilling undertone. "Your friend! The Scorpion has him!"

Hansen had awakened and now sat gaping stupidly at the strange scene which met his eyes.

Zuleika did not heed him.

"And oh, Steephen!" she cried, and tears shone in her eyes, "I have tried so hard to secure some more elixir but I could not."

"Never mind that," I finally found my speech. "Tell me about Gordon."

"He went back to Kamonos's alone, and Hassim and Ganra Singh took him captive and brought him to the Master's house. Tonight assemble a great host of the people of the Scorpion for the sacrifice."

"Sacrifice!" A grisly thrill of horror coursed down my spine. Was there no limit to the ghastliness of this business?

"Quick, Zuleika, where is this house of the Master's?"

"Soho 48. You must summon the police and send many men to surround it, but you must not go yourself—"

Hansen sprang up quivering for action, but I turned to him. My brain was clear now, or seemed to be, and racing unnaturally.

"Wait!" I turned back to Zuleika. "When is this sacrifice to take place?"

"At the rising of the moon."

"That is only a few hours before dawn. Time to save him, but if we raid the house they'll kill him before we can reach them. And God only knows how many diabolical things guard all approaches."

"I do not know," Zuleika whimpered. "I must go now, or the Master will kill me."

Something gave way in my brain at that; something like a flood of wild and terrible exultation swept over me.

"The Master will kill no one!" I shouted, flinging my arms on high. "Before ever the east turns red for dawn, the Master dies! By all things holy and unholy I swear it!"

Hansen stared wildly at me and Zuleika shrank back as I turned on her. To my dope-inspired brain had come a sudden burst of light, true and unerring.

I knew Kathulos was a mesmerist—that he understood fully the secret of dominating another's mind and soul. And I knew that at last I had hit upon the reason of his power over the girl. Mesmerism! As a snake fascinates and draws to him a bird, so the Master held Zuleika to him with unseen shackles. So absolute was his rule over her that it held even when she was out of his sight, working over great distances.

There was but one thing which would break that hold: the magnetic power of some other person whose control was stronger with her than Kathulos's. I laid my hands on her slim little shoulders and made her face me.

"Zuleika," I said commandingly, "here you are safe; you shall not return to Kathulos. There is no need of it. Now you are free."

But I knew I had failed before I ever started. Her eyes held a look of amazed, unreasoning fear and she twisted timidly in my grasp.

"Steephen, please let me go!" she begged. "I must—I must!"

I drew her over to the bed and asked Hansen for his handcuffs. He handed them to me, wonderingly, and I fastened one cuff to the bed-post and the other to her slim wrist. The girl whimpered but made no resistance, her limpid eyes seeking mine in mute appeal.

It cut me to the quick to enforce my will upon her in this apparently brutal manner but I steeled myself.

"Zuleika," I said tenderly, "you are now my prisoner. The Scorpion can not blame you for not returning to him when you are unable to do so—and before dawn you shall be free of his rule entirely."

I turned to Hansen and spoke in a tone which admitted of no argument.

"Remain here, just without the door, until I return. On no account allow any strangers to enter—that is, anyone whom you do not personally know. And I charge you, on your honor as a man, do not release this girl, no matter what she may say. If neither I nor Gordon have returned by ten o'clock tomorrow, take her to this address—that family once were friends of mine and will take care of a homeless girl. I am going to Scotland Yard."

"Steephen," Zuleika wailed, "you are going to the Master's lair? You will be killed. Send the police, do not go!"

I bent, drew her into my arms, felt her lips against mine, then tore myself away.

The fog plucked at me with ghostly fingers, cold as the hands of dead men, as I raced down the street. I had no plan, but one was forming in my mind, beginning to seethe in the stimulated cauldron that was my brain. I halted at the sight of a policeman pacing his beat, and beckoning him to me, scribbled a terse note on a piece of paper torn from a notebook and handed it to him.

"Get this to Scotland Yard; it's a matter of life and death and it has to do with the business of John Gordon."

At that name, a gloved hand came up in swift assent, but his assurance of haste died out behind me as I renewed my flight. The note stated briefly that Gordon was a prisoner at Soho 48 and advised an immediate raid in force—advised, nay, in Gordon's name, commanded it.

My reason for my actions was simple; I knew that the first noise of the raid sealed John Gordon's doom. Somehow I first must reach him and protect or free him before the police arrived.

The time seemed endless, but at last the grim gaunt outlines of the house that was Soho 48 rose up before me, a giant ghost in the fog. The hour grew late; few people dared the mists and the dampness as I came to a halt in the street before this forbidding building. No lights showed from the windows, either upstairs or down. It seemed deserted. But the lair of the scorpion often seems deserted until the silent death strikes suddenly.

Here I halted and a wild thought struck me. One way or another, the drama would be over by dawn. Tonight was the climax of my career, the ultimate top of life. Tonight I was the strongest link in the strange chain of events. Tomorrow it would not matter whether I lived or died. I drew the flask of elixir from my pocket and gazed at it. Enough for two more days if properly eked out. Two more days of life! Or—I needed stimulation as I never needed it before; the task in front of me was one no mere human could hope to accomplish. If I drank the entire remainder of the elixir, I had no idea as to the duration of its effect, but it would last the night through. And my legs were shaky; my mind had curious periods of utter vacuity; weakness of brain and body assailed me. I raised the flask and with one draft drained it.

For an instant I thought it was death. Never had I taken such an amount.

Sky and world reeled and I felt as if I would fly into a million vibrating fragments, like the bursting of a globe of brittle steel. Like fire, like hell-fire the elixir raced along my veins and I was a giant! monster! a superman!

Turning, I strode to the menacing, shadowy doorway. I had no plan; I felt the need of none. As a drunken man walks blithely into danger, I strode to the lair of the Scorpion, magnificently aware of my superiority, imperially confident of my stimulation and sure as the unchanging stars that the way would open before me.

Oh, there never was a superman like that who knocked commandingly on the door of Soho 48 that night in the rain and the fog!

I knocked four times, the old signal that we slaves had used to be admitted into the idol-room at Yun Shatu's. An aperture opened in the center of the door and slanted eyes looked warily out. They slightly widened as the owner recognized me, then narrowed wickedly.

"You fool!" I said angrily. "Don't you see the mark?"

I held my hand to the aperture.

"Don't you recognize me? Let me in, curse you."

I think the very boldness of the trick made for its success. Surely by now all the Scorpion's slaves knew of Stephen Costigan's rebellion, knew that he was marked for death. And the very fact that I came here, inviting doom, confused the doorman.

The door opened and I entered. The man who had admitted me was a tall, lank Chinaman I had known as a servant of Kathulos. He closed the door behind me and I saw we stood in a sort of vestibule, lighted by a dim lamp whose glow could not be seen from the street for the reason that the windows were heavily curtained. The Chinaman glowered at me undecided. I looked at him, tensed. Then suspicion flared in his eyes and his hand flew to his sleeve. But at the instant I was on him and his lean neck broke like a rotten bough between my hands.

I eased his corpse to the thickly carpeted floor and listened. No sound broke the silence. Stepping as stealthily as a wolf, fingers spread like talons, I stole into the next room. This was furnished in Oriental style, with couches and rugs and gold-worked drapery, but was empty of human life. I crossed it and went into the next one. Light flowed softly from the censers which were swung from the ceiling, and the Eastern rugs deadened the sound of my footfalls; I seemed to be moving through a castle of enchantment.

Every moment I expected a rush of silent assassins from the doorways or from behind the curtains or screen with their writhing dragons. Utter silence reigned. Room after room I explored and at last halted at the foot of the stairs. The inevitable censer shed an uncertain light, but most of the stairs were veiled in shadows. What horrors awaited me above?

But fear and the elixir are strangers and I mounted that stair of lurking terror as boldly as I had entered that house of terror. The upper rooms I found to be much like those below and with them they had this fact in common: they were empty of human life. I sought an attic but there seemed no door letting into one. Returning to the first floor, I made a search for an entrance into the basement, but again my efforts were fruitless. The amazing truth was borne in upon me: except for myself and that dead man who lay sprawled so grotesquely in the outer vestibule, there were no men in that house, dead or living.

I could not understand it. Had the house been bare of furniture I should have reached the natural conclusion that Kathulos had fled—but no signs of flight met my eye. This was unnatural, uncanny. I stood in the great shadowy library and pondered. No, I had made no mistake in the house. Even if the broken corpse in the vestibule were not there to furnish mute testimony, everything in the room pointed toward the presence of the Master. There were the artificial palms, the lacquered screen, the tapestries, even the idol, though now no incense smoke rose before it. About the walls were ranged long shelves of books, bound in strange and costly fashion—books in every language in the world, I found from a swift examination, and on every subject—outré and bizarre, most of them.

Remembering the secret passage in the Temple of Dreams, I investigated the heavy mahogany table which stood in the center of the room. But nothing resulted. A sudden blaze of fury surged up in me, primitive and unreasoning. I snatched a statuette from the table and dashed it against the shelf-covered wall. The noise of its breaking would surely bring the gang from their hiding-place. But the result was much more startling than that!

The statuette struck the edge of a shelf and instantly the whole section of shelves with their load of books swung silently outward, revealing a narrow doorway! As in the other secret door, a row of steps led downward. At another time I would have shuddered at the thought of descending, with the horrors of the other tunnel fresh in my mind, but inflamed as I was by the elixir, I strode forward without an instant's hesitancy.

Since there was no one in the house, they must be somewhere in the tunnel or in whatever lair to which the tunnel led. I stepped through the doorway, leaving the door open; the police might find it that way and follow me, though somehow I felt as if mine would be a lone hand from the start to grim finish.

I went down a considerable distance and then the stair debouched into a level corridor some twenty feet wide—a remarkable thing. In spite of the width, the ceiling was rather low and from it hung small, curiously shaped lamps which flung a dim light. I stalked hurriedly along the corridor like old Death seeking victims, and as I went I noted the work of the thing. The floor was of great broad flags and the walls seemed to be of huge blocks of evenly set stone. This passage was clearly no work of modern days; the slaves of Kathulos never tunneled there. Some secret way of mediaeval times, I thought—and after all, who knows what catacombs lie below London, whose secrets are greater and darker than those of Babylon and Rome?

On and on I went, and now I knew that I must be far below the earth. The air was dank and heavy, and cold moisture dripped from the stones of walls and ceiling. From time to time I saw smaller passages leading away in the darkness but I determined to keep to the larger main one.

A ferocious impatience gripped me. I seemed to have been walking for hours and still only dank damp walls and bare flags and guttering lamps met my eyes. I kept a close watch for sinister-appearing chests or the like—saw no such things.

Then as I was about to burst into savage curses, another stair loomed up in the shadows in front of me.

19. Dark Fury

"The ringed wolf glared the circle round
  Through baleful, blue-lit eye,
Not unforgetful of his debt.
Quoth he, 'I'll do some damage yet
  Or ere my turn to die!'"

—MUNDY

Like a lean wolf I glided up the stairs. Some twenty feet up there was a sort of landing from which other corridors diverged, much like the lower one by which I had come. The thought came to me that the earth below London must be honeycombed with such secret passages, one above the other.

Some feet above this landing the steps halted at a door, and here I hesitated, uncertain as to whether I should chance knocking or not. Even as I meditated, the door began to open. I shrank back against the wall, flattening myself out as much as possible. The door swung wide and a Moor came through. Only a glimpse I had of the room beyond, out of the corner of my eye, but my unnaturally alert senses registered the fact that the room was empty.

And on the instant, before he could turn, I smote the Moor a single deathly blow behind the angle of the jawbone and he toppled headlong down the stairs, to lie in a crumpled heap on the landing, his limbs tossed grotesquely about.

My left hand caught the door as it started to slam shut and in an instant I was through and standing in the room beyond. As I had thought, there was no occupant of this room. I crossed it swiftly and entered the next. These rooms were furnished in a manner before which the furnishings of the Soho house paled into insignificance. Barbaric, terrible, unholy—these words alone convey some slight idea of the ghastly sights which met my eyes. Skulls, bones and complete skeletons formed much of the decorations, if such they were. Mummies leered from their cases and mounted reptiles ranged the walls. Between these sinister relics hung African shields of hide and bamboo, crossed with assagais and war daggers. Here and there reared obscene idols, black and horrible.

And in between and scattered about among these evidences of savagery and barbarism were vases, screens, rugs and hangings of the highest Oriental workmanship; a strange and incongruous effect.

I had passed through two of these rooms without seeing a human being, when I came to stairs leading upward. Up these I went, several flights, until I came to a door in a ceiling. I wondered if I were still under the earth. Surely the first stairs had led into a house of some sort. I raised the door cautiously. Starlight met my eyes and I drew myself warily up and out. There I halted. A broad flat roof stretched away on all sides and beyond its rim on all sides glimmered the lights of London. Just what building I was on, I had no idea, but that it was a tall one I could tell, for I seemed to be above most of the lights I saw. Then I saw that I was not alone.

Over against the shadows of the ledge that ran around the roof's edge, a great menacing form bulked in starlight. A pair of eyes glinted at me with a light not wholly sane; the starlight glanced silver from a curving length of steel. Yar Khan the Afghan killer fronted me in the silent shadows.

A fierce wild exultation surged over me. Now I could begin to pay the debt I owed Kathulos and all his hellish band! The dope fired my veins and sent waves of inhuman power and dark fury through me. A spring and I was on my feet in a silent, deathly rush.

Yar Khan was a giant, taller and bulkier than I. He held a tulwar, and from the instant I saw him I knew that he was full of the dope to the use of which he was addicted—heroin.

As I came in he swung his heavy weapon high in air, but ere he could strike I seized his sword wrist in an iron grip and with my free hand drove smashing blows into his midriff.

Of that hideous battle, fought in silence above the sleeping city with only the stars to see, I remember little. I remember tumbling back and forth, locked in a death embrace. I remember the stiff beard rasping my flesh as his dope-fired eyes gazed wildly into mine. I remember the taste of hot blood in my mouth, the tang of fearful exultation in my soul, the onrushing and upsurging of inhuman strength and fury.

God, what a sight for a human eye, had anyone looked upon that grim roof where two human leopards, dope maniacs, tore each other to pieces!

I remember his arm breaking like rotten wood in my grip and the tulwar falling from his useless hand. Handicapped by a broken arm, the end was inevitable, and with one wild uproaring flood of might, I rushed him to the edge of the roof and bent him backward far out over the ledge. An instant we struggled there; then I tore loose his hold and hurled him over, and one single shriek came up as he hurtled into the darkness below.

I stood upright, arms hurled up toward the stars, a terrible statue of primordial triumph. And down my breast trickled streams of blood from the long wounds left by the Afghan's frantic nails, on neck and face.

Then I turned with the craft of the maniac. Had no one heard the sound of that battle? My eyes were on the door through which I had come, but a noise made me turn, and for the first time I noticed a small affair like a tower jutting up from the roof. There was no window there, but there was a door, and even as I looked that door opened and a huge black form framed itself in the light that streamed from within. Hassim!

He stepped out on the roof and closed the door, his shoulders hunched and neck outthrust as he glanced this way and that. I struck him senseless to the roof with one hate-driven smash. I crouched over him, waiting some sign of returning consciousness; then away in the sky, close to the horizon, I saw a faint red tint. The rising of the moon!

Where in God's name was Gordon? Even as I stood undecided, a strange noise reached me. It was curiously like the droning of many bees.

Striding in the direction from which it seemed to come, I crossed the roof and leaned over the ledge. A sight nightmarish and incredible met my eyes.

Some twenty feet below the level of the roof on which I stood, there was another roof, of the same size and clearly a part of the same building. On one side it was bounded by the wall; on the other three sides a parapet several feet high took the place of a ledge.

A great throng of people stood, sat and squatted, close-packed on the roof—and without exception they were *Negroes*!

There were hundreds of them, and it was their low-voiced
conversation which I had heard. But what held my gaze was that
upon which their eyes were fixed.

About the center of the roof rose a sort of teocalli some ten
feet high, almost exactly like those found in Mexico and on
which the priests of the Aztecs sacrificed human victims. This,
allowing for its infinitely smaller scale, was an exact type of
those sacrificial pyramids. On the flat top of it was a curiously
carved altar, and beside it stood a lank, dusky form whom even
the ghastly mask he wore could not disguise to my gaze—
Santiago, the Haiti voodoo fetish man. On the altar lay John
Gordon, stripped to the waist and bound hand and foot, but
conscious.

I reeled back from the roof edge, rent in twain by indecision.
Even the stimulus of the elixir was not equal to this. Then a
sound brought me about to see Hassim struggling dizzily to his
knees. I reached him with two long strides and ruthlessly
smashed him down again. Then I noticed a queer sort of
contrivance dangling from his girdle. I bent and examined it. It
was a mask similar to that worn by Santiago. Then my mind
leaped swift and sudden to a wild desperate plan, which to my
dope-ridden brain seemed not at all wild or desperate. I stepped
softly to the tower and, opening the door, peered inward. I saw
no one who might need to be silenced, but I saw a long silken
robe hanging upon a peg in the wall. The luck of the dope fiend! I
snatched it and closed the door again. Hassim showed no signs
of consciousness but I gave him another smash on the chin to
make sure and, seizing his mask, hurried to the ledge.

A low guttural chant floated up to me, jangling, barbaric,
with an undertone of maniacal blood-lust. The Negroes, men
and women, were swaying back and forth to the wild rhythm of
their death chant. On the teocalli Santiago stood like a statue of
black basalt, facing the east, dagger held high—a wild and
terrible sight, naked as he was save for a wide silken girdle and
that inhuman mask on his face. The moon thrust a red rim above
the eastern horizon and a faint breeze stirred the great black
plumes which nodded above the voodoo man's mask. The chant
of the worshipers dropped to a low, sinister whisper.

I hurriedly slipped on the death mask, gathered the robe close
about me and prepared for the descent. I was prepared to drop
the full distance, being sure in the superb confidence of my
insanity that I would land unhurt, but as I climbed over the ledge

I found a steel ladder leading down. Evidently Hassim, one of the voodoo priests, intended descending this way. So down I went, and in haste, for I knew that the instant the moon's lower rim cleared the city's skyline, that motionless dagger would descend into Gordon's breast.

Gathering the robe close about me so as to conceal my white skin, I stepped down upon the roof and strode forward through rows of black worshipers who shrank aside to let me through. To the foot of the teocalli I stalked and up the stairs that ran about it, until I stood beside the death altar and marked the dark red stains upon it. Gordon lay on his back, his eyes open, his face drawn and haggard, but his gaze dauntless and unflinching.

Santiago's eyes blazed at me through the slits of his mask, but I read no suspicion in his gaze until I reached forward and took the dagger from his hand. He was too much astonished to resist, and the black throng fell suddenly silent. That he saw my hand was not that of a Negro it is certain, but he was simply struck speechless with astonishment. Moving swiftly I cut Gordon's bonds and hauled him erect. Then Santiago with a shriek leaped upon me—shrieked again and, arms flung high, and pitched headlong from the teocalli with his own dagger buried to the hilt in his breast.

Then the black worshipers were on us with a screech and a roar—leaping on the steps of the teocalli like black leopards in the moonlight, knives flashing, eyes gleaming whitely.

I tore mask and robe from me and answered Gordon's exclamation with a wild laugh. I had hoped that by virtue of my disguise I might get us both safely away but now I was content to die there at his side.

He tore a great metal ornament from the altar, and as the attackers came he wielded this. A moment we held them at bay and then they flowed over us like a black wave. This to me was Valhalla! Knives stung me and blackjacks smashed against me, but I laughed and drove my iron fists in straight, steam-hammer smashes that shattered flesh and bone. I saw Gordon's crude weapon rise and fall, and each time a man went down. Skulls shattered and blood splashed and the dark fury swept over me. Nightmare faces swirled about me and I was on my knees; up again and the faces crumpled before my blows. Through far mists I seemed to hear a hideous familiar voice raised in imperious command.

Gordon was swept away from me but from the sounds I knew

that the work of death still went on. The stars reeled through fogs of blood, but hell's exaltation was on me and I reveled in the dark tides of fury until a darker deeper tide swept over me and I knew no more.

20. Ancient Horror

"Here now in his triumph where all things falter
    Stretched out on the spoils that his own hand spread,
As a God self-slain on his own strange altar,
    Death lies dead."

—SWINBURNE

Slowly I drifted back into life—slowly, slowly. A mist held me and in the mist I saw a Skull—

I lay in a steel cage like a captive wolf, and the bars were too strong, I saw, even for my strength. The cage seemed to be set in a sort of niche in the wall and I was looking into a large room. This room was under the earth, for the floor was of stone flags and the walls and ceiling were composed of gigantic blocks of the same material. Shelves ranged the walls, covered with weird appliances, apparently of a scientific nature, and more were on the great table that stood in the center of the room. Beside this sat Kathulos.

The Sorcerer was clad in a snaky yellow robe, and those hideous hands and that terrible head were more pronouncedly reptilian than ever. He turned his great yellow eyes toward me, like pools of livid fire, and his parchment-thin lips moved in what probably passed for a smile.

I staggered erect and gripped the bars, cursing.

"Gordon, curse you, where is Gordon?"

Kathulos took a test-tube from the table, eyed it closely and emptied it into another.

"Ah, my friend awakes," he murmured in his voice—the voice of a living dead man.

He thrust his hands into his long sleeves and turned fully to me.

"I think in you," he said distinctly, "I have created a Frankenstein monster. I made of you a superhuman creature to serve my wishes and you broke from me. You are the bane of my might, worse than Gordon even. You have killed valuable servants and interfered with my plans. However, your evil comes to an end tonight. Your friend Gordon broke away but he is being hunted through the tunnels and can not escape.

"You," he continued with the sincere interest of the scientist, "are a most interesting subject. Your brain must be formed differently from any other man that ever lived. I will make a close study of it and add it to my laboratory. How a man, with the apparent need of the elixir in his system, has managed to go on for two days still stimulated by the last draft is more than I can understand."

My heart leaped. With all his wisdom, little Zuleika had tricked him and he evidently did not know that she had filched a flask of the life-giving stuff from him.

"The last draft you had from me," he went on, "was sufficient only for some eight hours. I repeat, it has me puzzled. Can you offer any suggestion?"

I snarled wordlessly. He sighed.

"As always the barbarian. Truly the proverb speaks: 'Jest with the wounded tiger and warm the adder in your bosom before you seek to lift the savage from his savagery.'"

He meditated awhile in silence. I watched him uneasily. There was about him a vague and curious difference—his long fingers emerging from the sleeves drummed on the chair arms and some hidden exultation strummed at the back of his voice, lending it unaccustomed vibrancy.

"And you might have been a king of the new regime," he said suddenly. "Aye, the new—new and inhumanly old!"

I shuddered as his dry cackling laugh rasped out.

He bent his head as if listening. From far off seemed to come a hum of guttural voices. His lips writhed in a smile.

"My black children," he murmured. "They tear my enemy Gordon to pieces in the tunnels. They, Mr. Costigan, are my real henchmen and it was for their edification tonight that I laid John Gordon on the sacrificial stone. I would have preferred to have made some experiments with him, based on certain scientific theories, but my children must be humored. Later under my tutelage they will outgrow their childish superstitions and throw aside their foolish customs, but now they must be led gently by the hand.

"How do you like these under-the-earth corridors, Mr. Costigan?" he switched suddenly. "You thought of them—what? No doubt that the white savages of your Middle Ages built them? Faugh! These tunnels are older than your world! They were brought into being by mighty kings, too many eons ago for your mind to grasp, when an imperial city towered where now this crude village of London stands. All trace of that metropolis has crumbled to dust and vanished, but these corridors were built by more than human skill—ha ha! Of all the teeming thousands who move daily above them, none knows of their existence save my servants—and not all of them. Zuleika, for instance, does not know of them, for of late I have begun to doubt her loyalty and shall doubtless soon make of her an example."

At that I hurled myself blindly against the side of the cage, a red wave of hate and fury tossing me in its grip. I seized the bars and strained until the veins stood out on my forehead and the muscles bulged and crackled in my arms and shoulders. And the bars bent before my onslaught—a little but no more, and finally the power flowed from my limbs and I sank down trembling and weakened. Kathulos watched me imperturbably.

"The bars hold," he announced with something almost like relief in his tone. "Frankly, I prefer to be on the opposite side of them. You are a human ape if there was ever one."

He laughed suddenly and wildly.

"But why do you seek to oppose me?" he shrieked unexpectedly. "Why defy me, who am Kathulos, the Sorcerer, great even in the days of the old empire? Today, invincible! A magician, a scientist, among ignorant savages! Ha ha!"

I shuddered, and sudden blinding light broke in on me. Kathulos himself was an addict, and was fired by the stuff of his choice! What hellish concoction was strong enough, terrible enough to thrill the Master and inflame him, I do not know, nor do I wish to know. Of all the uncanny knowledge that was his, I, knowing the man as I did, count this the most weird and grisly.

"You, you paltry fool!" he was ranting, his face lit supernaturally. "Know you who I am? Kathulos of Egypt! Bah! They knew me in the old days! I reigned in the dim misty sea lands ages and ages before the sea rose and engulfed the land. I died, not as men die; the magic draft of life everlasting was ours! I drank deep and slept. Long I slept in my lacquered case! My flesh withered and grew hard; my blood dried in my veins. I became as one dead. But still within me burned the spirit of life, sleeping but anticipating the awakening. The great cities crumbled to dust. The sea drank the land. The tall shrines and the lofty spires sank beneath the green waves. All this I knew as I slept, as a man knows in dreams. Kathulos of Egypt? Faugh! *Kathulos of Atlantis!*"

I uttered a sudden involuntary cry. This was too grisly for sanity.

"Aye, the magician, the Sorcerer.

"And down the long years of savagery, through which the barbaric races struggled to rise without their masters, the legend came of the day of empire, when one of the Old Race would rise up from the sea. Aye, and lead to victory the black people who were our slaves in the old days.

"These brown and yellow people, what care I for them? The blacks were the slaves of my race, and I am their god today. They will obey me. The yellow and the brown peoples are fools—I make them my tools and the day will come when my black warriors will turn on them and slay at my word. And you, you white barbarians, whose ape-ancestors forever defied my race and me, your doom is at hand! And when I mount my universal throne the only whites shall be white slaves!

"The day came as prophesied, when my case, breaking free from the halls where it lay—where it had lain when Atlantis was still sovran of the world—where since her empery it had sunk into the green fathoms—when my case, I say, was smitten by the deep sea tides and moved and stirred, and thrust aside the clinging seaweed that masks temples and minarets, and came floating up past the lofty sapphire and golden spires, up through the green waters, to float upon the lazy waves of the sea.

"Then came a white fool carrying out the destiny of which he was not aware. The men on his ship, true believers, knew that the time had come. And I—the air entered my nostrils and I awoke from the long, long sleep. I stirred and moved and lived. And rising in the night, I slew the fool that had lifted me from the ocean, and my servants made obeisance to me and took me into Africa, where I abode awhile and learned new languages and new ways of a new world and became strong.

"The wisdom of your dreary world—ha ha! I who delved

deeper in the mysteries of the old than any man dared go! All that men know today, I know, and my knowledge beside that which I have brought down the centuries is as a grain of sand beside a mountain! You should know something of that knowledge! By it I lifted you from one hell to plunge you into a greater! You fool, here at my hand is that which would lift you from this! Aye, would strike from you the chains whereby I have bound you!"

He snatched up a golden vial and shook it before my gaze. I eyed it as men dying in the desert must eye the distant mirages. Kathulos fingered it meditatively. His unnatural excitement seemed to have passed suddenly, and when he spoke again it was in the passionless, measured tones of the scientist.

"That would indeed be an experiment worth while—to free you of the elixir habit and see if your dope-riddled body would sustain life. Nine times out of ten the victim, with the need and stimulus removed, would die—but you are such a giant of a brute—"

He sighed and set the vial down.

"The dreamer opposes the man of destiny. My time is not my own or I should choose to spend my life pent in my laboratories, carrying out my experiments. But now, as in the days of the old empire when kings sought my counsel, I must work and labor for the good of the race at large. Aye, I must toil and sow the seed of glory against the full coming of the imperial days when the seas give up all their living dead."

I shuddered. Kathulos laughed wildly again. His fingers began to drum his chair arms and his face gleamed with the unnatural light once more. The red visions had begun to seethe in his skull again.

"Under the green seas they lie, the ancient masters, in their lacquered cases, dead as men reckon death, but only sleeping. Sleeping through the long ages as hours, awaiting the day of awakening! The old masters, the wise men, who foresaw the day when the sea would gulp the land, and who made ready. Made ready that they might rise again in the barbaric days to come. As did I. Sleeping they lie, ancient kings and grim wizards, who died as men die, before Atlantis sank. Who, sleeping, sank with her but who shall arise again!

"Mine the glory! I rose first. And I sought out the site of old cities, on shores that did not sink. Vanished, long vanished. The barbarian tide swept over them thousands of years ago as the green waters swept over their elder sister of the deeps. On some, the deserts stetch bare. Over some, as here, young barbarian cities rise."

He halted suddenly. His eyes sought one of the dark openings that marked a corridor. I think his strange intuition warned him of some impending danger but I do not believe that he had any inkling of how dramatically our scene would be interrupted.

As he looked, swift footsteps sounded and a man appeared suddenly in the doorway—a man disheveled, tattered and bloody. *John Gordon!* Kathulos sprang erect with a cry, and Gordon, gasping as from superhuman exertion, brought down the revolver he held in his hand and fired point-blank. Kathulos staggered, clapping his hand to his breast, and then, groping wildly, reeled to the wall and fell against it. A doorway opened and he reeled through, but as Gordon leaped fiercely across the chamber, a blank stone surface met his gaze, which yielded not to his savage hammerings.

He whirled and ran drunkenly to the table where lay a bunch of keys the Master had dropped there.

"The vial!" I shrieked. "Take the vial!" And he thrust it into his pocket.

Back along the corridor through which he had come sounded a faint clamor growing swiftly like a wolf-pack in full cry. A few precious seconds spent with fumbling for the right key, then the cage door swung open and I sprang out. A sight for the gods we were, the two of us! Slashed, bruised and cut, our garments hanging in tatters—my wounds had ceased to bleed, but now as I moved they began again, and from the stiffness of my hands I knew that my knuckles were shattered. As for Gordon, he was fairly drenched in blood from crown to foot.

We made off down a passage in the opposite direction from the menacing noise, which I knew to be the black servants of the Master in full pursuit of us. Neither of us was in good shape for running, but we did our best. Where we were going I had no idea. My superhuman strength had deserted me and I was going now on will-power alone. We switched off into another corridor and we had not gone twenty steps until, looking back, I saw the first of the black devils round the corner.

A desperate effort increased our lead a trifle. But they had seen us, were in full view now, and a yell of fury broke from them to be succeeded by a more sinister silence as they bent all efforts to overhauling us.

There a short distance in front of us we saw a stair loom suddenly in the gloom. If we might reach that—but we saw something else.

Against the ceiling, between us and the stairs, hung a huge thing like an iron grille, with great spikes along the bottom—a portcullis. And even as we looked, without halting in our panting strides, it began to move.

"They're lowering the portcullis!" Gordon croaked, his blood-streaked face a mask of exhaustion and will.

Now the blacks were only ten feet behind us—now the huge grate, gaining momentum, with a creak of rusty, unused mechanism, rushed downward. A final spurt, a gasping straining nightmare of effort—and Gordon, sweeping us both along in a wild burst of pure nerve-strength, hurled us under and through, and the gate crashed behind us!

A moment we lay gasping, not heeding the frenzied horde who raved and screamed on the other side of the gate. So close had that final leap been, that the great spikes in their descent had torn shreds from our clothing.

The blacks were thrusting at us with daggers through the bars, but we were out of reach and it seemed to me that I was content to lie there and die of exhaustion. But Gordon weaved unsteadily erect and hauled me with him.

"Got to get out," he croaked; "go to warn—Scotland Yard—honeycombs in heart of London—high explosives—arms—ammunition."

We blundered up the steps, and in front of us I seemed to hear a sound of metal grating against metal. The stairs ended abruptly, on a landing that terminated in a blank wall. Gordon hammered against this and the inevitable secret doorway opened. Light streamed in, through the bars of a sort of grille. Men in the uniform of London police were sawing at these with hacksaws, and even as they greeted us, an opening was made through which we crawled.

"You're hurt, sir!" One of the men took Gordon's arm.

My companion shook him off.

"There's no time to lose! Out of here, as quick as we can go!"

I saw that we were in a basement of some sort. We hastened up the steps and out into the early dawn which was turning the east scarlet. Over the tops of smaller houses I saw in the distance a great gaunt building on the roof of which, I felt instinctively, that wild drama had been enacted the night before.

"That building was leased some months ago by a mysterious Chinaman," said Gordon, following my gaze. "Office building originally—the neighborhood deteriorated and the building stood vacant for some time. The new tenant added several stories to it but left it apparently empty. Had my eye on it for some time."

This was told in Gordon's jerky swift manner as we started hurriedly along the sidewalk. I listened mechanically, like a man in a trance. My vitality was ebbing fast and I knew that I was going to crumple at any moment.

"The people living in the vicinity had been reporting strange sights and noises. The man who owned the basement we just left heard queer sounds emanating from the wall of the basement and called the police. About that time I was racing back and forth among those cursed corridors like a hunted rat and I heard the police banging on the wall. I found the secret door and opened it but found it barred by a grating. It was while I was telling the astounded policemen to procure a hacksaw that the pursuing Negroes, whom I had eluded for the moment, came into sight and I was forced to shut the door and run for it again. By pure luck I found you and by pure luck managed to find the way back to the door.

"Now we must get to Scotland Yard. If we strike swiftly, we may capture the entire band of devils. Whether I killed Kathulos or not I do not know, or if he can be killed by mortal weapons. But to the best of my knowledge all of them are now in those subterranean corridors and—"

At that moment the world shook! A brain-shattering roar seemed to break the sky with its incredible detonation; houses tottered and crashed to ruins; a mighty pillar of smoke and flame burst from the earth and on its wings great masses of debris soared skyward. A black fog of smoke and dust and falling timbers enveloped the world, a prolonged thunder seemed to rumble up from the center of the earth as of walls and ceilings falling, and amid the uproar and the screaming I sank down and knew no more.

21. The Breaking of the Chain

"And like a soul belated,
    In heaven and hell unmated,
    By cloud and mist abated,
        Comes out of darkness morn."
                                            —SWINBURNE

There is little need to linger on the scenes of horror of that
terrible London morning. The world is familiar with and knows
most of the details attendant to the great explosion which wiped
out a tenth of that great city with a resultant loss of lives and
property. For such a happening some reason must needs be
given; the tale of the deserted building got out, and many wild
stories were circulated. Finally, to still the rumors, the report
was unofficially given out that this building had been the
rendezvous and secret stronghold of a gang of international
anarchists, who had stored its basement full of high explosives
and who had supposedly ignited these accidentally. In a way
there was a good deal to this tale, as you know, but the threat
that had lurked there far transcended any anarchist.

All this was told to me, for when I sank unconscious,
Gordon, attributing my condition to exhaustion and a need of
the hashish to the use of which he thought I was addicted, lifted
me and with the aid of the stunned policemen got me to his
rooms before returning to the scene of the explosion. At his
rooms he found Hansen, and Zuleika handcuffed to the bed as I
had left her. He released her and left her to tend to me, for all
London was in a terrible turmoil and he was needed elsewhere.

When I came to myself at last, I looked up into her starry eyes
and lay quiet, smiling up at her. She sank down upon my bosom,

107

nestling my head in her arms and covering my face with her kisses.

"Steephen!" she sobbed over and over, as her tears splashed hot on my face.

I was scarcely strong enough to put my arms about her but I managed it, and we lay there for a space, in silence except for the girl's hard, racking sobs.

"Zuleika, I love you," I murmured.

"And I love you, Steephen," she sobbed. "Oh, it is so hard to part now—but I'm going with you, Steephen; I can't live without you!"

"My dear child," said John Gordon, entering the room suddenly, "Costigan's not going to die. We will let him have enough hashish to tide him along, and when he is stronger we will take him off the habit slowly."

"You don't understand, sahib; it is not hashish Steephen must have. It is something which only the Master knew, and now that he is dead or is fled, Steephen can not get it and must die."

Gordon shot a quick, uncertain glance at me. His fine face was drawn and haggard, his clothes sooty and torn from his work among the debris of the explosion.

"She's right, Gordon," I said languidly. "I'm dying. Kathulos killed the hashish-craving with a concoction he called the elixir. I've been keeping myself alive on some of the stuff that Zuleika stole from him and gave me, but I drank it all last night."

I was aware of no craving of any kind, no physical or mental discomfort even. All my mechanism was slowing down fast; I had passed the stage where the need of the elixir would tear and rend me. I felt only a great lassitude and a desire to sleep. And I knew that the moment I closed my eyes, I would die.

"A strange dope, that elixir," I said with growing languor. "It burns and freezes and then at last the craving kills easily and without torment."

"Costigan, curse it," said Gordon desperately, "you can't go like this! That vial I took from the Egyptian's table—what is in it?"

"The Master swore it would free me of my curse and probably kill me also," I muttered. "I'd forgotten about it. Let me have it; it can no more than kill me and I'm dying now."

"Yes, quick, let me have it!" exclaimed Zuleika fiercely, springing to Gordon's side, her hands passionately outstretched. She returned with the vial which he had taken from his pocket, and knelt beside me, holding it to my lips, while she murmured to me gently and soothingly in her own language.

I drank, draining the vial, but feeling little interest in the whole matter. My outlook was purely impersonal, at such a low ebb was my life, and I can not even remember how the stuff tasted. I only remember feeling a curious sluggish fire burn faintly along my veins, and the last thing I saw was Zuleika crouching over me, her great eyes fixed with a burning intensity on me. Her tense little hand rested inside her blouse, and remembering her vow to take her own life if I died I tried to lift a hand and disarm her, tried to tell Gordon to take away the dagger she had hidden in her garments. But speech and action failed me and I drifted away into a curious sea of unconsciousness.

Of that period I remember nothing. No sensation fired my sleeping brain to such an extent as to bridge the gulf over which I drifted. They say I lay like a dead man for hours, scarcely breathing, while Zuleika hovered over me, never leaving my side an instant, and fighting like a tigress when anyone tried to coax her away to rest. Her chain was broken.

As I carried the vision of her into that dim land of nothingness, so her dear eyes were the first thing which greeted my returning consciousness. I was aware of a greater weakness than I thought possible for a man to feel, as if I had been an invalid for months, but the life in me, faint though it was, was sound and normal, caused by no artificial stimulation. I smiled up at my girl and murmured weakly:

"Throw away your dagger, little Zuleika; I'm going to live."

She screamed and fell on her knees beside me, weeping and laughing at the same time. Women are strange beings, of mixed and powerful emotions, truly.

Gordon entered and grasped the hand which I could not lift from the bed.

"You're a case for an ordinary human physician now, Costigan," he said. "Even a layman like myself can tell that. For the first time since I've known you, the look in your eyes is entirely sane. You look like a man who has had a complete nervous breakdown, and needs about a year of rest and quiet. Great heavens, man, you've been through enough, outside your dope experience, to last you a lifetime."

"Tell me first," said I, "was Kathulos killed in the explosion?"

"I don't know," answered Gordon somberly. "Apparently

tne entire system of subterranean passages was destroyed. I know my last bullet—the last bullet that was in the revolver which I wrested from one of my attackers—found its mark in the Master's body, but whether he died from the wound, or whether a bullet can hurt him, I do ñot know. And whether in his death agonies he ignited the tons and tons of high explosives which were stored in the corridors, or whether the Negroes did it unintentionally, we shall never know.

"My God, Costigan, did you ever see such a honeycomb? And we know not how many miles in either direction the passages reached. Even now Scotland Yard men are combing the subways and basements of the town for secret openings. All known openings, such as the one through which we came and the one in Soho 48, were blocked by falling walls. The office building was simply blown to atoms."

"What about the men who raided Soho 48?"

"The door in the library wall had been closed. They found the Chinaman you killed, but searched the house without avail. Lucky for them, too, else they had doubtless been in the tunnels when the explosion came, and perished with the hundreds of Negroes who must have died then."

"Every Negro in London must have been there."

"I dare say. Most of them are voodoo worshipers at heart and the power the Master wielded was incredible. They died, but what of him? Was he blown to atoms by the stuff which he had secretly stored, or crushed when the stone walls crumbled and the ceilings came thundering down?"

"There is no way to search among those subterranean ruins, I suppose?"

"None whatever. When the walls caved in, the tons of earth upheld by the ceiling also came crashing down, filling the corridors with dirt and broken stone, blocking them forever. And on the surface of the earth, the houses which the vibration shook down were heaped high in utter ruins. What happened in those terrible corridors must remain forever a mystery."

My tale draws to a close. The months that followed passed uneventfully, except for the growing happiness which to me was paradise, but which would bore you were I to relate it. But one day Gordon and I again discussed the mysterious happenings that had had their being under the grim hand of the Master.

"Since that day," said Gordon, "the world has been quiet. Africa has subsided and the East seems to have returned to her ancient sleep. There can be but one answer—living or dead, Kathulos was destroyed that morning when his world crashed about him."

"Gordon," said I, "what is the answer to that greatest of all mysteries?"

My friend shrugged his shoulders.

"I have come to believe that mankind eternally hovers on the brinks of secret oceans of which it knows nothing. Races have lived and vanished before our race rose out of the slime of the primitive, and it is likely still others will live upon the earth after ours has vanished. Scientists have long upheld the theory that the Atlanteans possessed a higher civilization than our own, and on very different lines. Certainly Kathulos himself was proof that our boasted culture and knowledge were nothing beside that of whatever fearful civilization produced him.

"His dealings with you alone have puzzled all the scientific world, for none of them has been able to explain how he could remove the hashish craving, stimulate you with a drug so infinitely more powerful, and then produce another drug which entirely effaced the effects of the other."

"I have him to thank for two things," I said slowly; "the regaining of my lost manhood—and Zuleika. Kathulos, then, is dead, as far as any mortal thing can die. But what of those others—those 'ancient masters' who still sleep in the sea?"

Gordon shuddered.

"As I said, perhaps mankind loiters on the brink of unthinkable chasms of horror. But a fleet of gunboats is even now patrolling the oceans unobtrusively, with orders to destroy instantly any strange case that may be found floating—to destroy it and its contents. And if my word has any weight with the English government and the nations of the world, the seas will be so patrolled until doomsday shall let down the curtain on the races of today."

"At night I dream of them, sometimes," I muttered, "sleeping in their lacquered cases, which drip with strange seaweed, far down among the green surges—where unholy spires and strange towers rise in the dark ocean."

"We have been face to face with an ancient horror," said Gordon somberly, "with a fear too dark and mysterious for the human brain to cope with. Fortune has been with us; she may not again favor the sons of men. It is best that we be ever on our guard. The universe was not made for humanity alone; life takes strange phases and it is the first instinct of nature for the different species to destroy each other. No doubt we seemed as horrible to the Master as he did to us. We have scarcely tapped the chest of secrets which nature has stored, and I shudder to think of what that chest may hold for the human race."

"That's true," said I, inwardly rejoicing at the vigor which was beginning to course through my wasted veins, "but men will meet obstacles as they come, as men have always risen to meet them. Now, I am beginning to know the full worth of life and love, and not all the devils from all the abysses can hold me."

Gordon smiled.

"You have it coming to you, old comrade. The best thing is to forget all that dark interlude, for in that course lies light and happiness."

LORD OF THE DEAD

The onslaught was as unexpected as the stroke of an unseen cobra. One second Steve Harrison was plodding profanely but prosaically through the darkness of the alley—the next, he was fighting for his life with the snarling, mouthing fury that had fallen on him, talon and tooth. The thing was obviously a man, though in the first few dazed seconds Harrison doubted even this fact. The attacker's style of fighting was appallingly vicious and beast-like, even to Harrison who was accustomed to the foul battling of the underworld.

The detective felt the other's teeth in his flesh, and yelped profanely. But there was a knife, too; it ribboned his coat and shirt, and drew blood, and only blind chance that locked his fingers about a sinewy wrist, kept the point from his vitals. It was dark as the backdoor of Erebus. Harrison saw his assailant only as a slightly darker chunk in the blackness. The muscles under his grasping fingers were taut and steely as piano wire, and there was a terrifying suppleness about the frame writhing against his which filled Harrison with panic.

The big detective had seldom met a man his equal in strength; this denizen of the dark not only was as strong as he, but was more lithe, quicker and tougher than a civilized man ought to be.

They rolled over into the mud of the alley, biting, kicking and slugging, and though the unseen enemy grunted each time one of Harrison's maul-like fists thudded against him, he showed no

signs of weakening. His wrist was like a woven mass of steel
wires, threatening momentarily to writhe out of Harrison's
clutch. His flesh crawling with fear of the cold steel, the detective
grasped that wrist with both his own hands, and tried to break it.
A blood-thirsty howl acknowledged this futile attempt, and a
voice, which had been mouthing in an unknown tongue, hissed
in Harrison's ear: "Dog! You shall die in the mud, as I died in the
sand! You gave my body to the vultures! I give yours to the rats
of the alley! *Wellah!*"

A grimy thumb was feeling for Harrison's eye, and fired to
desperation, the detective heaved his body backward, bringing
up his knee with bone-crushing force. The unknown gasped and
rolled clear, squalling like a cat. Harrison staggered up, lost his
balance, caromed against a wall. With a scream and a rush, the
other was up and at him. Harrison heard the knife whistle and
chunk into the wall beside him, and he lashed out blindly with all
the power of his massive shoulders. He landed solidly, felt his
victim shoot off his feet backward, and heard him crash
headlong into the mud. Then Steve Harrison, for the first time in
his life, turned his back on a single foe and ran lumberingly but
swiftly up the alley.

His breath came pantingly; his feet splashed through refuse
and clanged over rusty cans. Momentarily he expected a knife in
his back. "Hogan!" he bawled desperately. Behind him sounded
the quick lethal patter of flying feet.

He catapulted out of the black alley mouth head on into
Patrolman Hogan who had heard his urgent bellow and was
coming on the run. The breath went out of the patrolman in an
agonized gasp, and the two hit the sidewalk together.

Harrison did not take time to rise. Ripping the Colt .38
Special from Hogan's holster, he blazed away at a shadow that
hovered for an instant in the black mouth of the alley.

Rising, he approached the dark entrance, the smoking gun in
his hand. No sound came from the Stygian gloom.

"Give me your flashlight," he requested, and Hogan rose, one
hand on his capacious belly, and proffered the article. The white
beam showed no corpse stretched in the alley mud.

"Got away," muttered Harrison.

"Who?" demanded Hogan with some spleen. "What is this,
anyway? I hear you bellowin' 'Hogan!' like the devil had you by
the seat of the britches, and the next thing you ram me like a
chargin' bull. What—"

"Shut·up, and let's explore this alley," snapped Harrison. "I didn't mean to run into you. Something jumped me—"

"I'll say somethin' did." The patrolman surveyed his companion in the uncertain light of the distant corner lamp. Harrison's coat hung in ribbons; his shirt was slashed to pieces, revealing his broad hairy chest which heaved from his exertions. Sweat ran down his corded neck, mingling with blood from gashes on arms, shoulders and breast muscles. His hair was clotted with mud, his clothes smeared with it.

"Must have been a whole gang," decided Hogan.

"It was one man," said Harrison; "one man or one gorilla; but it talked. Are you coming?"

"I am not. Whatever it was, it'll be gone now. Shine that light up the alley. See? Nothin' in sight. It wouldn't be waitin' around for us to grab it by the tail. You better get them cuts dressed. I've warned you against short cuts through dark alleys. Plenty men have grudges against you."

"I'll go to Richard Brent's place," said Harrison. "He'll fix me up. Go along with me, will you?"

"Sure, but you better let me—"

"Whatever it is, no!" growled Harrison, smarting from cuts and wounded vanity. "And listen, Hogan—don't mention this, see? I want to work it out for myself. This is no ordinary affair."

"It must not be—when *one* critter licks the tar out of Iron Man Harrison," was Hogan's biting comment; whereupon Harrison cursed under his breath.

Richard Brent's house stood just off Hogan's beat—one lone bulwark of respectability in the gradually rising tide of deterioration which was engulfing the neighborhood, but of which Brent, absorbed in his studies, was scarcely aware.

Brent was in his relic-littered study, delving into the obscure volumes which were at once his vocation and his passion. Distinctly the scholar in appearance, he contrasted strongly with his visitors. But he took charge without undue perturbation, summoning to his aid a half course of medical studies.

Hogan, having ascertained that Harrison's wounds were little more than scratches, took his departure, and presently the big detective sat opposite his host, a long whiskey glass in his massive hand.

Steve Harrison's height was above medium, but it seemed dwarfed by the breadth of his shoulders and the depth of his chest. His heavy arms hung low, and his head jutted aggressively forward. His low, broad brow, crowned with heavy black hair, suggested the man of action rather than the thinker, but his cold blue eyes reflected unexpected depths of mentality.

"'—As I died in the sand,'" he was saying. "That's what he yammered. Was he just a plain nut—or what the hell?"

Brent shook his head, absently scanning the walls, as if seeking inspiration in the weapons, antique and modern, which adorned it.

"You could not understand the language in which he spoke before?"

"Not a word. All I know is, it wasn't English and it wasn't Chinese. I do know the fellow was all steel springs and whale bone. It was like fighting a basketfull of wild cats. From now on I pack a gun regular. I haven't toted one recently, things have been so quiet. Always figured I was a match for several ordinary humans with my fists, anyway. But this devil wasn't an ordinary human; more like a wild animal."

He gulped his whiskey loudly, wiped his mouth with the back of his hand, and leaned toward Brent with a curious glint in his cold eyes.

"I wouldn't be saying this to anybody but you," he said with a strange hesitancy. "And maybe you'll think I'm crazy—but— well, I've bumped off several men in my life. Do you suppose— well, the Chinese believe in vampires and ghouls and walking dead men—and with all this talk about being dead, and me killing him—do you suppose—"

"Nonsense!" exclaimed Brent with an incredulous laugh. "When a man's dead, he's dead. He can't come back."

"That's what I've always thought," muttered Harrison. "But what the devil *did* he mean about me feeding him to the vultures?"

"I will tell you!" A voice hard and merciless as a knife edge cut their conversation.

Harrison and Brent wheeled, the former starting out of his chair. At the other end of the room one of the tall shuttered windows stood open for the sake of the coolness. Before this now stood a tall rangy man whose ill-fitting garments could not conceal the dangerous suppleness of his limbs, nor the breadth of his hard shoulders. Those cheap garments, muddy and blood-stained, seemed incongruous with the fierce dark hawk-like face, the flame of the dark eyes. Harrison grunted explosively, meeting the concentrated ferocity of that glare.

"You escaped me in the darkness," muttered the stranger, rocking slightly on the balls of his feet as he crouched, cat-like, a wicked curved dagger gleaming in his hand. "Fool! Did you dream I would not follow you? Here is light; you shall not escape again!"

"Who the devil are you?" demanded Harrison, standing in an unconscious attitude of defense, legs braced, fists poised.

"Poor of wit and scant of memory!" sneered the other. "You do not remember Amir Amin Izzedin, whom you slew in the Valley of the Vultures, thirty years ago! But I remember! From my cradle I remember. Before I could speak or walk, I knew that I was Amir Amin, and I remembered the Valley of Vultures. But only after deep shame and long wandering was full knowledge revealed to me. In the smoke of Shaitan I saw it! You have changed your garments of flesh, Ahmed Pasha, you Bedouin dog, but you can not escape me. By the Golden Calf!"

With a feline shriek he ran forward, dagger on high. Harrison sprang aside, surprisingly quick for a man of his bulk, and ripped an archaic spear from the wall. With a wordless yell like a warcry, he rushed, gripping it with both hands as if it were a rifle with bayonet fixed. Amir Amin wheeled toward him lithely, swaying his pantherish body to avoid the onrushing point. Too late Harrison realized his mistake—knew he would be spitted on the long knife as he plunged past the elusive Oriental. But he could not check his headlong impetus. And then Amir Amin's foot slipped on a sliding rug. The spear head ripped through his muddy coat, ploughed along his ribs, bringing a spurting stream of blood. Knocked off balance, he slashed wildly, and then Harrison's bull-like shoulder smashed into him, carrying them both to the floor.

Amir Amin was up first, minus his knife. As he glared wildly about for it, Brent, temporarily stunned by the unaccustomed violence, went into action. From the racks on the wall the scholar had taken a shotgun, and he wore a look of grim determination. As he lifted it, Amir Amin yelped and plunged recklessly through the nearest window. The crash of splintering glass mingled with the thunderous roar of the shotgun. Brent, rushing to the window, blinking in the powder fumes, saw a shadowy form dart across the shadowy lawn, under the trees, and vanish. He turned back into the room, where Harrison was rising, swearing luridly.

"Twice in one night is too danged much! Who is this nut,

anyway? I never saw him before!"

"A Druse!" stuttered Brent. "His accent—his mention of the golden calf—his hawk-like appearance—I am sure he is a Druse."

"What the hell is a Druse?" bellowed Harrison, in a spasm of irritation. His bandages had been torn and his cuts were bleeding again.

"They live in a mountain district in Syria," answered Brent; "a tribe of fierce fighters—"

"I can tell that," snarled Harrison. "I never expected to meet anybody that could lick me in a stand-up fight, but this devil's got me buffaloed. Anyway, it's a relief to know he's a living human being. But if I don't watch my step, I won't be. I'm staying here tonight, if you've got a room where I can lock all the doors and windows. Tomorrow I'm going to see Woon Sun."

2

Few men ever traversed the modest curio shop that opened on dingy River Street and passed through the cryptic curtain-hung door at the rear of that shop, to be amazed at what lay beyond: luxury in the shape of gilt-worked velvet hangings, silken cushioned divans, tea-cups of tinted porcelain on toy-like tables of lacquered ebony, over all which was shed a soft colored glow from electric bulbs concealed in gilded lanterns.

Steve Harrison's massive shoulders were as incongruous among those exotic surroundings as Woon Sun, short, sleek, clad in close-fitting black silk, was adapted to them.

The Chinaman smiled, but there was iron behind his suave mask.

"And so—" he suggested politely.

"And so I want your help," said Harrison abruptly. His nature was not that of a rapier, fencing for an opening, but a hammer smashing directly at its objective.

"I know that you know every Oriental in the city. I've described this bird to you. Brent says he's a Druse. You couldn't be ignorant of him. He'd stand out in any crowd. He doesn't belong with the general run of River Street gutter rats. He's a wolf."

"Indeed he is," murmured Woon Sun. "It would be useless to try to conceal from you the fact that I know this young barbarian. His name is Ali ibn Suleyman."

121

"He called himself something else," scowled Harrison.

"Perhaps. But he is Ali ibn Suleyman to his friends. He is, as your friend said, a Druse. His tribe live in stone cities in the Syrian mountains—particularly about the mountain called the Djebel Druse."

"Muhammadans, eh?" rumbled Harrison. "Arabs?"

"No; they are, as it were, a race apart. They worship a calf cast of gold, believe in reincarnation, and practise heathen rituals abhorred by the Moslems. First the Turks and now the French have tried to govern them, but they have never really been conquered."

"I can believe it, alright," muttered Harrison. "But why did he call me 'Ahmed Pasha'? What's he got it in for *me* for?"

Woon Sun spread his hands helplessly.

"Well, anyway," growled Harrison, "I don't want to keep on dodging knives in back alleys. I want you to fix it so I can get the drop on him. Maybe he'll talk sense, if I can get the cuffs on him. Maybe I can argue him out of this idea of killing me, whatever it is. He looks more like a fanatic than a criminal. Anyway, I want to find out just what it's all about."

"What could I do?" murmured Woon Sun, folding his hands on his round belly, malice gleaming from under his dropping lids. "I might go further and ask, why *should* I do anything for you?"

"You've stayed inside the law since coming here," said Harrison. "I know that curio shop is just a blind; you're not making any fortune out of it. But I know, too, that you're not mixed up with anything crooked. You had your dough when you came here—plenty of it—and how you got it is no concern of mine.

"But, Woon Sun," Harrison leaned forward and lowered his voice, "do you remember that young Eurasian Josef La Tour? I was the first man to reach his body, the night he was killed in Osman Pasha's gambling den. I found a note book on him, and I kept it. Woon Sun, your name was in that book!"

An electric silence impregnated the atmosphere. Woon Sun's smooth yellow features were immobile, but red points glimmered in the shoe-button blackness of his eyes.

"La Tour must have been intending to blackmail you," said Harrison. "He'd worked up a lot of interesting data. Reading that note book, I found that your name wasn't always Woon Sun; found out where you got your money, too."

The red points had faded in Woon Sun's eyes; those eyes seemed glazed; a greenish pallor overspread the yellow face.

"You've hidden yourself well, Woon Sun," muttered the detective. "But double-crossing your society and skipping with all their money was a dirty trick. If they ever find you, they'll feed you to the rats. I don't know but what it's my duty to write a letter to a mandarin in Canton, named—"

"Stop!" The Chinaman's voice was unrecognizable. "Say no more, for the love of Buddha! I will do as you ask. I have this Druse's confidence, and can arrange it easily. It is now scarcely dark. At midnight be in the alley known to the Chinese of River Street as the Alley of Silence. You know the one I mean? Good. Wait in the nook made by the angle of the walls, near the end of the alley, and soon Ali ibn Suleyman will walk past it, ignorant of your presence. Then if you dare, you can arrest him."

"I've got a gun this time," grunted Harrison. "Do this for me, and we'll forget about La Tour's note book. But no double-crossing, or—"

"You hold my life in your fingers," answered Woon Sun. "How can I double-cross you?"

Harrison grunted skeptically, but rose without further words, strode through the curtained door and through the shop, and let himself into the street. Woon Sun watched inscrutably the broad shoulders swinging aggressively through the swarms of stooped, hurrying Orientals, men and women, who thronged River Street at that hour; then he locked the shop door and hurried back through the curtained entrance into the ornate chamber behind. And there he halted, staring.

Smoke curled up in a blue spiral from a satin divan, and on that divan lounged a young woman—a slim, dark supple creature, whose night-black hair, full red lips and scintillant eyes hinted at blood more exotic than her costly garments suggested. Those red lips curled in malicious mockery, but the glitter of her dark eyes belied any suggestion of humor, however satirical, just as their vitality belied the languor expressed in the listlessly drooping hand that held the cigarette.

"Joan!" The Chinaman's eyes narrowed to slits of suspicion. "How did you get in here?"

"Through that door over there, which opens on a passage which in turn opens on the alley that runs behind this building. Both doors were locked—but long ago I learned how to pick locks."

"But why—?"

"I saw the brave detective come here. I have been watching him for some time now—though he does not know it." The girl's vital eyes smoldered yet more deeply for an instant.

"Have you been listening outside the door?" demanded Woon Sun, turning grey.

"I am no eavesdropper. I did not have to listen. I can guess why he came—and you promised to help him?"

"I don't know what you are talking about," answered Woon Sun, with a secret sigh of relief.

"You lie!" The girl came tensely upright on the divan, her convulsive fingers crushing her cigarette, her beautiful face momentarily contorted. Then she regained control of herself, in a cold resolution more dangerous than spitting fury. "Woon Sun," she said calmly, drawing a stubby black automatic from her mantle, "how easily and with what good will could I kill you where you stand—but I do not wish to. We shall remain friends. See, I replace the gun—but do not tempt me, my friend. Do not try to eject me or to use violence with me. Here, sit down and take a cigarette. We will talk this over calmly."

"I do not know what you wish to talk over," said Woon Sun, sinking down on a divan and mechanically taking the cigarette she offered, as if hypnotized by the glitter of her magnetic black eyes—and the knowledge of the hidden pistol. All his Oriental immobility could not conceal the fact that he feared this young pantheress—more than he feared Harrison. "The detective came here merely on a friendly call," he said. "I have many friends among the police. If I were found murdered they would go to much trouble to find and hang the guilty person."

"Who spoke of killing?" protested Joan, snapping a match on a pointed, henna-tinted nail, and holding the tiny flame to Woon Sun's cigarette. At the instant of contact their faces were close together, and the Chinaman drew back from the strange intensity that burned in her dark eyes. Nervously he drew on the cigarette, inhaling deeply.

"I have been your friend," he said. "You should not come here threatening me with a pistol. I am a man of no small importance on River Street. You, perhaps, are not as secure as you suppose. The time may come when you will need a friend like me—"

He was suddenly aware that the girl was not answering him, or even heeding his words. Her own cigarette smoldered

unheeded in her fingers, and through the clouds of smoke her
eyes burned at him with the terrible eagerness of a beast of prey.
With a gasp he jerked the cigarette from his lips and held it to his
nostrils.

"She-devil!" It was a shriek of pure terror. Hurling the
smoking stub from him, he lurched to his feet where he swayed
dizzily on legs suddenly grown numb and dead. His fingers
groped toward the girl with strangling motions. "Poison—
dope—the black lotos—"

She rose, thrust an open hand against the flowered breast of
his silk jacket and shoved him back down on the divan. He fell
sprawling and lay in a limp attitude, his eyes open, but glazed
and vacant. She bent over him, tense and shuddering with the
intensity of her purpose.

"You are my slave," she hissed, as a hypnotizer impells his
suggestions upon his subject. "You have no will but my will.
Your conscious brain is asleep, but your tongue is free to tell the
truth. Only the truth remains in your drugged brain. Why did
Detective Harrison come here?"

"To learn of Ali ibn Suleyman, the Druse," muttered Woon
Sun, in a curious, lifeless sing-song.

"You promised to betray the Druse to him?"

"I promised but I lied," the monotonous voice continued.
"The detective goes at midnight to the Alley of Silence, which is
the Gateway to the Master. Many bodies have gone feet-first
through that gateway. It is the best place to dispose of his corpse.
I will tell the Master he came to spy upon him, and thus gain
honor for myself, as well as ridding myself of any enemy. The
white barbarian will stand in the nook between the walls,
awaiting the Druse as I bade him. He does not know that a trap
can be opened in the angle of the walls behind him and a hand
strike with a hatchet. My secret will die with him."

Apparently Joan was indifferent as to what the secret might
be, since she questioned the drugged man no further. But the
expression on her beautiful face was not pleasant.

"No, my yellow friend," she murmured. "Let the white
barbarian go to the Alley of Silence—aye, but it is not a yellow-
belly who will come to him in the darkness. He shall have his
desire. He shall meet Ali ibn Suleyman; and after him, the
worms that writhe in darkness!"

Taking a tiny jade vial from her bosom, she poured wine
from a porcelain jug into an amber goblet, and shook into the

liquor the contents of the vial. Then she put the goblet into Woon Sun's limp fingers and sharply ordered him to drink, guiding the beaker to his lips. He gulped the wine mechanically, and immediately slumped sidewise on the divan and lay still.

"You will wield no hatchet this night," she muttered. "When you awaken many hours from now, my desire will have been accomplished—and you will need fear Harrison no longer, either—whatever may be his hold upon you."

She seemed struck by a sudden thought and halted as she was turning toward the door that opened on the corridor.

"'Not as secure as I suppose'—" she muttered, half aloud. "What could he have meant by that?" A shadow, almost of apprehension, crossed her face. Then she shrugged her shoulders. "Too late to make him tell me now. No matter. The Master does not suspect—and what if he did? He's no Master of mine. I waste too much time—"

She stepped into the corridor, closing the door behind her. Then when she turned, she stopped short. Before her stood three grim figures, tall, gaunt, black-robed, their shaven vulture-like heads nodding in the dim light of the corridor.

In that instant, frozen with awful certainty, she forgot the gun in her bosom. Her mouth opened for a scream, which died in a gurgle as a bony hand was clapped over her lips.

3

The alley, nameless to white men, but known to the teeming swarms of River Street as the Alley of Silence, was as devious and cryptic as the characteristics of the race which frequented it. It did not run straight, but, slanting unobstrusedly off River Street, wound through a maze of tall, gloomy structures, which, to outward seeming at least, were tenements and warehouses, and crumbling forgotten buildings apparently occupied only by rats, where boarded-up windows stared blankly.

As River Street was the heart of the Oriental quarter, so the Alley of Silence was the heart of River Street, though apparently empty and deserted. At least that was Steve Harrison's idea, though he could give no definite reason why he ascribed so much importance to a dark, dirty, crooked alley that seemed to go nowhere. The men at headquarters twitted him, telling him that he had worked so much down in the twisty mazes of rat-haunted River Street that he was getting a Chinese twist in his mind.

He thought of this, as he crouched impatiently in the angle formed by the last crook of that unsavory alley. That it was past midnight he knew from a stealthy glance at the luminous figures on his watch. Only the scurrying of rats broke the silence. He was well hidden in a cleft formed by two jutting walls, whose slanting planes came together to form a triangle opening on the alley. Alley architecture was as crazy as some of the tales which crept forth from its dank blackness. A few paces further on the

127

alley ended abruptly at the cliff-like blankness of a wall, in which showed no windows and only a boarded-up door.

This Harrison knew only by a vague luminance which filtered greyly into the alley from above. Shadows lurked along the angles darker than the Stygian pits, and the boarded-up door was only a vague splotch in the sheer of the wall. An empty warehouse, Harrison supposed, abandoned and rotting through the years. Probably it fronted on the bank of the river, ledged by crumbling wharfs, forgotten and unused in the years since the river trade and activity had shifted into a newer part of the city.

He wondered if he had been seen ducking into the alley. He had not turned directly off River Street, with its slinking furtive shapes that drifted silently past all night long. He had come in from a wandering side street, working his way between leaning walls and jutting corners until he came out into the dark winding alley. He had not worked the Oriental quarter for so long, not to have absorbed some of the stealth and wariness of its inhabitants.

But midnight was past, and no sign of the man he hunted. Then he stiffened. Someone was coming up the alley. But the gait was a shuffling step; not the sort he would have connected with a man like Ali ibn Suleyman. A tall stooped figure loomed vaguely in the gloom and shuffled on past the detective's covert. His trained eye, even in the dimness, told Harrison that the man was not the one he sought.

The unknown went straight to the blank door and knocked three times with a long interval between the raps. Abruptly a red disk glowed in the door. Words were hissed in Chinese. The man on the outside replied in the same tongue, and his words came clearly to the tensed detective: *"Erlik Khan!"* Then the door unexpectedly opened inward, and he passed through, illumined briefly in the reddish light which streamed through the opening. Then darkness followed the closing of the door, and silence reigned again in the alley of its name.

But crouching in the shadowed angle, Harrison felt his heart pound against his ribs. He had recognized the fellow who passed through the door as a Chinese killer with a price on his head; but it was not that recognition which sent the detective's blood pumping through his veins. It was the pass-word muttered by the evil-visaged visitant: "Erlik Khan!" It was like the materialization of a dim nightmare dream; like the confirmation of an evil legend.

For more than a year rumors had crept snakily out of the black alleys and crumbling doorways behind which the mysterious yellow people moved phantom-like and inscrutable. Scarcely rumors, either; that was a term too concrete and definite to be applied to the maunderings of dope-fiends, the ravings of madmen, the whimpers of dying men—disconnected whispers that died on the midnight wind. Yet through these disjointed mutterings had wound a dread name, fearsomely repeated, in shuddering whispers: *"Erlik Khan!"*

It was a phrase always coupled with dark deeds; it was like a black wind moaning through midnight trees; a hint, a breath, a myth, that no man could deny or affirm. None knew if it were the name of a man, a cult, a course of action, a curse, or a dream. Through its associations it became a slogan of dread: a whisper of black water lapping at rotten piles; of blood dripping on slimy stones; of death whimpers in dark corners; of stealthy feet shuffling through the haunted midnight to unknown dooms.

The men at headquarters had laughed at Harrison when he swore that he sensed a connection between various scattered crimes. They had told him, as usual, that he had worked too long among the labyrinths of the Oriental district. But that very fact made him more sensitive to furtive and subtle impressions than were his mates. And at times he had seemed almost to sense a vague and monstrous Shape that moved behind a web of illusion.

And now, like the hiss of an unseen serpent in the dark, had come to him at least as much concrete assurance as was contained in the whispered words: *"Erlik Khan!"*

Harrison stepped from his nook and went swiftly toward the boarded door. His feud with Ali ibn Suleyman was pushed into the background. The big dick was an opportunist; when chance presented itself, he seized it first and made plans later. And his instinct told him that he was on the threshold of something big.

A slow, almost imperceptible drizzle had begun. Overhead, between the towering black walls, he got a glimpse of thick grey clouds, hanging so low they seemed to merge with the lofty roofs, dully reflecting the glow of the city's myriad lights. The rumble of distant traffic came to his ears faintly and faraway. His environs seemed curiously strange, alien and aloof. He might have been stealing through the gloom of Canton, or forbidden Peking—or of Babylon, or Egyptian Memphis.

Halting before the door, he ran his hands lightly over it, and

over the boards which apparently sealed it. And he discovered
that some of the bolt-heads were false. It was an ingenious trick
to make the door appear inaccessible to the casual glance.

Setting his teeth, with a feeling as of taking a blind plunge in
the dark, Harrison rapped three times as he had heard the killer,
Fang Yim, rap. Almost instantly a round hole opened in the
door, level with his face, and framed dimly in a red glow he
glimpsed a yellow Mongoloid visage. Sibilant Chinese hissed at
him.

Harrison's hat was pulled low over his eyes, and his coat
collar, turned up against the drizzle, concealed the lower part of
his features. But the disguise was not needed. The man inside the
door was no one Harrison had ever seen.

"Erlik Khan!" muttered the detective. No suspicion shadowed the slant eyes. Evidently white men had passed through
that door before. It swung inward, and Harrison slouched
through, shoulders hunched, hands thrust deep in his coat
pockets, the very picture of a waterfront hoodlum. He heard the
door closed behind him, and found himself in a small square
chamber at the end of a narrow corridor. He noted that the door
was furnished with a great steel bar, which the Chinaman was
now lowering into place in the heavy iron sockets set on each
side of the portal, and the hole in the center was covered by a
steel disk, working on a hinge. Outside of a squatting-cushion
beside the door for the doorman, the chamber was without
furnishings.

All this Harrison's trained eye took in at a glance, as he
slouched across the chamber. He felt that he would not be
expected, as a denizen of whatever resort the place proved to be,
to remain long in the room. A small red lantern, swinging from
the ceiling, lighted the chamber, but the corridor seemed to be
without lumination, save such as was furnished by the aforesaid
lantern.

Harrison slouched on down the shadowy corridor, giving no
evidence of the tensity of his nerves. He noted, with sidelong
glances, the firmness and newness of the walls. Obviously a great
deal of work had recently been done on the interior of this
supposedly deserted building.

Like the alley outside, the corridor did not run straight.
Ahead of him it bent at an angle, around which shown a mellow
stream of light, and beyond this bend Harrison heard a light

padding step approaching. He grabbed at the nearest door, which opened silently under his hand, and closed as silently behind him. In pitch darkness he stumbled over steps, nearly falling, catching at the wall, and cursing the noise he made. He heard the padding step halt outside the door; then a hand pushed against it. But Harrison had his forearm and elbow braced against the panel. His groping fingers found a bolt and he slid it home, wincing at the faint scraping it made. A voice hissed something in Chinese, but Harrison made no answer. Turning, he groped his way hurriedly down the stairs.

Presently his feet struck a level floor, and in another instant he bumped into a door. He had a flashlight in his pocket, but he dared not use it. He fumbled at the door and found it unlocked. The edges, sill and jambs seemed to be padded. The walls, too, seemed to be specially treated, beneath his sensitive fingers. He wondered with a shiver what cries and noises those walls and padded doors were devised to drown.

Shoving open the door, he blinked in a flood of soft reddish light, and drew his gun in a panic. But no shouts or shots greeted him, and as his eyes became accustomed to the light, he saw that he was looking into a great basement-like room, empty except for three huge packing cases. There were doors at either end of the room, and along the sides, but they were all closed. Evidently he was some distance under the ground.

He approached the packing cases, which had apparently but recently been opened, their contents not yet removed. The boards of the lids lay on the floor beside them, with wads of excelsior and tow packing.

"Booze?" he muttered to himself. "Dope? Smugglers?"

He scowled down into the nearest case. A single layer of tow sacking covered the contents, and he frowned in puzzlement at the outlines under that sacking. Then suddenly, with his skin crawling, he snatched at the sacking and pulled it away—and recoiled, choking in horror. Three yellow faces, frozen and immobile, stared sightlessly up at the swinging lamp. There seemed to be another layer underneath—

Gagging and sweating, Harrison went about his grisly task of verifying what he could scarcely believe. And then he mopped away the beads of perspiration.

"Three packing cases full of dead Chinamen!" he whispered shakily. "Eighteen yellow stiffs! Great cats! Talk about wholesale murder! I thought I'd bumped into so many hellish sights that nothing could upset me. But this is piling it on *too* thick!"

It was the stealthy opening of a door which roused him from his morbid meditations. He wheeled, galvanized. Before him crouched a monstrous and brutish shape, like a creature out of a nightmare. The detective had a glimpse of a massive, half-naked torso, a bullet-like shaven head split by a toothy and slavering grin—then the brute was upon him.

Harrison was no gunman; all his instincts were of the strong-arm variety. Instead of drawing his gun, he dashed his right mauler into that toothy grin, and was rewarded by a jet of blood. The creature's head snapped back at an agonized angle, but his bony fingers had locked on the detective's lapels. Harrison drove his left wrist-deep into his assailant's midriff, causing a green tint to overspread the coppery face, but the fellow hung on, and with a wrench, pulled Harrison's coat down over his shoulders. Recognizing a trick meant to imprison his arms, Harrison did not resist the movement, but rather aided it, with a headlong heave of his powerful body that drove his lowered head hard against the yellow man's breastbone, and tore his own arms free of the clinging sleeves.

The giant staggered backward, gasping for breath, holding the futile garment like a shield before him, and Harrison, inexorable in his attack, swept him back against the wall by the sheer force of his rush, and smashed a bone-crushing left and right to his jaw. The yellow giant pitched backward, his eyes already glazed; his head struck the wall, fetching blood in streams, and he toppled face-first to the floor where he lay twitching, his shaven head in a spreading pool of blood.

"A Mongol strangler!" panted Harrison, glaring down at him. "What kind of a nightmare is this, anyway?"

It was just at that instant that a blackjack, wielded from behind, smashed down on his head; the lights went out.

4

Some misplaced connection with his present condition caused Steve Harrison to dream fitfully of the Spanish Inquisition just before he regained consciousness. Possibly it was the clank of steel chains. Drifting back from a land of enforced dreams, his first sensation was that of an aching head, and he touched it tenderly and swore bitterly.

He was lying on a concrete floor. A steel band girdled his waist, hinged behind, and fastened before with a heavy steel lock. To that band was riveted a chain, the other one end of which was made fast to a ring in the wall. A dim lantern suspended from the ceiling lighted the room, which seemed to have but one door and no window. The door was closed.

Harrison noted other objects in the room, and as he blinked and they took definite shape, he was aware of an icy premonition, too fantastic and monstrous for credit. Yet the objects at which he was staring were incredible, too.

There was an affair with levers and windlasses and chains. There was a chain suspended from the ceiling, and some objects that looked like iron fire tongs. And in one corner there was a massive, grooved block, and beside it leaned a heavy broad-edged axe. The detective shuddered in spite of himself, wondering if he were in the grip of some damnable medieval dream. He could not doubt the significance of those objects. He had seen their duplicates in museums—

Aware that the door had opened, he twisted about and glared at the figure dimly framed there—a tall, shadowy form, clad in night-black robes. This figure moved like a shadow of Doom into the chamber, and closed the door. From the shadow of a hood, two icy eyes glittered eerily, framed in a dim yellow oval of a face.

For an instant the silence held, broken suddenly by the detective's irate bellow.

"What the hell is this? Who are you? Get this chain off me!"

A scornful silence was the only answer, and under the unwinking scrutiny of those ghostly eyes, Harrison felt cold perspiration gather on his forehead and among the hairs on the backs of his hands.

"You fool!" At the peculiar hollow quality of the voice, Harrison started nervously. "You have found your doom!"

"Who are you?" demanded the detective.

"Men call me Erlik Kahn, which signifies Lord of the Dead," answered the other. A trickle of ice meandered down Harrison's spine, not so much from fear, but because of the grisly thrill in the realization that at last he was face to face with the materialization of his suspicions.

"So Erlik Khan is a man, after all," grunted the detective. "I'd begun to believe that it was the name of a Chinese society."

"I am no Chinese," returned Erlik Khan. "I am a Mongol—direct descendant of Genghis Khan, the great conqueror, before whom all Asia bowed."

"Why tell me this?" growled Harrison, concealing his eagerness to hear more.

"Because you are soon to die," was the tranquil reply, "and I would have you realize that it is into the hands of no common gangster scum you have blundered.

"I was head of a lamasery in the mountains of Inner Mongolia, and, had I been able to attain my ambitions, would have rebuilt a lost empire—aye, the old empire of Genghis Khan. But I was opposed by various fools, and barely escaped with my life.

"I came to America, and here a new purpose was born in me: that of forging all secret Oriental societies into one mighty organization to do my bidding and reach unseen tentacles across the seas into hidden lands. Here, unsuspected by such blundering fools as you, have I built my castle. Already I have accomplished much. Those who oppose me die suddenly, or—

you saw those fools in the packing cases in the cellar. They are members of the Yat Soy, who thought to defy me."

"Judas!" muttered Harrison. "A whole tong scuppered!"

"Not dead," corrected Erlik Khan. "Merely in a cataleptic state, induced by certain drugs introduced into their liquor by trusted servants. They were brought here in order that I might convince them of their folly in opposing me. I have a number of underground crypts like this one, wherein are implements and machines calculated to change the mind of the most stubborn."

"Torture chambers under River Street!" muttered the detective. "Damned if this isn't a nightmare!"

"You, who have puzzled so long amidst the mazes of River Street, are you surprized at the mysteries within its mysteries?" murmured Erlik Khan. "Truly, you have but touched the fringes of its secrets. Many men do my bidding—Chinese, Syrians, Mongols, Hindus, Arabs, Turks, Egyptians."

"Why?" demanded Harrison. "Why should so many men of such different and hostile religions serve you—"

"Behind all differences of religion and belief," said Erlik Khan, "lies the eternal *Oneness* that is the essence and root-stem of the East. Before Muhammad was, or Confucius, or Gautama, there were signs and symbols, ancient beyond belief, but common to all sons of the Orient. There are cults stronger and older than Islam or Buddhism—cults whose roots are lost in the blackness of the dawn ages, before Babylon was, or Atlantis sank.

"To an adept, these young religions and beliefs are but new cloaks, masking the reality beneath. Even to a dead man I can say no more. Suffice to know that I, whom men call Erlik Khan, have power above and behind the powers of Islam or of Buddha."

Harrison lay silent, meditating over the Mongol's words, and presently the latter resumed: "You have but yourself to blame for your plight. I am convinced that you did not come here tonight to spy upon me—poor, blundering, barbarian fool, who did not even guess my existence. I have learned that you came in your crude way, expecting to trap a servant of mine, the Druse Ali ibn Suleyman."

"You sent him to kill me," growled Harrison.

A scornful laugh put his teeth on edge.

"Do you fancy yourself so important? I would not turn aside to crush a blind worm. Another put the Druse on your trail—a deluded person, a miserable, egoistic fool, who even now is paying the price of folly.

"Ali ibn Suleyman is, like many of my henchmen, an outcast from his people, his life forfeit.

"Of all virtues, the Druses most greatly esteem the elementary one of physical courage. When a Druse shows cowardice, none taunts him, but when the warriors gather to drink coffee, some one spills a cup on his *abba*. That is his death-sentence. At the first opportunity, he is obliged to go forth and die as heroically as possible.

"Ali ibn Suleyman failed on a mission where success was impossible. Being young, he did not realize that his fanatical tribe would brand him as a coward because, in failing, he had not got himself killed. But the cup of shame was spilled on his robe. Ali was young; he did not wish to die. He broke a custom of a thousand years; he fled the Djebel Druse and became a wanderer over the earth.

"Within the past year he joined my followers, and I welcomed his desperate courage and terrible fighting ability. But recently the foolish person I mentioned decided to use him to further a private feud, in no way connected with my affairs. That was unwise. My followers live but to serve me, whether they realize it or not.

"Ali goes often to a certain house to smoke opium, and this person caused him to be drugged with the dust of the black lotos, which produces a hypnotic condition, during which the subject is amenable to suggestions, which, if continually repeated, carry over into the victim's waking hours.

"The Druses believe that when a Druse dies, his soul is instantly reincarnated in a Druse baby. The great Druse hero, Amir Amin Izzedin, was killed by the Arab shaykh Ahmed Pasha, the night Ali ibn Suleyman was born. Ali has always believed himself to be the reincarnated soul of Amir Amin, and mourned because he could not revenge his former self on Ahmed Pasha, who was killed a few days after he slew the Druse chief.

"All this the *person* ascertained, and by means of the black lotos, known as the Smoke of Shaitan, convinced the Druse that you, detective Harrison, were the reincarnation of his old enemy Shaykh Ahmed Pasha. It took time and cunning to convince him, even in his drugged condition, that an Arab shaykh could be reincarnated in an American detective, but the *person* was very clever, and so at last Ali was convinced, and disobeyed my orders—which were never to molest the police, unless they got in my way, and then only according to my directions. For I do not woo publicity. He must be taught a lesson.

"Now I must go. I have spent too much time with you already. Soon one will come who will lighten you of your earthly burdens. Be consoled by the realization that the foolish person who brought you to this pass is expiating her crime likewise. In fact, separated from you but by that padded partition. Listen!"

From somewhere near rose a feminine voice, incoherent but urgent.

"The foolish one realizes her mistake," smiled Erlik Khan benevolently. "Even through these walls pierce her lamentations. Well, she is not the first to regret foolish actions in these crypts. And now I must be gone. Those foolish Yat Soys will soon begin to awaken."

"Wait, you devil!" roared Harrison, struggling up against his chain. "What—"

"Enough, enough!" There was a touch of impatience in the Mongol's tone. "You weary me. Get you to your meditations, for your time is short. Farewell, Mr. Harrison—*not* au revoir."

The door closed silently, and the detective was left alone with his thoughts which were far from pleasant. He cursed himself for falling into that trap; cursed his peculiar obsession for always working alone. None knew of the tryst he had tried to keep; he had divulged his plans to no one.

Beyond the partition the muffled sobs continued. Sweat began to bead Harrison's brow. His nerves, untouched by his own plight, began to throb in sympathy with that terrified voice.

Then the door opened again, and Harrison, twisting about, knew with numbing finality that he looked on his executioner. It was a tall, gaunt Mongol, clad only in sandals and a trunk-like garment of yellow silk, from the girdle of which depended a bunch of keys. He carried a great bronze bowl and some objects that looked like joss sticks. These he placed on the floor near Harrison, and squatting just out of the captive's reach, began to arrange the evil-smelling sticks in a sort of pyramidal shape in the bowl. And Harrison, glaring, remembered a half-forgotten horror among the myriad dim horrors of River Street: a corpse he had found in a sealed room where acrid fumes still hovered over a charred bronze bowl—the corpse of a Hindu, shriveled and crinkled like old leather—mummified by a lethal smoke that killed and shrunk the victim like a poisoned rat.

From the other cell came a shriek so sharp and poignant that Harrison jumped and cursed. The Mongol halted in his task, a match in his hand. His parchment-like visage split in a leer of appreciation, disclosing the withered stump of a tongue; the man was a mute.

The cries increased in intensity, seemingly more in fright than in pain, yet an element of pain was evident. The mute, rapt in his evil glee, rose and leaned nearer the wall, cocking his ear as if unwilling to miss any whimper of agony from that torture cell. Saliva dribbled from the corner of his loose mouth; he sucked his breath in eagerly, unconsciously edging nearer the wall— Harrison's foot shot out, hooked suddenly and fiercely about the lean ankle. The Mongol threw wild arms aloft, and toppled into the detective's waiting arms.

It was with no scientific wrestling hold that Harrison broke the executioner's neck. His pent-up fury had swept away everything but a berserk madness to grip and rend and tear in primitive passion. Like a grizzly he grappled and twisted, and felt the vertebrae give way like rotten twigs.

Dizzy with glutted fury he struggled up, still gripping the limp shape, gasping incoherent blasphemy. His fingers closed on the keys dangling at the dead man's belt, and ripping them free, he hurled the corpse savagely to the floor in a paroxysm of excess ferocity. The thing struck loosely and lay without twitching, the sightless face grinning hideously back over the yellow shoulder.

Harrison mechanically tried the keys in the lock at his waist. An instant later, freed of his shackles, he staggered in the middle of the cell, almost overcome by the wild rush of emotion—hope, exultation, and the realization of freedom. He snatched up the grim axe that leaned against the darkly stained block, and could have yelled with bloodthirsty joy as he felt the perfect balance of the weighty weapon, and saw the dim light gleaming on its flaring razor-edge.

An instant's fumbling with the keys at the lock, and the door opened. He looked out into a narrow corridor, dimly lighted, lined with closed doors. From one next to his, the distressing cries were coming, muffled by the padded door and the specially treated walls.

In his berserk wrath he wasted no time in trying his keys on that door. Heaving up the sturdy axe with both hands, he swung it crashing against the panels, heedless of the noise, mindful only of his frenzied urge to violent action. Under his flailing strokes the door burst inward and through its splintered ruins he lunged, eyes glaring, lips asnarl.

He had come into a cell much like the one he had just quitted. There was a rack—a veritable medieval devil-machine—and in its cruel grip writhed a pitiful white figure—a girl, clad only in a scanty chemise. A gaunt Mongol bent over the handles, turning them slowly. Another was engaged in heating a pointed iron over a small brazier.

This he saw at a glance, as the girl rolled her head toward him and cried out in agony. Then the Mongol with the iron ran at him silently, the glowing, white-hot steel thrust forward like a spear. In the grip of red fury though he was, Harrison did not lose his head. A wolfish grin twisting his thin lips, he side stepped, and split the torturer's head as a melon is split. Then as the corpse tumbled down, spilling blood and brains, he wheeled cat-like to meet the onslaught of the other.

The attack of this one was silent as that of the other. They too were mutes. He did not lunge in so recklessly as his mate, but his caution availed him little as Harrison swung his dripping axe. The Mongol threw up his left arm, and the curved edge sheared through muscle and bone, leaving the limb hanging by a shred of flesh. Like a dying panther the torturer sprang in turn, driving in his knife with the fury of desperation. At the same instant the bloody axe flailed down. The thrusting knife point tore through Harrison's shirt, ploughed through the flesh over his breast-bone, and as he flinched involuntarily, the axe turned in his hand and struck flat, crushing the Mongol's skull like an egg shell.

Swearing like a pirate, the detective wheeled this way and that, glaring for new foes. Then he remembered the girl on the rack.

And then he recognized her at last. "Joan La Tour! What in the name—"

"Let me go!" she wailed. "Oh, for God's sake, let me go!"

The mechanism of the devilish machine balked him. But he saw that she was tied by heavy cords on wrists and ankles, and cutting them, he lifted her free. He set his teeth at the thought of the ruptures, dislocated joints and torn sinews that she might have suffered, but evidently the torture had not progressed far enough for permanent injury. Joan seemed none the worse, physically, for her experience, but she was almost hysterical. As he looked at the cowering, sobbing figure, shivering in her scanty garment, and remembered the perfectly poised, sophisticated, and self-sufficient beauty as he had known her, he shook his head in amazement. Certainly Erlik Khan knew how to bend his victims to his despotic will.

"Let us go," she pleaded between sobs. "They'll be back—they will have heard the noise—"

"Alright," he grunted; "but where the devil are we?"

"I don't know," she whimpered. "Somewhere in the house of Erlik Khan. His Mongol mutes brought me here earlier tonight, through passages and tunnels connecting various parts of the city with this place."

"Well, come on," said he. "We might as well go somewhere."

Taking her hand he led her out into the corridor, and glaring about uncertainly, he spied a narrow stair winding upward. Up this they went, to be halted soon by a padded door, which was not locked. This he closed behind him, and tried to lock, but without success. None of his keys would fit the lock.

"I don't know whether our racket was heard or not," he grunted, "unless somebody was nearby. This building is fixed to drown noise. We're in some part of the basement, I reckon."

"We'll never get out alive," whimpered the girl. "You're wounded—I saw blood on your shirt—"

"Nothing but a scratch," grunted the big detective, stealthily investigating with his fingers the ugly ragged gash that was soaking his torn shirt and waist-band with steadily seeping blood. Now that his fury was beginning to cool, he felt the pain of it.

Abandoning the door, he groped upward in thick darkness, guiding the girl of whose presence he was aware only by the contact of a soft little hand trembling in his. Then he heard her sobbing convulsively.

"This is all my fault! I got you into this! The Druse, Ali ibn Suleyman—"

"I know," he grunted; "Erlik Khan told me. But I never suspected that you were the one who put this crazy heathen up to knifing me. Was Erlik Khan lying?"

"No," she whimpered. "My brother—Josef. Until tonight I thought you killed him."

He started convulsively.

"*Me*? I didn't do it! I don't know who did. Somebody shot him over my shoulder—aiming at me, I reckon, during that raid on Osman Pasha's joint."

"I know, now," she muttered. "But I'd always believed you

lied about it. I thought you killed him, yourself. Lots of people think that, you know. I wanted revenge. I hit on what looked like a sure scheme. The Druse doesn't know me. He's never seen me, awake. I bribed the owner of the opium-joint that Ali ibn Suleyman frequents, to drug him with the black lotus. Then I would do my work on him. It's much like hypnotism.

"The owner of the joint must have talked. Anyway, Erlik Khan learned how I'd been using Ali ibn Suleyman, and he decided to punish me. Maybe he was afraid the Druse talked too much while he was drugged.

"I know too much, too, for one not sworn to obey Erlik Khan. I'm part Oriental and I've played in the fringe of River Street affairs until I've got myself tangled up in them. Josef played with fire, too, just as I've been doing, and it cost him his life. Erlik Khan told me tonight who the real murderer was. It was Osman Pasha. He wasn't aiming at you. He intended to kill Josef.

"I've been a fool, and now my life is forfeit. Erlik Khan is the king of River Street."

"He won't be long," growled the detective. "We're going to get out of here somehow, and then I'm coming back with a squad and clean out this damned rat hole. I'll show Erlik Khan that this is America, not Mongolia. When I get through with him—"

He broke off short as Joan's fingers closed on his convulsively. From somewhere below them sounded a confused muttering. What lay above, he had no idea, but his skin crawled at the thought of being trapped on that dark twisting stair. He hurried, almost dragging the girl, and presently encountered a door that did not seem to be locked.

Even as he did so, a light flared below, and a shrill yelp galvanized him. Far below he saw a cluster of dim shapes in a red glow of a torch or lantern. Rolling eyeballs flashed whitely, steel glimmered.

Darting through the door and slamming it behind them, he sought for a frenzied instant for a key that would fit the lock and not finding it, seized Joan's wrist and ran down the corridor that wound among black velvet hangings. Where it led he did not know. He had lost all sense of direction. But he did know that death grim and relentless was on their heels.

Looking back, he saw a hideous crew swarm up into the corridor: yellow men in silk jackets and baggy trousers, grasping knives. Ahead of him loomed a curtain-hung door. Tearing aside the heavy satin hangings, he hurled the door open and leaped through, drawing Joan after him, slamming the door behind them. And stopped dead, an icy despair gripping at his heart.

5

They had come into a vast hall-like chamber, such as he had never dreamed existed under the prosaic roofs of any Western city.

Gilded lanterns, on which writhed fantastic carven dragons, hung from the fretted ceiling, shedding a golden lustre over velvet hangings that hid the walls. Across these black expanses other dragons twisted, worked in silver, gold and scarlet. In an alcove near the door reared a squat idol, bulky, taller than a man, half hidden by a heavy lacquer screen, an obscene, brutish travesty of nature, that only a Mongolian brain could conceive. Before it stood a low altar, whence curled up a spiral of incense smoke.

But Harrison at the moment gave little heed to the idol. His attention was riveted on the robed and hooded form which sat cross-legged on a velvet divan at the other end of the hall—they had blundered full into the web of the spider. About Erlik Khan, in subordinate attitudes sat a group of Orientals, Chinese, Syrians and Turks.

The paralysis of surprize that held both groups was broken by a peculiarly menacing cry from Erlik Khan, who reared erect, his hand flying to his girdle. The others sprang up, yelling and fumbling for weapons. Behind him, Harrison heard the clamor of their pursuers just beyond the door. And in that instant he recognized and accepted the one desperate alternative to instant capture. He sprang for the idol, thrust Joan into the alcove behind it, and squeezed after her. Then he turned at bay. It was the last stand—trail's end. He did not hope to escape; his motive was merely that of a wounded wolf which drags itself into a corner where its killers must come at it from in front.

The green stone bulk of the idol blocked the entrance of the alcove save for one side, where there was a narrow space between its misshapen hip and shoulder, and the corner of the wall. The space on the other side was too narrow for a cat to have squeezed through, and the lacquer screen stood before it. Looking through the interstices of this screen, Harrison could see the whole room, into which the pursuers were now storming. The detective recognized their leader as Fang Yim, the hatchet-man.

A furious babble rose, dominated by Erlik Khan's voice, speaking English, the one common language of those mixed breeds.

"They hide behind the god; drag them forth."

"Let us rather fire a volley," protested a dark-skinned powerfully built man whom Harrison recognized—Ak Bogha, a Turk, his fez contrasting with his full dress suit. "We risk our lives, standing here in full view; he can shoot through that screen."

"Fool!" The Mongol's voice rasped with anger. "He would have fired already if he had a gun. Let no man pull a trigger. They can crouch behind the idol, and it would take many shots to smoke them out. We are not now in the Crypts of Silence. A volley would make too much noise; one shot might not be heard in the streets. But one shot will not suffice. He has but an axe; rush in and cut him down!"

Without hesitation Ak Bogha ran forward, followed by the others. Harrison shifted his grip on his axe haft. Only one man could come at him at a time—

Ak Bogha was in the narrow strait between idol and wall before Harrison moved from behind the great green bulk. The Turk yelped in fierce triumph and lunged, lifting his knife. He blocked the entrance; the men crowding behind him had only a glimpse, over his straining shoulder, of Harrison's grim face and blazing eyes.

Full into Ak Bogha's face Harrison thrust the axe head, smashing nose, lips and teeth. The Turk reeled, gasping and choking with blood, and half blinded, but struck again, like the slash of a dying panther. The keen edge sliced Harrison's face from temple to jaw, and then the flailing axe crushed in Ak Bogha's breastbone and sent him reeling backward, to fall dying.

The men behind him gave back suddenly. Harrison, bleeding like a stuck hog, again drew back behind the idol. They could not see the white giant who lurked at bay in the shadow of the god, but they saw Ak Bogha gasping his life out on the bloody floor before the idol, like a gory sacrifice, and the sight shook the nerve of the fiercest.

And now, as matters hovered at a deadlock, and the Lord of the Dead seemed himself uncertain, a new factor introduced itself into the tense drama. A door opened and a fantastic figure swaggered through. Behind him Harrison heard Joan gasp incredulously.

It was Ali ibn Suleyman who strode down the hall as if he trod his own castle in the mysterious Djebel Druse. No longer the garments of western civilization clothed him. On his head he wore a silken *kafiyeh* bound about the temples with a broad gilded band. Beneath his voluminous, girdled *abba* showed silver-heeled boots, ornately stitched. His eye-lids were painted with *kohl*, causing his eyes to glitter even more lethally than ordinarily. In his hand was a long curved scimitar.

Harrison mopped the blood from his face and shrugged his shoulders. Nothing in the house of Erlik Khan could surprize him any more, not even this picturesque shape which might have just swaggered out of an opium dream of the East.

The attention of all was centered on the Druse as he strode down the hall, looking even bigger and more formidable in his native costume than he had in western garments. He showed no more awe of the Lord of the Dead than he showed of Harrison. He halted directly in front of Erlik Khan, and spoke without meekness.

"Why was it not told me that mine enemy was a prisoner in the house?" he demanded in English, evidently the one language he knew in common with the Mongol.

"You were not here," Erlik Khan answered brusquely, evidently liking little the Druse's manner.

"Nay, I but recently returned, and learned that the dog who was once Ahmed Pasha stood at bay in this chamber. I have

donned my proper garb for this occasion." Turning his back full
on the Lord of the Dead, Ali ibn Suleyman strode before the
idol.

"Oh, infidel!" he called, "come forth and meet my steel!
Instead of the dog's death which is your due, I offer you
honorable battle—your axe against my sword. Come forth, ere I
hale you thence by your beard!"

"I haven't any beard," grunted the detective. "Come in and
get me!"

"Nay," scowled Ali ibn Suleyman; "when you were Ahmed
Pasha, you were a man. Come forth, where we can have room to
wield our weapons. If you slay me, you shall go free. I swear by
the Golden Calf!"

"Could I dare trust him?" muttered Harrison.

"A Druse keeps his word," whispered Joan. "But there is
Erlik Khan—"

"Who are you to make promises?" called Harrison. "Erlik
Khan is master here."

"Not in the matter of my private feud!" was the arrogant
reply. "I swear by my honor that no hand but mine shall be lifted
against you, and that if you slay me, you shall go free. Is it not so,
Erlik Khan?"

"Let it be as you wish," answered the Mongol, spreading his
hands in a gesture of resignation.

Joan grasped Harrison's arm convulsively, whispering
urgently: "Don't trust him! He won't keep his word! He'll betray
you and Ali both! He's never intended that the Druse should kill
you—it's his way of punishing Ali, by having some one else kill
you! Don't—don't—"

"We're finished anyway," muttered Harrison, shaking the
sweat and blood out of his eyes. "I might as well take the chance.
If I don't they'll rush us again, and I'm bleeding so that I'll soon
be too weak to fight. Watch your chance, girl, and try to get
away while everybody's watching Ali and me." Aloud he called:
"I have a woman here, Ali. Let her go before we start fighting."

"To summon the police to your rescue?" demanded Ali. "No!
She stands or falls with you. Will you come forth?"

"I'm coming," gritted Harrison. Grasping his axe, he moved
out of the alcove, a grim and ghastly figure, blood masking his
face and soaking his torn garments. He saw Ali ibn Suleyman
gliding toward him, half crouching, the scimitar in his hand a
broad curved glimmer of blue light. He lifted his axe, fighting

down a sudden wave of weakness—there came a muffled dull report, and at the same instant he felt a paralyzing impact against his head. He was not aware of falling, but realized that he was lying on the floor, conscious but unable to speak or move.

A wild cry rang in his dulled ears and Joan La Tour, a flying white figure, threw herself down beside him, her fingers frantically fluttering over him.

"Oh, you dogs, dogs!" she was sobbing. "You've killed him!" She lifted her head to scream: "Where is your honor now, Ali ibn Suleyman?"

From where he lay Harrison could see Ali standing over him, scimitar still poised, eyes flaring, mouth gaping, an image of horror and surprise. And beyond the Druse the detective saw the silent group clustered about Erlik Khan; and Fang Yim was holding an automatic with a strangely misshapen barrel—a Maxim silencer. One muffled shot would not be noticed from the street.

A fierce and frantic cry burst from Ali ibn Suleyman.

"Aie, my honor! My pledged word! My oath on the Golden Calf! You have broken it! You have shamed me to an infidel! You robbed me both of vengeance and honor! Am I a dog, to be dealt with thus! *Ya Maruf!*"

His voice soared to a feline screech, and wheeling, he moved like a blinding blur of light. Fang Yim's scream was cut short horribly in a ghastly gurgle, as the scimitar cut the air in a blue flame. The Chinaman's head shot from his shoulders on a jetting fountain of blood and thudded on the floor, grinning awfully in the golden light. With a yell of terrible exultation, Ali ibn Suleyman leapt straight toward the hooded shape on the divan. Fezzed and turbaned figures ran in between. Steel flashed, showering sparks, blood spurted, and men screamed. Harrison saw the Druse scimitar flame bluely through the lamplight full on Erlik Khan's coifed head. The hood fell in halves, and the Lord of the Dead rolled to the floor, his fingers convulsively clenching and unclenching.

The others swarmed about the maddened Druse, hacking and stabbing. The figure in the wide-sleeved *abba* was the center of a score of licking blades, of a gasping, blaspheming, clutching knot of straining bodies. And still the dripping scimitar flashed and flamed, shearing through flesh, sinew and bone, while under the stamping feet of the living rolled mutilated corpses. Under the impact of struggling bodies, the altar was overthrown, the smoldering incense scattered over the rugs. The next instant flame was licking at the hangings. With a rising roar and a rush the fire enveloped one whole side of the room, but the battlers heeded it not.

Harrison was aware that someone was pulling and tugging at him, someone who sobbed and gasped, but did not slacken their effort. A pair of slender hands were locked in his tattered shirt, and he was being dragged bodily through billowing smoke that blinded and half strangled him. The tugging hands grew weaker, but did not release their hold, as their owner fought on in a heart-breaking struggle. Then suddenly the detective felt a rush of clean wind, and was aware of concrete instead of carpeted wood under his shoulders.

He was lying in a slow drizzle on a sidewalk, while above him towered a wall reddened in a mounting glare. On the other side loomed broken docks, and beyond them the lurid glow was reflected on water. He heard the screams of fire sirens, and felt the gathering of a chattering, shouting crowd about him.

Life and movement slowly seeping back into his numbed veins, he lifted his head feebly, and saw Joan La Tour crouched beside him, oblivious to the rain as to her scanty attire. Tears were streaming down her face, and she cried out as she saw him move. "Oh, you're not dead—I thought I felt life in you, but I dared not let *them* know—"

"Just creased my scalp," he mumbled thickly. "Knocked me out for a few minutes—seen it happen that way before—you dragged me out—"

"While they were fighting. I thought I'd never find an outer door—here come the firemen at last!"

"The Yat Soys!" he gasped, trying to rise. "Eighteen Chinamen in that basement—my God, they'll be roasted!"

"We can't help it!" panted Joan La Tour. "We were fortunate to save ourselves. Oh!"

The crowd surged back, yelling, as the roof began to cave in, showering sparks. And through the crumpling walls, by some miracle, reeled an awful figure—Ali ibn Suleyman. His clothing hung in smoldering, bloody ribbons, revealing the ghastly wounds beneath. He had been slashed almost to pieces. His head-cloth was gone, his hair crisped, his skin singed and blackened where it was not blood-smeared. His scimitar was gone, and blood streamed down his arm over the fingers that gripped a dripping dagger.

"Aie!" he cried in a ghastly croak. "I see you, Ahmed Pasha, through the fire and mist! You live, in spite of Mongol treachery! That is well! Only by the hand of Ali ibn Suleyman, who was Amir Amin Izzedin, shall you die! I have washed my honor in blood, and it is spotless!

> *"'I am a son of Maruf,*
> *Of the mountain of sanctuary;*
> *When my sword is rusty*
> *I make it bright*
> *With the blood of my enemies!"*

Reeling, he pitched face-first, stabbing at Harrison's feet as he fell; then rolling on his back he lay motionless, staring sightlessly up at the flame-lurid skies.

NAMES IN THE BLACK BOOK

"Three unsolved murders in a week are not so unusual—for River Street," grunted Steve Harrison, shifting his muscular bulk restlessly in his chair.

His companion lighted a cigarette and Harrison observed that her slim hand was none too steady. She was exotically beautiful, a dark, supple figure, with the rich colors of purple Eastern nights and crimson dawns in her dusky hair and red lips. But in her dark eyes Harrison glimpsed the shadow of fear. Only once before had he seen fear in those marvelous eyes, and the memory made him vaguely uneasy.

"It's your business to solve murders," she said.

"Give me a little time. You can't rush things, when you're dealing with the people of the Oriental quarter."

"You have less time than you think," she answered cryptically. "If you do not listen to me, you'll never solve these killings."

"I'm listening."

"But you won't believe. You'll say I'm hysterical—seeing ghosts and shying at shadows."

"Look here, Joan," he exclaimed impatiently. "Come to the point. You called me to your apartment and I came because you said you were in deadly danger. But now you're talking riddles about three men who were killed last week. Spill it plain, won't you?"

"Do you remember Erlik Khan?" she asked abruptly.

Involuntarily his hand sought his face, where a thin scar ran from temple to jaw-rim.

"I'm not likely to forget him," he said. "A Mongol who called himself Lord of the Dead. His idea was to combine all the Oriental criminal societies in America in one big organization, with himself at the head. He might have done it, too, if his own men hadn't turned on him."

"Erlik Khan has returned," she said.

"What!" His head jerked up and he glared at her incredulously. "What are you talking about? I saw him die, and so did you!"

"I saw his hood fall apart as Ali ibn Suleyman struck with his keen-edged scimitar," she answered. "I saw him roll to the floor and lie still. And then the house went up in flames, and the roof fell in, and only charred bones were ever found among the ashes. Nevertheless, Erlik Khan has returned."

Harrison did not reply, but sat waiting for further disclosures, sure they would come in an indirect way. Joan La Tour was half Oriental, and partook of many of the characteristics of her subtle kin.

"How did those three men die?" she asked, though he was aware that she knew as well as he.

"Li-crin, the Chinese merchant, fell from his own roof," he grunted. "People on the street heard him scream and then saw him come hurtling down. Might have been an accident—but middle-aged Chinese merchants don't go climbing around on roofs at midnight.

"Ibrahim ibn Achmet, the Syrian curio dealer, was bitten by a cobra. That might have been an accident too, only I know somebody dropped the snake on him through the skylight.

"Jacob Kossova, the Levantine exporter, was simply knifed in a back alley. Dirty jobs, all of them, and no apparent motive on the surface. But motives are hidden deep, in River Street. When I find the guilty parties I'll uncover the motives."

"And those murders suggest nothing to you?" exclaimed the girl, tense with suppressed excitement. "You do not see the link that connects them? You do not grasp the point they all have in common? Listen—all these men were formerly associated in one way or another with Erlik Khan!"

"Well?" he demanded. "That doesn't mean that Erlik Khan's spook killed them! We found plenty of bones in the ashes of the house, but there were members of his gang in other parts of the city. His gigantic organization went to pieces, after his death for lack of a leader, but the survivors were never uncovered. Some of these might be paying off old grudges."

"Then why did they wait so long to strike? It's been a year since we saw Erlik Khan die. I tell you, the Lord of the Dead himself, alive or dead, has returned and is striking down these men for one reason or another. Perhaps they refuse to do his bidding once more. Five were marked for death. Three have fallen."

"How do you know that?" said he.

"Look!" From beneath the cushions of the divan on which she sat she drew something, and rising, came and bent beside him while she unfolded it.

It was a square piece of parchment-like substance, black and glossy. On it were written five names, one below the other, in a bold flowing hand—and in crimson, like spilled blood. Through the first three names a crimson bar had been drawn. They were the names of Li-chin, Ibrahim ibn Achmet, and Jacob Kossova. Harrison grunted explosively. The last two names, as yet unmarred, were those of Joan La Tour and Stephen Harrison.

"Where did you get this?" he demanded.

"It was shoved under my door last night, while I slept. If all the doors and windows had not been locked, the police would have found it pinned to my corpse this morning."

"But still I don't see what connection—"

"It is a page from the Black Book of Erlik Khan!" she cried. "The book of the dead! I have seen it, when I was a subject of his in the old days. There he kept accounts of his enemies, alive and dead. I saw that book, open, the very day of the night Ali ibn Suleyman killed him—a big book with jade-hinged ebony covers and glossy black parchment pages. Those names were not in it then; they have been written in since Erlik Khan died—and that is Erlik Khan's handwriting!"

If Harrison was impressed he failed to show it.

"Does he keep his books in English?"

"No, in a Mongolian script. This is for our benefit. And I know we are hopelessly doomed. Erlik Khan never warned his victims unless he was sure of them."

"Might be a forgery," grunted the detective.

"No! No man could imitate Erlik Khan's hand. He wrote

those names himself. He has come back from the dead! Hell could not hold a devil as black as he!" Joan was losing some of her poise in her fear and excitement. She ground out the half-consumed cigarette and broke the cover of a fresh carton. She drew forth a slim white cylinder and tossed the package on the table. Harrison took it up and absently extracted one for himself.

"Our names are in the Black Book! It is a sentence of death from which there is no appeal!" She struck a match and was lifting it, when Harrison struck the cigarette from her with a startled oath. She fell back on the divan, bewildered at the violence of his action, and he caught up the package and began gingerly to remove the contents.

"Where'd you get these things?"

"Why, down at the corner drug store, I guess," she stammered. "That's where I usually—"

"Not these you didn't," he grunted. "These fags have been specially treated. I don't know what it is, but I've seen one puff of the stuff knock a man stone dead. Some kind of a hellish Oriental drug mixed with the tobacco. You were out of your apartment while you were phoning me—"

"I was afraid my wire was tapped," she answered. "I went to a public booth down the street."

"And it's my guess somebody entered your apartment while you were gone and switched cigarettes on you. I only got a faint whiff of the stuff when I started to put that fag in my mouth, but it's unmistakable. Smell it yourself. Don't be afraid. It's deadly only when ignited."

She obeyed, and turned pale.

"I told you! We were the direct cause of Erlik Khan's overthrow! If you hadn't smelt that drug, we'd both be dead now, as he intended!"

"Well," he grunted, "it's a cinch somebody's after you, anyway. I still say it can't be Erlik Khan, because nobody could live after the lick on the head I saw Ali ibn Suleyman hand him, and I don't believe in ghosts. But you've got to be protected until I run down whoever is being so free with his poisoned cigarettes."

"What about yourself? Your name's in his book too."

"Never mind me," Harrison growled pugnaciously. "I reckon I can take care of myself." He looked capable enough, with his cold blue eyes, and the muscles bulging in his coat. He had shoulders like a bull.

"This wing's practically isolated from the rest of the building," he said, "and you've got the third floor to yourself?"

"Not only the third floor of the wing," she answered. "There's no one else on the third floor anywhere in the building at present."

"That makes it fine!" he exclaimed irritably. "Somebody could sneak in and cut your throat without disturbing anyone. That's what they'll try, too, when they realize the cigarettes didn't finish you. You'd better move to a hotel."

"That wouldn't make any difference," she answered, trembling. Her nerves obviously were in a bad way. "Erlik Khan would find me, anywhere. In a hotel, with people coming and going all the time, and the rotten locks they have on the doors, with transoms and fire escapes and everything, it would just be that much easier for him."

"Well, then, I'll plant a bunch of cops around here."

"That wouldn't do any good, either. Erlik Khan has killed again and again in spite of the police. They do not understand his ways."

"That's right," he muttered uncomfortably aware of a conviction that to summon men from headquarters would merely be signing those men's death warrants, without accomplishing anything else. It was absurd to suppose that the dead Mongol fiend was behind these murderous attacks, yet— Harrison's flesh crawled along his spine at the memory of things that had taken place in River Street—things he had never reported, because he did not wish to be thought either a liar or a madman. The dead do not return—but what seems absurd on Thirty-ninth Boulevard takes on a different aspect among the haunted labyrinths of the Oriental quarter.

"Stay with me!" Joan's eyes were dilated, and she caught Harrison's arm with hands that shook violently. "We can defend these rooms! While one sleeps the other can watch! Do not call the police; their blunders would doom us. You have worked in the quarter for years, and are worth more than the whole police force. The mysterious instincts that are a part of my Eastern heritage are alert to danger. I feel peril for us both, near, creeping closer, gliding around us like serpents in the darkness!"

"But I can't stay here," he scowled worriedly. "We can't

barricade ourselves and wait for them to starve us out. I've got to hit back—find out who's behind all this. The best defense is a good offense. But I can't leave you here unguarded, either. Damn!" He clenched his big fists and shook his head like a baffled bull in his perplexity.

"There is one man in the city besides yourself I could trust," she said suddenly. "One worth more than all the police. With him guarding me, I could sleep safely."

"Who is he?"

"Khoda Khan."

"That fellow? Why, I thought he'd skipped months ago."

"No; he's been hiding in Levant Street."

"But he's a confounded killer himself!"

"No, he isn't; not according to his standards, which mean as much to him as yours do to you. He's an Afghan who was raised in a code of blood-feud and vengeance. He's as honorable according to his creed of life as you or I. And he's my friend. He'd die for me."

"I reckon that means you've been hiding him from the law," said Harrison with a searching glance which she did not seek to evade. He made no further comment. River Street is not South Park Avenue. Harrison's own methods were not always orthodox, but they generally got results.

"Can you reach him?" he asked abruptly. She nodded.

"Alright. Call him and tell him to beat it up here. Tell him he won't be molested by the police, and after the brawl's over, he can go back into hiding. But after that it's open season if I catch him. Use your phone. Wire may be tapped, but we'll have to take the chance. I'll go downstairs and use the booth in the office. Lock the door, and don't open it to anybody until I get back."

When the bolts clicked behind him, Harrison turned down the corridor toward the stairs. The apartment house boasted no elevator. He watched all sides warily as he went. A peculiarity of architecture had, indeed, practically isolated that wing. The wall opposite Joan's doors was blank. The only way to reach the other suites on that floor was to descend the stair and ascend another on the other side of the building.

As he reached the stair he swore softly; his heel had crunched a small vial on the first step. With some vague suspicion of a planted poison trap he stooped and gingerly investigated the splintered bits and the spilled contents. There was a small pool of colorless liquid which gave off a pungent, musky odor, but there seemed nothing lethal about it.

"Some damned Oriental perfume Joan dropped, I reckon," he decided. He descended the twisting stair without further delay and was presently in the booth in the office which opened on the street; a sleepy clerk dozed behind the desk.

Harrison got the chief of police on the wire and began abruptly.

"Say, Hoolihan, you remember that Afghan, Khoda Khan, who knifed a Chinaman about three months ago? Yes, that's the one. Well, listen: I'm using him on a job for a while, so tell your men to lay off, if they see him. Pass the word along *pronto*. Yes, I know it's very irregular; so's the job I hold down. In this case it's the choice of using a fugitive from the law, or seeing a law-abiding citizen murdered. Never mind what it's all about. This is my job, and I've got to handle it my own way. All right; thanks."

He hung up the receiver, thought vigorously for a few minutes, and then dialed another number that was definitely not related to the police station. In place of the chief's booming voice there sounded at the other end of the wire a squeaky whine framed in the argot of the underworld.

"Listen, Johnny," said Harrison with his customary abruptness, "you told me you thought you had a lead on the Kossova murder. What about it?"

"It wasn't no lie, boss!" The voice at the other end trembled with excitement. "I got a tip, and it's big!—*big!* I can't spill it over the phone, and I don't dare stir out. But if you'll meet me at Shan Yang's hop joint, I'll give you the dope. It'll knock you loose from your props, believe me it will!"

"I'll be there in an hour," promised the detective. He left the booth and glanced briefly out into the street. It was a misty night, as so many River Street nights are. Traffic was only a dim echo from some distant, busier section. Drifting fog dimmed the street lamps, shrouding the forms of occasional passers-by. The stage was set for murder; it only awaited the appearance of the actors in the dark drama.

Harrison mounted the stairs again. They wound up out of the office and up into the third story wing without opening upon the second floor at all. The architecture, like much of it in or near the Oriental section, was rather unusual. People of the quarter were notoriously fond of privacy, and even apartment houses were built with this passion in mind. His feet made no sound on the

thickly carpeted stairs, though a slight crunching at the top step
reminded him of the broken vial again momentarily. He had
stepped on the splinters.

He knocked at the locked door, answered Joan's tense
challenge and was admitted. He found the girl more self-
possessed.

"I talked with Khoda Khan. He's on his way here now. I
warned him that the wire might be tapped—that our enemies
might know as soon as I called him, and try to stop him on his
way here."

"Good," grunted the detective. "While I'm waiting for him I'll
have a look at your suite."

There were four rooms, drawing room in front, with a large
bedroom behind it, and behind that two smaller rooms, the
maid's bedroom and the bathroom. The maid was not there,
because Joan had sent her away at the first intimation of danger
threatening. The corridor ran parallel with the suite, and the
drawing room, large bedroom and bathroom opened upon it.
That made three doors to consider. The drawing room had one
big east window, overlooking the street, and one on the south.
The big bedroom had one south window, and the maid's room
one south and one west window. The bathroom had one
window, a small one in the west wall, overlooking a small court
bounded by a tangle of alleys and board-fenced backyards.

"Three outside doors and six windows to be watched, and
this the top story," muttered the detective. "I still think I ought
to get some cops here." But he spoke without conviction. He was
investigating the bathroom when Joan called him cautiously
from the drawing room, telling him that she thought she had
heard a faint scratching outside the door. Gun in hand he
opened the bathroom door and peered out into the corridor. It
was empty. No shape of horror stood before the drawing room
door. He closed the door, called reassuringly to the girl, and
completed his inspection, grunting approval. Joan La Tour was
a daughter of the Oriental quarter. Long ago she had provided
against secret enemies as far as special locks and bolts could
provide. The windows were guarded with heavy iron-braced
shutters, and there was no trapdoor, dumb waiter nor skylight
anywhere in the suite.

"Looks like you're ready for a siege," he commented.

"I am. I have canned goods laid away to last for weeks. With
Khoda Khan I can hold the fort indefinitely. If things get too hot

for you, you'd better come back here yourself—if you can. It's safer than the police station—unless they burn the house down."

A soft rap on the door brought them both round.

"Who is it?" called Joan warily.

"I, Khoda Khan, *Sahiba*," came the answer in a low-pitched, but strong and resonant voice. Joan sighed deeply and unlocked the door. A tall figure bowed with a stately gesture and entered.

Khoda Khan was taller than Harrison, and though he lacked something of the American's sheer bulk, his shoulders were equally broad, and his garments could not conceal the hard lines of his limbs, the tigerish suppleness of his motions. His garb was a curious combination of costume, which is common in River Street. He wore a turban which well set off his hawk nose and black beard, and a long silk coat hung nearly to his knees. His trousers were conventional, but a silk sash girdled his lean waist, and his foot-gear was Turkish slippers.

In any costume it would have been equally evident that there was something wild and untamable about the man. His eyes blazed as no civilized man's ever did, and his sinews were like coiled springs under his coat. Harrison felt much as he would have felt if a panther had padded into the room, for the moment placid but ready at an instant's notice to go flying into flaming-eyed, red-taloned action.

"I thought you'd left the country," he said.

The Afghan smiled, a glimmer of white amidst the dark tangle of his beard.

"Nay, *sahib*. That son of a dog I knifed did not die."

"You're lucky he didn't," commented Harrison. "If you kill him you'll hang, sure."

"*Inshallah*," agreed Khoda Khan cheerfully. "But it was a matter of *izzat*—honor. The dog fed me swine's flesh. But no matter. The *memsahib* called me and I came."

"Alright. As long as she needs your protection the police won't arrest you. But when the matter's finished, things stand as they were. I'll give you time to hide again, if you wish, and then I'll try to catch you as I have in the past. Or if you want to surrender and stand trial, I'll promise you as much leniency as possible."

"You speak fairly," answered Khoda Khan. "I will protect the *memsahib*, and when our enemies are dead, you and I will begin our feud anew."

"Do you know anything about these murders?"

"Nay, *sahib*. The *memsahib* called me, saying Mongol dogs threatened her. I came swiftly, over the roofs, lest they seek to ambush me. None molested me. But here is something I found outside the door."

He opened his hand and exhibited a bit of silk, evidently torn from his sash. On it lay a crushed object that Harrison did not recognize. But Joan recoiled with a low cry.

"God! A black scorpion of Assam!"

"Aye—whose sting is death. I saw it running up and down before the door, seeking entrance. Another man might have stepped upon it without seeing it, but I was on my guard, for I smelled the Flower of Death as I came up the stairs. I saw the thing at the door and crushed it before it could sting me."

"What do you mean by the Flower of Death?" demanded Harrison.

"It grows in the jungles where these vermin abide. Its scent attracts them as wine draws a drunkard. A trail of the juice had somehow been laid to this door. Had the door been opened before I slew it, it would have darted in and struck whoever happened to be in its way."

Harrison swore under his breath, remembering the faint scratching noise Joan had heard outside the door.

"I get it now! They put a bottle of that juice on the stairs where it was sure to be stepped on. I did step on it, and broke it, and got the liquid on my shoe. Then I tracked down the stairs, leaving the scent wherever I stepped. Came back upstairs, stepped in the stuff again and tracked it on through the door. Then somebody downstairs turned that scorpion loose—the devil! That means they've been in this house since I was downstairs!—may be hiding somewhere here now! But somebody had to come into the office to put the scorpion on the trail—I'll ask the clerk—"

"He sleeps like the dead," said Khoda Khan. "He did not waken when I entered and mounted the stairs. What matters if the house is full of Mongols? These doors are strong, and I am alert!" From beneath his coat he drew the terrible Khyber knife—a yard long, with an edge like a razor. "I have slain *men* with this," he announced, grinning like a bearded mountain devil. "Pathans, Indians, a Russian or so. These Mongols are dogs on whom the good steel will be shamed."

"Well," grunted Harrison. "I've got an appointment that's overdue now. I feel queer walking out and leaving you two to fight these devils alone. But there'll be no safety for us until I've smashed this gang at its root, and that's what I'm out to do."

"They'll kill you as you leave the building," said Joan with conviction.

"Well, I've got to risk it. If you're attacked call the police anyway, and call me, at Shan Yang's joint. I'll come back here some time before dawn. But I'm hoping the tip I expect to get will enable me to hit straight at whoever's after us."

He went down the hallway with an eery feeling of being watched and scanned the stairs as if he expected to see it swarming with black scorpions, and he shied wide of the broken glass on the step. He had an uncomfortable sensation of duty ignored, in spite of himself, though he knew that his two companions did not want the police, and that in dealing with the East it is better to heed the advice of the East.

The clerk still sagged behind his desk. Harrison shook him without avail. The man was not asleep; he was drugged. But his heartbeat was regular, and the detective believed he was in no danger. Anyway, Harrison had no more time to waste. If he kept Johnny Kleck waiting too long, the fellow might become panicky and bolt, to hide in some rat-run for weeks.

He went into the street, where the lamps gleamed luridly through the drifting river mist, half expecting a knife to be thrown at him, or to find a cobra coiled on the seat of his automobile. But he found nothing his suspicion anticipated, even though he lifted the hood and the rumble-seat to see if a bomb had been planted. Satisfying himself at last, he climbed in and the girl watching him through the slits of a third-story shutter sighed relievedly to see him roar away unmolested.

Khoda Khan had gone through the rooms, giving approval in his beard of the locks, and having extinguished the lights in the other chambers he returned to the drawing room, where he turned out all lights except one small desk lamp. It shed a pool of light in the center of the room, leaving the rest in shadowy vagueness.

"Darkness baffles rogues as well as honest men," he said sagely, "and I see like a cat in the dark."

He sat cross-legged near the door that let into the bedroom, which he left partly open. He merged with the shadows so that all of him Joan could make out with any distinctness was his turban and the glimmer of his eyes as he turned his head.

"We will remain in this room, *sahiba*," he said. "Having failed with poison and reptile, it is certain that men will next be sent. Lie down on that divan and sleep, if you can. I will keep watch."

Joan obeyed, but she did not sleep. Her nerves seemed to thrum with tautness. The silence of the house oppressed her, and the few noises of the street made her start.

Khoda Khan sat motionless as a statue, imbued with the savage patience and immobility of the hills that bred him. Grown to manhood on the raw barbaric edge of the world, where survival depended on personal ability, his senses were whetted keener than is possible for civilized men. Even Harrison's trained faculties were blunt in comparison. Khoda Khan could still smell the faint aroma of the Flower of Death, mingled with the acrid odor of the crushed scorpion. He heard and identified every sound in or outside the house—knew which were natural, and which were not.

He heard the sounds on the roof long before his warning hiss brought Joan upright on the divan. The Afghan's eyes glowed like phosphorus in the shadows and his teeth glimmered dimly in a savage grin. Joan looked at him inquiringly. Her civilized ears heard nothing. But he heard and with his ears followed the sounds accurately and located the place where they halted. Joan heard something then, a faint scratching somewhere in the building, but she did not identify it—as Khoda Khan did—as the forcing of the shutters on the bathroom window.

With a quick reassuring gesture to her, Khoda Khan rose and melted like a slinking leopard into the darkness of the bedroom. She took up a blunt-nosed automatic, with no great conviction of reliance upon it, and groped on the table for a bottle of wine, feeling an intense need of stimulants. She was shaking in every limb and cold sweat was gathering on her flesh. She remembered the cigarettes, but the unbroken seal on the bottle reassured her. Even the wisest have their thoughtless moments. It was not until she had begun to drink that the peculiar flavor made her realize that the man who had shifted the cigarettes might just as easily have taken a bottle of wine and left another in its place, a facsimile that included an unbroken seal. She fell back on the divan, gagging.

Khoda Khan wasted no time, because he heard other sounds, out in the hall. His ears told him, as he crouched by the bathroom door, that the shutters had been forced—done almost in silence a job that a white man would have made sound like an explosion in an iron foundry—and now the window was being jimmied. Then he heard something stealthy and bulky drop into the room. Then it was that he threw open the door and charged in like a typhoon, his long knife held low.

Enough light filtered into the room from outside to limn a powerful, crouching figure, with dim snarling yellow features. The intruder yelped explosively, started a motion—and then the long Khyber knife, driven by an arm nerved to the fury of the Himalayas, ripped him open from groin to breastbone.

Khoda Khan did not pause. He knew there was only one man in the room, but through the open window he saw a thick rope dangling from above. He sprang forward, grasped it with both hands and heaved backward like a bull. The men on the roof holding it released it to keep from being jerked headlong over the edge, and he tumbled backward, sprawling over the corpse, the loose rope in his hands. He yelped exultantly, then sprang up and glided to the door that opened into the corridor. Unless they had another rope, which was unlikely, the men on the roof were temporarily out of the fight.

He flung open the door and ducked deeply. A hatchet cut a great chip out of the jamb, and he stabbed upward once, then sprang over a writhing body in the corridor, jerking a big pistol from its hidden scabbard.

The bright light of the corridor did not blind him. He saw a second hatchet-man crouching by the bedroom door, and a man in the silk robes of a mandarin working at the lock of the drawing room door. He was between them and the stairs. As they wheeled toward him he shot the hatchet-man in the belly. An automatic spat in the hand of the mandarin, and Khoda Khan felt the wind of the bullet. The next instant his own gun roared again and the Manchu staggered, the pistol flying from a hand that was suddenly a dripping red pulp. Then he whipped a long knife from his robes with his left hand and came along the corridor like a hurricane, his eyes glaring and his silk garments whipping about him.

Khoda Khan shot him through the head and the mandarin fell so near his feet that the long knife stuck into the floor and quivered a matter of inches from the Afghan's slipper.

But Khoda Khan paused only long enough to pass his knife through the hatchet-man he had shot in the belly—for his fighting ethics were those of the savage Hills—and then he turned and ran back into the bathroom. He fired a shot through the window, though the men on the roof were making no further demonstration, and then ran through the bedroom, snapping on lights as he went.

"I have slain the dogs, *sahiba*!" he exclaimed. "By Allah, they have tasted lead and steel! Others are on the roof but they are helpless for the moment. But men will come to investigate the shots, that being the custom of the *sahibs*, so it is expedient that we decide on our further actions, and the proper lies to tell— *Allah*!"

Joan LaTour stood bolt upright, clutching the back of the divan. Her face was the color of marble, and the expression was rigid too, like a mask of horror carved in stone. Her dilated eyes blazed like weird black fire.

"Allah shield us against Shaitan the Damned!" ejaculated Khoda Khan, making a sign with his fingers that antedated Islam by some thousands of years. "What has happened to you, *sahiba*?"

He moved toward her, to be met by a scream that sent him cowering back, cold sweat starting out on his flesh.

"Keep back!" she cried in a voice he did not recognize. "You are a demon! You are all demons! I see you! I hear your cloven feet padding in the night! I see your eyes blazing from the shadows! Keep your taloned hands from me! *Aie*!" Foam flecked her lips as she screamed blasphemies in English and Arabic that made Khoda Khan's hair stand stiffly on end.

"*Sahiba*!" he begged, trembling like a leaf. "I am no demon! I am Khoda Khan! I—" His outstretched hand touched her, and with an awful shriek she turned and darted for the door, tearing at the bolts. He sprang to stop her, but in her frenzy she was even quicker than he. She whipped the door open, eluded his grasping hand and flew down the corridor, deaf to his anguished yells.

When Harrison left Joan's house, he drove straight to Shan Yang's dive, which, in the heart of River Street, masqueraded as a low-grade drinking joint. It was late. Only a few derelicts huddled about the bar, and he noticed that the barman was a Chinaman that he had never seen before. He stared impassively at Harrison, but jerked a thumb toward the back door, masked by dingy curtains, when the detective asked abruptly: "Johnny Kleck here?"

Harrison passed through the door, traversed a short dimly-lighted hallway and rapped authoritatively on the door at the other end. In the silence he heard rats scampering. A steel disk in the center of the door shifted and a slanted black eye glittered in the opening.

"Open the door, Shan Yang," ordered Harrison impatiently, and the eye was withdrawn, accompanied by the rattling of bolts and chains.

He pushed open the door and entered the room whose illumination was scarcely better than that of the corridor. It was a large, dingy, drab affair, lined with bunks. Fires sputtered in braziers, and Shan Yang was making his way to his accustomed seat behind a low counter near the wall. Harrison spent but a single casual glance on the familiar figure, the known dingy silk jacket worked in gilt dragons. Then he strode across the room to a door in the wall opposite the counter to which Shan Yang was making his way. This was an opium joint and Harrison knew it—knew those figures in the bunks were Chinamen sleeping the sleep of the smoke. Why he had not raided it, as he had raided and destroyed other opium-dens, only Harrison could have said. But law-enforcement on River Street is not the orthodox routine it is on Baskerville Avenue, for instance. Harrison's reasons were those of expediency and necessity. Sometimes certain conventions have to be sacrificed for the sake of more important gains—especially when the law-enforcement of a whole district (and in the Oriental quarter) rests on one's shoulders.

A characteristic smell pervaded the dense atmosphere, in spite of the reek of dope and unwashed bodies—the dank odor of the river, which hangs over the River Street dives or wells up from their floors like the black intangible spirit of the quarter itself. Shan Yang's dive, like many others, was built on the very bank of the river. The back room projected out over the water on rotting piles, at which the black river lapped hungrily.

Harrison opened the door, entered and pushed it to behind him, his lips framing a greeting that was never uttered. He stood dumbly, glaring.

He was in a small dingy room, bare except for a crude table and some chairs. An oil lamp on the table cast a smoky light. And in that light he saw Johnny Kleck. The man stood bolt upright against the far wall, his arms spread like a crucifix, rigid, his eyes glassy and staring, his mean, ratty features twisted in a frozen grin. He did not speak, and Harrison's gaze, traveling down him, halted with a shock. Johnny's feet did not touch the floor by several inches—

Harrison's big blue pistol jumped into his hand. Johnny Kleck was dead, that grin was a contortion of horror and agony. He was crucified to the wall by skewer-like dagger blades through his wrists and ankles, his ears spiked to the wall to keep his head upright. But that was not what had killed him. The bosom of Johnny's shirt was charred, and there was a round, blackened hole.

Feeling suddenly sick the detective wheeled, opened the door and stepped back into the larger room. The light seemed dimmer, the smoke thicker than ever. No mumblings came from the bunks; the fires in the braziers burned blue, with weird sputterings. Shan Yang crouched behind the counter. His shoulders moved as if he were tallying beads on an abacus.

"Shan Yang!" the detective's voice grated harshly in the murky silence. "Who's been in that room tonight besides Johnny Kleck?"

The man behind the counter straightened and looked full at him, and Harrison felt his skin crawl. Above the gilt-worked jacket an unfamiliar face returned his gaze. That was no Shan Yang; it was a man he had never seen—it was a Mongol. He started and stared about him as the men in the bunks rose with supple ease. They were not Chinese; they were Mongols to a man, and their slanted black eyes were not clouded by drugs.

With a curse Harrison sprang toward the outer door and with a rush they were on him. His gun crashed and a man staggered in mid-stride. Then the lights went out, the braziers were overturned, and in the stygian blackness hard bodies caromed against the detective. Long-nailed fingers clawed at his throat, thick arms locked about his waist and legs. Somewhere a sibilant voice was hissing orders.

Harrison's mauling left worked like a piston, crushing flesh and bone; his right wielded the gun barrel like a club. He forged toward the unseen door blindly, dragging his assailants by sheer strength. He seemed to be wading through a solid mass, as if the darkness had turned to bone and muscle about him. A knife licked through his coat, stinging his skin, and then he gasped as a silk cord looped about his neck, shutting off his wind, sinking deeper and deeper into the straining flesh. Blindly he jammed the muzzle against the nearest body and pulled the trigger. At the muffled concussion something fell away from him and the strangling agony lessened. Gasping for breath he groped and tore the cord away—then he was borne down under a rush of heavy bodies and something smashed savagely against his head. The darkness exploded in a shower of sparks that were instantly quenched in stygian blackness.

The smell of the river was in Steve Harrison's nostrils as he regained his addled senses, river-scent mingled with the odor of stale blood. The blood, he realized, when he had enough sense to realize anything, was clotted on his own scalp. His head swam and he tried to raise a hand to it, thereby discovering that he was bound hand and foot with cords that cut into the flesh. A candle was dazzling his eyes, and for awhile he could see nothing else. Then things began to assume their proper proportions, and objects grew out of nothing and became identifiable.

He was lying on a bare floor of new, unpainted wood, in a large square chamber, the walls of which were of stone, without paint or plaster. The ceiling was likewise of stone, with heavy, bare beams, and there was an open trap door almost directly above him, through which, in spite of the candle, he got a glimpse of stars. Fresh air flowed through that trap, bearing with it the river-smell stronger than ever. The chamber was bare of furniture, the candle stuck in a niche in the wall. Harrison swore, wondering if he was delirious. This was like an experience in a dream, with everything unreal and distorted.

He tried to struggle to a sitting position, but that made his head swim, so that he lay back and swore fervently. He yelled wrathfully, and a face peered down at him through the trap—a square, yellow face with beady slanted eyes. He cursed the face and it mocked him and was withdrawn. The noise of the door softly opening checked Harrison's profanity and he wriggled around to glare at the intruder.

And he glared in silence, feeling an icy prickling up and down his spine. Once before he had lain bound and helpless, staring up at a tall black-robed figure whose yellow eyes glimmered from the shadow of a dusky hood. But that man was dead; Harrison had seen him cut down by the scimitar of a maddened Druse.

"Erlik Khan!" The words were forced out of him. He licked lips suddenly dry.

"Aye!" It was the same ghostly, hollow voice that had chilled him in the old days. "Erlik Khan, the Lord of the Dead."

"Are you a man or a ghost?" demanded Harrison.

"I live."

"But I saw Ali ibn Suleyman kill you!" exclaimed the detective. "He slashed you across the head with a heavy sword that was sharp as a razor. He was a stronger man than I am. He struck with the full power of his arm. Your hood fell in two pieces—"

"And I fell like a dead man in my own blood," finished Erlik Khan. "But the steel cap I wore—as I wear now—under my hood, saved my life as it has more than once. The terrible stroke cracked it across the top and cut my scalp, fracturing my skull and causing concussion of the brain. But I lived, and some of my faithful followers, who escaped the sword of the Druse, carried me down through the subterranean tunnels which led from my house, and so I escaped the burning building. But I lay like a dead man for weeks, and it was not until a very wise man was brought from Mongolia that I recovered my senses, and sanity.

"But now I am ready to take up my work where I left off, though I must rebuild much. Many of my former followers had forgotten my authority. Some required to be taught anew who was master."

"And you've been teaching them," grunted Harrison, recovering his pugnacious composure.

"True. Some examples had to be made. One man fell off a roof, a snake bit another, yet another ran into knives in a dark alley. Then there was another matter. Joan La Tour betrayed me in the old days. She knows too many secrets. She had to die. So that she might taste agony in anticipation, I sent her a page from my book of the dead."

"Your devils killed Kleck," accused Harrison.

"Of course. All wires leading from the girl's apartment house are tapped. I myself heard your conversation with Kleck. That is why you were not attacked when you left the building. I saw that you were playing into my hands. I sent my men to take possession of Shan Yang's dive. He had no more use for his jacket, presently, so one donned it to deceive you. Kleck had somehow learned of my return; these stool pigeons are clever. But he had time to regret. A man dies hard with a white-hot point of iron bored through his breast."

Harrison said nothing and presently the Mongol continued.

"I wrote your name in my book because I recognized you as my most dangerous opponent. It was because of you that Ali ibn Suleyman turned against me.

"I am rebuilding my empire again, but more solidly. First I shall consolidate River Street, and create a political machine to rule the city. The men in office now do not suspect my existence. If all were to die, it would not be hard to find others to fill their places—men who are not indifferent to the clink of gold."

"You're mad," growled Harrison. "Control a whole city government from a dive in River Street?"

"It has been done," answered the Mongol tranquilly. "I will strike like a cobra from the dark. Only the men who obey my agent will live. He will be a white man, a figure-head whom men will think the real power, while I remain unseen. You might have been he, if you had a little more intelligence."

He took a bulky object from under his arm, a thick book with glossy black covers—ebony with green jade hinges. He riffled the night-hued pages and Harrison saw they were covered with crimson characters.

"My book of the dead," said Erlik Khan. "Many names have been crossed out. Many more have been added since I recovered my sanity. Some of them would interest you; they include names of the mayor, the chief of police, district attorney, a number of aldermen."

"That lick must have addled your brains permanently," snarled Harrison. "Do you think you can substitute a whole city government and get away with it?"

"I can and will. These men will die in various ways, and men of my own choice will succeed them in office. Within a year I will hold this city in the palm of my hand, and there will be none to interfere with me."

Lying staring up at the bizarre figure, whose features were, as always, shadowed beyond recognition by the hood, Harrison's flesh crawled with the conviction that the Mongol was indeed mad. His crimson dreams, always ghastly, were too grotesque and incredible for the visions of a wholly sane man. Yet he was dangerous as a maddened cobra. His monstrous plot must ultimately fail, yet he held the lives of many men in his hand. And Harrison, on whom the city relied for protection from whatever menace the Oriental quarter might spawn, lay bound and helpless before him. The detective cursed in fury.

"Always the man of violence," mocked Erlik Khan, with the suggestion of scorn in his voice. "Barbarian! Who lays his trust in guns and blades, who would check the stride of imperial power with blows of the naked fists! Brainless arm striking blind blows! Well, you have struck your last. Smell the river damp that creeps in through the ceiling? Soon it shall enfold you utterly and your dreams and aspirations will be one with the mist of the river."

"Where are we?" demanded Harrison.

"On an island below the city, where the marshes begin. Once there were warehouses here, and a factory, but they were abandoned as the city grew in the other direction, and have been crumbling into ruin for twenty years. I purchased the entire island through one of my agents, and am rebuilding to suit my own purposes an old stone mansion which stood here before the factory was built. None notices, because my own henchmen are the workmen, and no one ever comes to this marshy island. The house is invisible from the river, hidden as it is among the tangle of old rotting warehouses. You came here in a motor boat which was anchored beneath the rotting wharves behind Shan Yang's dive. Another boat will presently fetch my men who were sent to dispose of Joan La Tour."

"They may not find that so easy," commented the detective.

"Never fear. I know she summoned that hairy wolf, Khoda Khan, to her aid, and it's true that my men failed to slay him before he reached her. But I suppose it was a false sense of trust in the Afghan that caused you to make your appointment with Kleck. I rather expected you to remain with the foolish girl and try to protect her in your way."

Somewhere below them a gong sounded. Erlik Khan did not start, but there was a surprise in the lift of his head. He closed the black book.

"I have wasted enough time on you," he said. "Once before I bade you farewell in one of my dungeons. Then the fanaticism of a crazy Druse saved you. This time there will be no upset of my plans. The only men in this house are Mongols, who know no law but my will. I go, but you will not be lonely. Soon one will come to you."

And with a low, chilling laugh the phantom-like figure moved through the door and disappeared. Outside a lock clicked, and then there was stillness.

The silence was broken suddenly by a muffled scream. It came from somewhere below and was repeated half a dozen times. Harrison shuddered. No one who has ever visited an insane asylum could fail to recognize that sound. It was the shrieking of a mad woman. After these cries the silence seemed even more stifling and menacing.

Harrison swore to quiet his feelings, and again the velvet-capped head of the Mongol leered down at him through the trap.

"Grin, you yellow-bellied ape!" roared Harrison, tugging at his cords until the veins stood out on his temples. "If I could break these damned ropes I'd knock that grin around where your pigtail ought to be, you—" he went into minute details of the Mongol's ancestry, dwelling at length on the more scandalous phases of it, and in the midst of his noisy tirade he saw the leer change suddenly to a startled snarl. The head vanished from the trap and there came a sound like the blow of a butcher's cleaver.

Then another face was poked into the trap—a wild, bearded face, with blazing, bloodshot eyes, and surmounted by a disheveled turban.

"*Sahib!*" hissed the apparition.

"Khoda Khan!" ejaculated the detective, galvanized. "What the devil are you doing here?"

"Softly!" muttered the Afghan. "Let not the accursed ones hear!"

He tossed the loose end of a rope ladder down through the trap and came down in a rush, his bare feet making no sound as he hit the floor. He held his long knife in his teeth, and blood dripped from the point.

Squatting beside the detective he cut him free with reckless slashes that threatened to slice flesh as well as hemp. The Afghan was quivering with half-controlled passion. His teeth gleamed like a wolf's fangs amidst the tangle of his beard.

Harrison sat up, chafing his swollen wrists.

"Where's Joan? Quick, man, where is she?"

"Here! In this accursed den!"

"But—"

"That was she screaming a few minutes ago," broke in the Afghan, and Harrison's flesh crawled with a vague monstrous premonition.

"But that was a mad woman!" he almost whispered.

"The *sahiba* is mad," said Khoda Khan somberly. "Hearken, *sahib*, and then judge if the fault is altogether mine.

"After you left, the accursed ones let down a man from the roof on a rope. Him I knifed, and I slew three more who sought to force the doors. But when I returned to the *sahiba*, she knew me not. She fled from me into the street, and other devils must have been lurking nearby, because as she ran shrieking along the sidewalk, a big automobile loomed out of the fog and a Mongol stretched forth an arm and dragged her into the car, from under my very fingers. I saw his accursed yellow face by the light of a street lamp.

"Knowing she were better dead by a bullet than in their hands, I emptied my pistol after the car, but it fled like Shaitan the Damned from the face of Allah, and if I hit anyone in it, I know not. Then as I rent my garments and cursed the day of my birth—for I could not pursue it on foot—Allah willed that another automobile should appear. It was driven by a young man in evening clothes, returning from a revel, no doubt, and being cursed with curiosity he slowed down near the curb to observe my grief.

"So, praising Allah, I sprang in beside him and placing my knife point against his ribs bade him go with speed and he obeyed in great fear. The car of the damned ones was out of sight, but presently I glimpsed it again, and exhorted the youth to greater speed, so the machine seemed to fly like the steed of the Prophet. So, presently I saw the car halt at the river bank. I made the youth halt likewise, and he sprang out and fled in the other direction in terror.

"I ran through the darkness, hot for the blood of the accursed ones, but before I could reach the bank I saw the Mongols leave the car, carrying the *memsahib* who was bound and gagged, and they entered a motor-boat and headed out into the river toward an island which lay on the breast of the water like a dark cloud.

"I cast up and down on the shore like a madman, and was about to leap in and swim, though the distance was great, when I came upon a boat chained to a pile, but one driven by oars. I gave praise to Allah and cut the chain with my knife—see the nick in the edge?—and rowed after the accursed ones with great speed.

"They were far ahead of me, but Allah willed it that their engine should sputter and cease when they had almost reached the island. So I took heart, hearing them cursing in their heathen tongue, and hoped to draw along side and slay them all before they were aware of me. They saw me not in the darkness, nor heard my oars because of their own noises, but before I could reach them the accursed engine began again. So they reached a wharf on the marshy shore ahead of me, but they lingered to make the boat fast, so I was not too far behind them as they bore the *memsahib* through the shadows of the crumbling shacks which stood all about.

"Then I was hot to overtake and slay them, but before I could come up with them they had reached the door of a great stone house—this one, *sahib*—set in a tangle of rotting buildings. A steel fence surrounded it, with razor-edged spearheads set along the top but by Allah, that could not hinder a *lifter* of the Khyber! I went over it without so much as tearing my garments. Inside was a second wall of stone, but it stood in ruins.

"I crouched in the shadows near the house and saw that the windows were heavily barred and the doors strong. Moreover, the lower part of the house is full of armed men. So I climbed a corner of the wall, and it was not easy, but presently I reached the roof which at that part is flat, with a parapet. I expected a watcher, and so there was, but he was too busy taunting his captive to see or hear me until my knife sent him to hell. Here is his dagger; he bore no gun."

Harrison mechanically took the wicked, lean-bladed poniard.

"But what caused Joan to go mad?"

"*Sahib*, there was a broken wine bottle on the floor, and a goblet. I had no time to investigate it, but I know that wine must have been poisoned with the juice of the fruit called the black pomegranate. She can not have drunk much, or she would have died frothing and champing like a mad dog. But only a little will rob one of sanity. It grows in the jungles of Indo-China, and white men say it is a lie. But it is no lie; thrice I have seen men die after having drunk its juice, and more than once I have seen men, and women too, turn mad because of it. I have traveled in that hellish country where it grows."

"God!" Harrison's foundations were shaken by nausea. Then his big hands clenched into chunks of iron and baleful fire glimmered in his savage blue eyes. The weakness of horror and revulsion was followed by cold fury dangerous as the blood-hunger of a timber wolf.

"She may be already dead," he muttered thickly. "But dead or alive we'll send Erlik Khan to hell. Try that door."

It was of heavy teak, braced with bronze straps.

"It is locked," muttered the Afghan. "We will burst it."

He was about to launch his shoulder against it when he

stopped short, the long Khyber knife jumping into his fist like a
beam of light.

"Someone approaches!" he whispered, and a second later
Harrison's more civilized—and therefore duller—ears caught a
cat-like tread.

Instantly he acted. He shoved the Afghan behind the door
and sat down quickly in the center of the room, wrapped a piece
of rope about his ankles and then lay full length, his arms behind
and under him. He was lying on the other pieces of severed cord,
concealing them, and to the casual glance he resembled a man
lying bound hand and foot. The Afghan understood and grinned
hugely.

Harrison worked with the celerity of trained mind and
muscles that eliminates fumbling delay and bungling. He
accomplished his purpose in a matter of seconds and without
undue noise. A key grated in the lock as he settled himself, and
then the door swung open. A giant Mongol stood limned in the
opening. His head was shaven, his square features passionless as
the face of a copper idol. In one hand he carried a curiously
shaped ebony block, in the other a mace such as was borne by
the horsemen of Ghengis Khan—a straight-hafted iron
bludgeon with a round head covered with steel points, and a
knob on the other end to keep the hand from slipping.

He did not see Khoda Khan because when he threw back the
door, the Afghan was hidden behind it. Khoda Khan did not
stab him as he entered because the Afghan could not see into the
outer corridor, and had no way of knowing how many men were
following the first. But the Mongol was alone, and he did not
bother to shut the door. He went straight to the man lying on the
floor, scowling slightly to see the rope ladder hanging down
through the trap, as if it was not usual to leave it that way, but he
did not show any suspicion or call to the man on the roof.

He did not examine Harrison's cords. The detective
presented the appearance the Mongol had expected, and this
fact blunted his faculties as anything taken for granted is likely
to do. As he bent down, over his shoulder Harrison saw Khoda
Khan glide from behind the door as silently as a panther.

Leaning his mace against his leg, spiked head on the floor, the
Mongol grasped Harrison's shirt bosom with one hand, lifted
his head and shoulders clear of the floor, while he shoved the
block under his head. Like twin striking snakes the detective's

hands whipped from behind him and locked on the Mongol's bull throat.

There was no cry; instantly the Mongol's slant eyes distended and his lips parted in a grin of strangulation. With a terrific heave he reared upright, dragging Harrison with him, but not breaking his hold, and the weight of the big American pulled them both down again. Both yellow hands tore frantically at Harrison's iron wrists; then the giant stiffened convulsively and brief agony reddened his black eyes. Khoda Khan had driven his knife between the Mongol's shoulders so that the point cut through the silk over the man's breastbone.

Harrison caught up the mace, grunting with savage satisfaction. It was a weapon more suited to his temperament than the dagger Khoda Khan had given him. No need to ask its use; if he had been bound and alone when the executioner entered, his brains would now have been clotting its spiked ball and the hollowed ebon block which so nicely accommodated a human head. Erlik Khan's executions varied along the whole gamut from the exquisitely subtle to the crudely bestial.

"The door's open," said Harrison. "Let's go!"

There were no keys on the body. Harrison doubted if the key in the door would fit any other in the building, but he locked the door and pocketed the key, hoping that would prevent the body from being soon discovered.

They emerged into a dim-lit corridor which presented the same unfinished appearance as the room they had just left. At the other end stairs wound down into shadowy gloom, and they descended warily, Harrison feeling along the wall to guide his steps. Khoda Khan seemed to see like a cat in the dark; he went down silently and surely. But it was Harrison who discovered the door. His hand, moving along the convex surface, felt the smooth stone give way to wood—a short narrow panel, through which a man could just squeeze. When the wall was covered with tapestry—as he knew it would be when Erlik Khan completed his house—it would be sufficiently hidden for a secret entrance.

Khoda Khan, behind him, was growing impatient at the delay, when somewhere below them both heard a noise simultaneously. It might have been a man ascending the winding stairs and it might not, but Harrison acted instinctively. He pushed and the door opened inward on noiseless oiled springs. A groping foot discovered narrow steps inside. With a whispered word to the Afghan he stepped through and Khoda Khan followed. He pulled the door shut again and they stood in total blackness with a curving wall on either hand. Harrison struck a match and a narrow stairs was revealed, winding down.

"This place must be built like a castle," Harrison muttered, wondering at the thickness of the walls. The match went out and they groped down in darkness too thick for even the Afghan to pierce. And suddenly both halted in their tracks. Harrison estimated that they had reached the level of the second floor, and through the inner wall came the mutter of voices. Harrison groped for another door, or a peep-hole for spying, but he found nothing of the sort. But straining his ear close to the stone, he began to understand what was being said beyond the wall, and a long-drawn hiss between clenched teeth told him that Khoda Khan likewise understood.

The first voice was Erlik Khan's; there was no mistaking that hollow reverberance. It was answered by a piteous, incoherent whimpering that brought sweat suddenly out on Harrison's flesh.

"No," the Mongol was saying. "I have come back, not from hell as your barbarian superstitions suggest, but from a refuge unknown to your stupid police. I was saved from death by the steel cap I always wear beneath my coif. You are at a loss as to how you got here?"

"I don't understand!" It was the voice of Joan La Tour, half-hysterical but undeniably sane. "I remember opening a bottle of wine, and as soon as I drank I knew it was drugged. Then everything faded out—I don't remember anything except great black walls, and awful shapes skulking in the darkness. I ran through gigantic shadowy halls for a thousand years—"

"They were hallucinations of madness, of the juice of the black pomegranate," answered Erlik Khan. Khoda Khan was muttering blasphemously in his beard until Harrison admonished him to silence with a fierce dig of his elbow. "If you had drunk more you would have died like a rabid dog. As it was, you went insane. But I knew the antidote—possessed the drug that restored your sanity."

"Why?" the girl whimpered bewilderedly.

"Because I did not wish you to die like a candle blown out in the dark, my beautiful white orchid. I wish you to be fully sane so as to taste to the last dregs the shame and agony of death, subtle and prolonged. For the exquisite, an exquisite death.

For the coarse-fibered, the death of an ox, such as I have decreed for your friend Harrison."

"That will be more easily decreed than executed," she retorted with a flash of spirit.

"It is already accomplished," the Mongol asserted imperturbably. "The executioner has gone to him, and by this time Mr. Harrison's head resembles a crushed egg."

"Oh, God!" At the sick grief and pain in that moan Harrison winced and fought a frantic desire to shout out denial and reassurance.

Then she remembered something else to torture her.

"Khoda Khan! What have you done with Khoda Khan?"

The Afghan's fingers clamped like iron on Harrison's arm at the sound of his name.

"When my men brought you away they did not take time to deal with him," replied the Mongol. "They had not expected to take you alive, and when fate cast you into their hands, they came away in haste. He matters little. True, he killed four of my best men, but that was merely the deed of a wolf. He has no mentality. He and the detective were much alike—mere masses of brawn, brainless, helpless against intellect like mine. Presently I shall attend to him. His corpse shall be thrown on a dung-heap with a dead pig."

"Allah!" Harrison felt Khoda Khan trembling with fury. "Liar! I will feed his yellow guts to the rats!"

Only Harrison's grip on his arm kept the maddened Moslem from attacking the stone wall in an effort to burst through to his enemy. The detective was running his hand over the surface, seeking a door, but only blank stone rewarded him. Erlik Khan had not had time to provide his unfinished house with as many secrets as his rat-runs usually possessed.

They heard the Mongol clap his hands authoritatively, and they sensed the entrance of men into the room. Staccato commands followed in Mongolian, there was a sharp cry of pain or fear, and then silence followed the soft closing of a door. Though they could not see, both men knew instinctively that the chamber on the other side of the wall was empty. Harrison almost strangled with a panic of helpless rage. He was penned in these infernal walls and Joan La Tour was being borne away to some abominable doom.

"*Wallah!*" the Afghan was raving. "They have taken her away to slay her! Her life and our *izzat* is at stake! By the

Prophet's beard and my feet! I will burn this accursed house! I will slake the fire with Mongol blood! In Allah's name, *sahib*, let us do something!"

"Come on!" snarled Harrison. "There must be another door somewhere!"

Recklessly they plunged down the winding stair, and about the time they had reached the first floor level, Harrison's groping hand felt a door. Even as he found the catch, it moved under his fingers. Their noise must have been heard through the wall, for the panel opened, and a shaven head was poked in, framed in the square of light. The Mongol blinked in the darkness, and Harrison brought the mace down on his head, experiencing a vengeful satisfaction as he felt the skull give way beneath the iron spikes. The man fell face down in the narrow opening and Harrison sprang over his body into the outer room before he took time to learn if there were others. But the chamber was untenanted. It was thickly carpeted, the walls hung with black velvet tapestries. The doors were of bronze-bound teak, with gilt-worked arches. Khoda Khan presented an incongruous contrast, bare-footed, with draggled turban and red-smeared knife.

But Harrison did not pause to philosophise. Ignorant as he was of the house, one way was as good as another. He chose a door at random and flung it open, revealing a wide corridor carpeted and tapestried like the chamber. At the other end, through wide satin curtains that hung from roof to floor, a file of men was just disappearing—tall, black-silk clad Mongols, heads bent somberly, like a train of dusky ghosts. They did not look back.

"Follow them!" snapped Harrison. "They must be headed for the execution—"

Khoda Khan was already sweeping down the corridor like a vengeful whirlwind. The thick carpet deadened their footfalls, so even Harrison's big shoes made no noise. There was a distinct feeling of unreality, running silently down that fantastic hall—it was like a dream in which natural laws are suspended. Even in that moment Harrison had time to reflect that this whole night had been like a nightmare, possible only in the Oriental quarter, its violence and bloodshed like an evil dream. Erlik Khan had loosed the forces of chaos and insanity; murder had gone mad, and its frenzy was imparted to all actions and men caught in its maelstrom.

Khoda Khan would have burst headlong through the curtains—he was already drawing breath for a yell, and lifting his knife, if Harrison had not seized him. The Afghan's sinews were like cords under the detective's hands, and Harrison doubted his own ability to restrain him forcibly, but a vestige of sanity remained to the hillman.

Pushing him back, Harrison gazed between the curtains. There was a great double-valved door there, but it was partly open, and he looked into the room beyond. Khoda Khan's beard was jammed hard against his neck as the Afghan glared over his shoulder.

It was a large chamber, hung like the others with black velvet on which golden dragons writhed. There were thick rugs, and lanterns hanging from the ivory-inlaid ceiling cast a red glow that made for illusion. Black-robed men ranged along the wall might have been shadows but for their glittering eyes.

On a throne-like chair of ebony sat a grim figure, motionless as an image except when its loose robes stirred in the faintly moving air. Harrison felt the short hairs prickle at the back of his neck, just as a dog's hackles rise at the sight of an enemy. Khoda Khan muttered some incoherent blasphemy.

The Mongol's throne was set against a side wall. No one stood near him as he sat in solitary magnificence, like an idol brooding on human doom. In the center of the room stood what looked uncomfortably like a sacrificial altar—a curiously carved block of stone that might have come out of the heart of the Gobi. On that stone lay Joan La Tour, white as a marble statue, her arms outstretched like a crucifix, her hands and feet extending over the edges of the block. Her dilated eyes stared upward as one lost to hope, aware of doom and eager only for death to put an end to agony. The physical torture had not yet begun, but a gaunt half-naked brute squatted on his haunches at the end of the altar, heating the point of a bronze rod in a dish full of glowing coals.

"Damn!" It was half curse, half sob of fury bursting from Harrison's lips. Then he was hurled aside and Khoda Khan burst into the room like a flying dervish, bristling beard, blazing eyes, knife and all. Erlik Khan came erect with a startled guttural as the Afghan came tearing down the room like a headlong hurricane of destruction. The torturer sprang up just in time to meet the yard-long knife lashing down, and it split his skull down through the teeth.

"*Aie!*" It was a howl from a score of Mongol throats.

"*Allaho akabar!*" yelled Khoda Khan, whirling the red knife about his head. He threw himself on the altar, slashing at Joan's bonds with a frenzy that threatened to dismember the girl.

Then from all sides the black-robed figures swarmed in, not noticing in their confusion that the Afghan had been followed by another grim figure who came with less abandon but with equal ferocity.

They were aware of Harrison only when he dealt a prodigious sweep of his mace, right and left, bowling men over like ten-pins, and reached the altar through the gap made in the bewildered throng. Khoda Khan had freed the girl and he wheeled, spitting like a cat, his bared teeth gleaming and each hair of his beard stiffly on end.

"*Allah!*" he yelled—spat in the faces of the oncoming Mongols—crouched as if to spring into the midst of them—then whirled and rushed headlong at the ebony throne.

The speed and unexpectedness of the move were stunning. With a choked cry Erlik Khan fired and missed at point-blank range—and then the breath burst from Khoda Khan in an ear-splitting yell as his knife plunged into the Mongol's breast and the point sprang a hand's breadth out of his black-clad back.

The impetus of his rush unchecked, Khoda Khan hurtled into the falling figure, crashing it back on to the ebony throne which splintered under the impact of the two heavy bodies. Bounding up, wrenching his dripping knife free, Khoda Khan whirled it high and howled like a wolf.

"*Ya Allah!* Wearer of steel caps! Carry the taste of my knife in your guts to hell with you!"

There was a long hissing intake of breath as the Mongols stared wide-eyed at the black-robed, red-smeared figure crumpled grotesquely among the ruins of the broken throne; and in the instant that they stood like frozen men, Harrison caught up Joan and ran for the nearest door, bellowing: "Khoda Khan! This way! Quick!"

With a howl and a whickering of blades the Mongols were at his heels. Fear of steel in his back winged Harrison's big feet, and Khoda Khan ran slantingly across the room to meet him at the door.

"Haste, *sahib!* Down the corridor! I will cover your retreat!"

"No! Take Joan and run!" Harrison literally threw her into the Afghan's arms and wheeled back in the doorway, lifting the mace. He was as berserk in his own way as was Khoda Khan, frantic with the madness that sometimes inspired men in the midst of combat.

The Mongols came on as if they, too, were blood-mad. They jammed the door with square snarling faces and squat silk-clad bodies before he could slam it shut. Knives licked at him, and gripping the mace with both hands, he wielded it like a flail, working awful havoc among the shapes that strove in the doorway, wedged by the pressure from behind. The lights, the upturned snarling faces that dissolved in crimson ruin beneath his flailing, all swam in a red mist. He was not aware of his individual identity. He was only a man with a club, transported back fifty thousand years, a hairy-breasted, red-eyed primitive, wholly possessed by the crimson instinct for slaughter.

He felt like howling his incoherent exultation with each swing of his bludgeon that crushed skulls and splattered blood into his face. He did not feel the knives that found him, hardly realizing it when the men facing him gave back, daunted at the havoc he was wreaking. He did not close the door then; it was blocked and choked by a ghastly mass of crushed and red-dripping flesh.

He found himself running down the corridor, his breath coming in great gulping gasps, following some dim instinct of preservation or realization of duty that made itself heard amidst the red dizzy urge to grip his foes and strike, strike, strike, until he was himself engulfed in the crimson waves of death. In such moments the passion to die—die fighting—is almost equal to the will to live.

In a daze, staggering, bumping into walls and caroming off them, he reached the further end of the corridor where Khoda Khan was struggling with a lock. Joan was standing now, though she reeled on her feet, and seemed on the point of collapse. The mob was coming down the long corridor full cry behind him. Drunkenly Harrison thrust Khoda Khan aside and whirling the blood-fouled mace around his head, struck a stupendous blow that shattered the lock, burst the bolts out of their sockets and caved in the heavy panels as if they had been cardboard. The next instant they were through and Khoda Khan slammed the ruins of the door which sagged on its hinges, but somehow held together. There were heavy metal brackets on each jamb, and Khoda Khan found and dropped an iron bar in place just as the mob surged against it.

Through the shattered panels they howled and thrust their knives, but Harrison knew until they hewed away enough wood to enable them to reach in and dislodge it, the bar across the door would hold the splintered barrier in place. Recovering some of his wits, and feeling rather sick, he herded his companions ahead of him with desperate haste. He noticed, briefly, that he was stabbed in the calf, thigh, arm and shoulder. Blood soaked his ribboned shirt and ran down his limbs in streams. The Mongols were hacking at the door, snarling like jackals over carrion.

The apertures were widening, and through them he saw other Mongols running down the corridor with rifles; just as he wondered why they did not shoot through the door, then saw the reason. They were in a chamber which had been converted into a magazine. Cartridge cases were piled high along the wall, and there was at least one box of dynamite. But he looked in vain for rifles or pistols. Evidently they were stored in another part of the building.

Khoda Khan was jerking the bolts on an opposite door, but he paused to glare about and yelping *"Allah!"* he pounced on an open case, snatched something out—wheeled, yelled a curse and threw back his arm, but Harrison grabbed his wrist.

"Don't throw that, you idiot! You'll blow us all to hell! They're afraid to shoot into this room, but they'll have that door down in a second or so, and finish us with their knives. Help Joan!"

It was a hand grenade Khoda Khan had found—the only one in an otherwise empty case, as a glance assured Harrison. The detective threw the door open, slammed it shut behind them as they plunged out into the starlight, Joan reeling, half carried by the Afghan. They seemed to have emerged at the back of the house. They ran across an open space, hunted creatures looking for a refuge. There was a crumbling stone wall, about breast-high to a man, and they ran through a wide gap in it, only to halt, a groan burst from Harrison's lips. Thirty steps behind the ruined wall rose the steel fence of which Khoda Khan had spoken, a barrier ten feet high, topped with keen points. The door crashed open behind them and a gun spat venomously. They were in a trap. If they tried to climb the fence the Mongols had but to pick them off like monkeys shot off a ladder.

"Down behind the wall!" snarled Harrison, forcing Joan

behind an uncrumbled section of the stone barrier. "We'll make 'em pay for it, before they take us!"

The door was crowded with snarling faces, now leering in triumph. There were rifles in the hands of a dozen. They knew their victims had no fire-arms, and could not escape, and they themselves could use rifles without fear. Bullets began to splatter on the stone, then with a long-drawn yell Khoda Khan bounded to the top of the wall, ripping out the pin of the hand grenade with his teeth.

"*La illaha illulah; Muhammad rassoul ullah!*" he yelled, and hurled the bomb—not at the group which howled and ducked, but over their heads, into the magazine!

The next instant a rending crash tore the guts out of the night and a blinding blaze of fire ripped the darkness apart. In that glare Harrison had a glimpse of Khoda Khan, etched against the flame, hurtling backward, arms out-thrown—then there was utter blackness in which roared the thunder of the fall of the house of Erlik Khan as the shattered walls buckled, the beams splintered, the roof fell in and story after story came crashing down on the crumpled foundations.

How long Harrison lay like dead he never knew, blinded, deafened and paralyzed; covered by falling debris. His first realization was that there was something soft under him, something that writhed and whimpered. He had a vague feeling he ought not to hurt this soft something, so he began to shove the broken stones and mortar off him. His arm seemed dead, but eventually he excavated himself and staggered up, looking like a scarecrow in his rags. He groped among the rubble, grasped the girl and pulled her up.

"Joan!" His own voice seemed to come to him from a great distance; he had to shout to make her hear him. Their eardrums had been almost split by the concussion.

"Are you hurt?" He ran his one good hand over her to make sure.

"I don't think so," she faltered dazedly. "What—what happened?"

"Khoda Khan's bomb exploded the dynamite. The house fell in on the Mongols. We were sheltered by that wall; that's all that saved us."

The wall was a shattered heap of broken stone, half covered by rubble—a waste of shattered masonry with broken beams thrust up through the litter, and shards of walls reeling drunkenly. Harrison fingered his broken arm and tried to think, his head swimming.

"Where is Khoda Khan?" cried Joan, seeming finally to shake off her daze.

"I'll look for him." Harrison dreaded what he expected to find. "He was blown off the wall like a straw in a wind."

Stumbling over broken stones and bits of timber, he found the Afghan huddled grotesquely against the steel fence. His fumbling fingers told him of broken bones—but the man was still breathing. Joan came stumbling toward him, to fall beside Khoda Khan and flutter her quick fingers over him, sobbing hysterically.

"He's not like civilized man!" she exclaimed, tears running down her stained, scratched face. "Afghans are harder than cats to kill. If we could get him medical attention he'll live. Listen!" She caught Harrison's arm with galvanized fingers; but he had heard it too—the sputter of a motor that was probably a police launch, coming to investigate the explosion.

Joan was tearing her scanty garments to pieces to staunch the blood that seeped from the Afghan's wounds, when miraculously Khoda Khan's pulped lips moved. Harrison, bending close, caught fragments of words: "The curse of Allah—Chinese dog— swine's flesh—my *izzat*."

"You needn't worry about your *izzat*," grunted Harrison, glancing at the ruins which hid the mangled figures that had been Mongolian terrorists. "After this night's work you'll not go to jail—not for all the Chinamen in River Street."

TAVEREL MANOR*

*With Richard A. Lupoff.

1

Sir Haldred Taverel sat up in bed, conscious only of a bewildered, crawling horror. He raised his hands to his head, trying to collect his scattered faculties, as a man will do when wakened suddenly out of a deep slumber.

He had dreamed—or was it a dream, that hideous yellow face which had floated before him? Sir Haldred shuddered. The memory of those glaring inhuman eyes and the loose bestial mouth was startlingly vivid. But he could not tell if the memory were that of a dream or—

He began piecing the fragments of jumbled memory together, the while his eyes wandered about the great room with its costly and somber furnishings. While his eyes sought for stealthy movements among the antique hangings he recalled the events of the last few months.

The death of a distant relative had lifted the young lord from the position of a small country nobleman whose family fortune had gone to seed, to one of comparative affluence. Within a short week, Sir Haldred had found himself snatched out of his boyhood environment and the transition had left him dizzy and not altogether pleased, after the novelty had worn off. From pleasant south England he had come to this wild and desolate northern Coast to be the sole occupant of this grim old castle which tradition proclaimed was haunted by the ghosts of past crimes.

Not the sole occupant either—there was Lo Kung, the one servant the place boasted, left there by the previous owner. Lo Kung, Sir Haldred reflected, was a suitable attachment to the castle, for he was thin, silent and ghostly—though the young man could not rid himself of a feeling of familiarity about the man which he could not place—a tantalizing something in the stooped shoulders or in the soft sibilant voice of the Oriental.

But Lo Kung had assured him that they had never met before; had firmly maintained it, in that courteous, impersonal manner of his. And yet why had he acted so strangely the day Sir Haldred arrived? He had opened the door in response to the bell, had stepped aside and motioned the young man in, then had suddenly stopped short as if struck, standing perfectly motionless for an instant. His eyes had seemed to burn Sir Haldred through the heavy colored spectacles the Chinaman always wore, but his immobile face, with its queer thin pointed beard, had given no sign.

Sir Haldred's shoulder twitched under his thin silk pajamas as he recalled his life at Taverel Manor—short, to date, but far from merry. He had had few visitors; had spent most of his time wandering about the grim old castle trying to get used to the silence, the air of unseen watchers, the feeling of stealthy footsteps—

Suddenly he sprang from bed with an exclamation of impatience. Either he had dreamed it, or there had been a man in his room a few minutes before—a man? Perhaps not a man but some creature with a hideous yellow face, that no more resembled Lo Kung or any other Chinaman he had ever seen, than he resembled Sir Haldred himself. Imagine a hairless ape, with parchment-hued skin—Sir Haldred crossed the room hurriedly and opened the door, feeling a little shiver of apprehension as the knob yielded to his efforts. He had left the door locked, or had intended to.

He hurried on down the darkened corridor, dimly lit by the moonlight which managed to filter through some of the curtained windows, and descended the stairs, into the utter blackness of the first floor. There was no sound, but he was angered at himself to find himself holding his breath. He wished that he had a weapon; this old house was getting on his nerves. Only that morning Lo Kung had mentioned the fact that he seemed pale, and had urged him to run down to London for a few days. Lo Kung had been urgent in his advice and now Sir

Haldred, remembering, found time to wonder at the feeling that had vibrated in his tone. He wished he had taken that advice, as he groped his way down the darkened stairs. He had no torchlight and the house boasted no electrical connection with the village power plant.

Now he had reached the foot of the stairs, which let into the lower hallway. Not a sound in the house—he fell heavily over something which lay sprawled near the foot of the stairs.

He sprang up, struck a match. He stared in open-mouthed bewildered horror while the match burned down to his fingers. Lo Kung lay at his feet and a glance sufficed to show that he was dead. The Chinaman had been frightfully mauled as if by some huge animal. Sir Haldred struck another match and bent closer. The spectacles had been knocked off and the dead eyes stared wide open. The young man's breath caught in a quick intake. He grasped the thin pointed beard; it came away in his hand. For a moment he stared unbelievingly, then a sudden sound brought him round.

Down at the end of the hall something had moved—there had sounded the stealthy pad of unshod feet—human or otherwise. Sir Haldred snatched up a heavy poker and strode down the hall, his face set in grim lines. The horrid drama for which that dark and silent house had formed a stage that night, was not yet over.

At the end of the hall there was a curious relic of a former owner's wanderings in strange lands—a grim pagan shrine. A tall, grotesquely carven pedestal stood behind a low stained altar; the pedestal set firmly against the end wall of the hall. On this pedestal sat a great idol, loathsome and horrific, a frightful caricature of mankind.

Here Sir Haldred halted, puzzled. His gaze was fixed on this idol. Suddenly his eyes flared with horror and unbelief; then the poker dropped from his nerveless hand and one terrible, brain-shattering scream burst from him, splitting the grisly stillness. Then silence fell again like a black fog, broken only by the nervous scampering of a rat who stole from his covert to view the dead man who lay by the stairs.

2

"But, my dear girl, how am I to aid you, if all Scotland Yard has failed?"

The girl addressed twined her white hands helplessly and her eyes wandered nervously about the bizarrely furnished room. Besides herself there were four persons in this room—another girl and a young man, her companions; the other two sat facing her and it was to them that she had just made her appeal. One of these men was a tall, broad-shouldered man, lean and sun-bronzed, with piercing gray eyes. The other was not so tall, but heavier, a powerfully built man, whose dark features were as immobile as an Indian's.

"You see, my dear," the taller man was saying gently, "I'm not really a detective; I'm connected with the British Secret Service in a way, it's true. But my proper field of endeavor is in the Orient—"

"That's one reason why I came to you!" the girl broke in. "The main reason was I had nowhere else to turn after the police gave it up—then because of the circumstances—"

"Sir Haldred Taverel meant a great deal to you, did he not?"

"We were engaged to be married," her voice broke in a dry sob. "Then this terrible affair came up—"

"Let me tell the full details, sis," interrupted the young man at her side. "They've read about it, of course, but there may be some points—

"You see, Mr. Gordon. Haldred Taverel was born and raised in our parish; we all grew up together and I know him like a brother. If it had been anybody else I might have thought he'd gotten into a jam and skipped, but not he! If he had he'd face the music. That's why I know something's rotten somewhere.

"I've been making inquirement around the neighborhood of the castle where he vanished and find it has a long unsavory history. Up to a hundred years ago, that branch of the Taverel family was a bad lot—nothing like our south country Taverels. They gradually died off and finally the castle was left vacant. Sir Rupert Taverel, the last of the direct line, roved around over the world most of his life, but a few months before his death, decided he'd repair the ancestral estate. He moved in with one servant, a Chinaman, and he hadn't been there but a few months when he fell from an upstairs window—or was thrown—and died instantly. There was some dark talk about it, but nothing that could be proved. There was no one else in the house at the time; the Chinese servant proved that he had been down at the tavern in the village. It seems pretty conclusive that Sir Rupert fell from his bedroom window while drunk or walking in his sleep. He was a hard bitter man, with a black past, and he left neither friends nor will.

"In the absence of a will, the estate reverted to Sir Haldred, a distant relative, but the next in line. He moved there, for that was the custom—the heir of the estate always lived at Taverel Manor, up to Sir Rupert, and he eventually came back.

"Then one night it happened. Haldred Taverel and his Chinese servant, the same man who had worked for Sir Rupert, vanished completely as if from the face of the earth!"

"There was no clue?" Gordon's keen brown face showed interest. "No trace to show if they had been murdered or had fled alive?"

"There were stains of blood on the floor near the stairs, in the lower hallway—the evidence of a struggle; a heavy poker lay across the altar of a peculiar shrine at the other end of the hall. Otherwise—nothing!

"Up in Haldred's bedroom, the clothing he had presumably worn the day before lay as carefully arranged as when he had removed them to go to bed. None of his belongings were missing, not even his watch or pocketbook. If he fled, he must have done so in his night clothes!

"The local police were baffled and Scotland Yard sent down

a man who had no better result. That was nearly a month ago. The police have given it up; they ransacked the castle from cellar to attic and found exactly nothing."

"Is the house occupied by anyone now?"

"Yes, a fellow named Hammerby turned up—staid, clerical-looking chap, with a sort of bill of sale from Joseph Taverel. Joseph is next in line and by Haldred's death—or disappearance—the estate fell to him. But Joseph can't come back to England without looking up a rope, for he fled the country some years ago after the brutal murder of a girl with whom he'd had an affair—pretty sordid case.

"The police were naturally interested, but Hammerby swore he didn't know where Joseph was, and knew nothing about the crime. Hammerby is an Englishman, but he's lived in America for about twenty years. He said he had business dealings with Joseph there, though he said the fellow went under a different name then.

"Joseph stole a lot of money from him in a business deal and when he was going to send him to the pen, Taverel told him—and proved to him—that he was one of the heirs of a large estate in England, and as he had just heard of his cousin's disappearance, he made over his rights in the Taverel estate to Hammerby. That is, in case it was proven Haldred was dead. Hammerby had a letter signed by Joseph in which he stated that Hammerby represented him and was to have full charge of the estate until it was proven absolutely that Haldred was alive. If he chanced to be alive, of course Hammerby was out. If dead, the estate went to Hammerby in payment of debts. Hammerby was taking a heavy chance, but somehow Joseph seemed pretty certain that Haldred was dead.

"Rather irregular, but of course Joseph couldn't come to attend to it himself, with the shadow of the gallows hanging over him. And the letter wasn't a forgery; comparison with examples of Joseph's handwriting showed the signature on Hammerby's letter to be genuine. As no one wanted to have anything to do with the house, Hammerby was allowed to move in, which he's done. He's to occupy the house, rent free, for the time being. If Haldred shows up, Hammerby has agreed to pay back rent and get out. If it's proved Haldred is dead, the house and money goes to Hammerby. Rather irregular, but stranger things have happened."

"And what sort of a man is this Hammerby?" asked Gordon curiously.

"Oh, a prim middle-aged chap, rather pedantic. The sort of middle-class Englishman who has money himself, but would trade his eyebrows for a title or anything approaching it. You know the sort; good chap but dry and tedious."

"Oh, we're getting off the main subject," cried the girl who had first spoken. "Mr. Gordon, you've been a friend of my family longer than I can remember! You'll do this for me, won't you? Just run up to Taverel Manor with us and have one look around! Please! I'm going to go insane if something isn't done!"

"To be sure I'll go, Marjory," said Gordon gently. "I'll be glad to help you all I can, though I fear I can do nothing. If the case has baffled the best minds of Scotland Yard, I'm afraid you need hope of nothing from a man who is used to working in the open. But run along now; Costigan and I have a good deal to do to get ready for the journey."

Marjory Harper silently held out her hands to him, tears coming into her soft gray eyes. Gordon patted her shoulder gently, and her brother and the other girl rising, he escorted them to the door. Costigan made no move to rise, and the boy, Harry Harper, glanced back at the dark somber figure where he sat cramming a pipe with tobacco.

"Queer sort of fellow, your friend," he murmured in a low voice to Gordon, as he stepped into the hallway.

Gordon nodded. "Silent, moody chap to those who don't know him. But a marvelous friend. Shot up and shell shocked in the war—took to dope and spent years in the Limehouse—underworld. Take all night to tell you his story, how I helped him break the habit and how he helped me break up a gang of desperate criminals. Run along now; Costigan and I will meet you at that antique shop downstairs in two hours. We're to motor up to Taverel Manor, I take it?"

John Gordon turned back into his apartment and shut the door.

"Rotten luck in way," he said with a slight frown. "I've known Marjory Harper and her brother ever since I used to dandle them on my knee. Fine kids and this piece of business is a shame. I can't refuse them—but what can I do? And this smuggling job taking up all my time."

Costigan puffed at his pipe before replying.

"Looks like we haven't done much on that job, Gordon."

"I know," the other cried, pacing the room like a great tiger. "It's the most baffling case I've ever worked on. Here we trace a ring of opium smugglers out of China and clear across Europe, only to be brought up short here! There's a leak somewhere, but I can't find where. It's like chasing a rat up to a fence, seeing him get through and then be unable to find the hole. Oh, pshaw! Let's forget it for a few days. I don't know in which direction to look— I'll probably accomplish just as much looking for smugglers up on the northern coast as I'm accomplishing here in London. It's infuriating—knowing the stuff flooding the country through some loophole, and yet we can't discover the loophole.

"What do you think about Sir Haldred Taverel's disappearance?" he whirled suddenly on his companion with that sudden shift of subjects which characterized John Gordon's conversation.

"I think he got into a bad spot and took it on the lam," answered Costigan, unconsciously slipping into the patois of the underworld. "Or maybe the slant-eye put the kibosh on him and got out from under."

"Then where's the corpse? And what became of the Chinaman?"

"Don't ask me." Costigan's indifferent manner masked all but his eyes which were beginning to burn with a feral light.

3

Mr. Thomas Hammerby blinked mildly at his visitors. Mr. Hammerby was a rather stout man of medium height, and would have appeared only about early middle life, had it not been for his snow-white locks which lent him a benevolent air, an appearance heightened by a pair of bright friendly eyes which gleamed from behind his spectacles.

"I hope," he said apologetically, "that Sir Haldred's friends do not look on me as an interloper—an intruder who has taken advantage of circumstances to obtain possession of the ancestral estate?"

"Not at all, Mr. Hammerby," he was assured by Marjory Harper. "We have come to make one more investigation of the premises, in hopes—"

Her voice faltered. Mr. Hammerby bowed, sympathetically.

"Please do not feel at all constrained by my presence, and don't hesitate to call on me if I can be of assistance. I need not tell you how I regret this lamentable occurrence, nor how I hope that Sir Haldred will turn up safely, though it would mean the loss of the estate to me."

Gordon did not conduct investigations after the popularly conceived idea of detectives. In the first place, he knew that any possible clues would have been discovered long ago by the regular police. In the second, he was secretly convinced that for some reason or other, Sir Haldred Taverel had secretly fled.

He looked at the faint reddish stains on the floor near the foot of the stairs and examined the strange shrine at the other end of the hall. This occupied his attention for some time.

"What do you make it, Costigan?"

"Thibetan," said the taciturn one briefly. "Hill country—devil worshippers, eh?"

"I think so," Gordon nodded. He was engrossed with the obscene idol which squatted upon the black carven pedestal. This idol was man-like in form, but with the face of a simian devil. It was cunningly fashioned of some ancient yellow stone, and was as large as a large man. Two semi-precious stones leered down for eyes.

"Human sacrifice," murmured Gordon, glancing down at the ancient stains on the low altar before the pedestal.

"Undoubtedly." It was Hammerby speaking in his pedantic schoolmaster fashion at the detective's elbow. "I think you are right, sir, in naming it Thibetan in origin—the work of some obscure mountain people, I should say, judging from my study of anthropology. It was brought from India by Captain Hilton Taverel in 1849, the villagers say, and has set here ever since. It must have taken a vast amount of labor and money to transport such a huge thing so far. But the Taverels never considered expense or trouble when they wanted something—or so I hear."

"It was on this altar that the poker was found," said Harry. "And Haldred's fingerprints were on it. That meant little, though. He might have had occasion to lay it on the altar and then forget about it, a day or a week before his disappearance."

Gordon nodded shortly; his interest appeared to have waned. He glanced at his watch.

"Getting late," he said. "We'd better be getting back to the village."

"I should be glad if you would spend the night here," said Hammerby.

Gordon shook his head before any of the others could speak.

"Thanks. I think it best to return to the inn. There's nothing we could do tonight—yet, wait a moment. I believe Costigan and I will take advantage of your offer, after all."

After Harry, Marjory and Joan had left, Gordon turned to his host.

"You knew this Joseph Taverel; what sort of man was he?"

"A scoundrel, sir!" Hammerby's eyes flashed and his mild countenance became suffused with anger. "A rascal of the first water! A fraud and a cheat in his business relations, he did not hesitate to dupe his partners and swindle those who trusted him.

"Only threats of the penitentiary induced him to settle with me. At the time I accosted him I had no idea of his relationship to any title or estate; I knew him only as John Walshire, contractor. He swore he was without funds, which was very likely, because of his dissipated habits and spendthrift ways, and he himself suggested that I take the estate as settlement."

"The debt must have been considerable," remarked Gordon.

"It was, I assure you!" exclaimed Hammerby.

"Isn't it rather lonely out here?"

"Why, not to a man of my tastes. Here I have leisure for study and meditation, and then," he flushed and smiled with a naive embarrassment, "I have always wanted to live in a castle! I was raised in a hovel, I am not ashamed to say it, and in my childhood I often dreamed of the day when, having risen to prosperity by my own efforts, I should live in a castle as fine as any.

"Sometimes our childhood dreams are strongest of all ambitions, Mr. Gordon; mine has been realized, I am happy to say, though I regret deeply the circumstances by which it has come to pass.

"Then, as to loneliness, there is the village in case I feel the need of human companionship, and though none of the villagers ever comes here, there is nothing to prevent me from going there. Then here are Mrs. Drake, my housekeeper, and Hanson, my man of all work.

"No, I assure you, Mr. Gordon, my days here are full of work and study and even if I am ousted within a few weeks, I shall always look back upon the time spent here with the greatest of pleasure.

"It is such a pity that Sir Haldred had to come to woe in order for me to acquire this place! But that is the way of the world; whether we wish to or not, we gain by others' losses."

"How far is it to the coast?" asked Gordon abruptly.

"About a half mile. You can hear the breakers against the rocks at high tide."

"Let's take a stroll to the shore, Costigan," Gordon rose. "I have a peculiar penchant for walking in the mist, and the thunder of these northern coasts attracts me."

"As you like, sir," said Hammerby. "You must pardon me for not accompanying you, but neither the cold night air nor the exertion is good for one in my condition. I will send Hanson to guide you, if you like."

"Oh, no need of that. It's a straightaway course to the cliffs, isn't it? We will make it all right. And you needn't wait up for us, because we may be some little time."

Not until the black bulk of Taverel Manor lay starkly in the fog behind them did either of the men speak. They strode stolidly forward through the heavy dank mist, their pipes glowing in unison to their strides. Far ahead they heard the faint booming of the sea. All about them the moors lay barren and desolate for as far as they could see in the fog.

"Joseph Taverel must have owed an enormous amount of money to our friend Hammerby," mused Gordon.

Costigan laughed. "I think so, myself. All that estate taken on a debt? Bah! Hammerby put the screws on Taverel and shook him down for his whole wad, if you ask me."

"Meaning that he blackmailed him—threatened him with prison? Like enough; I don't believe that Taverel proposed deeding the estate to Hammerby—I believe that was Hammerby's idea. He'd always wanted an estate in England; he saw where he could get one for perhaps half the value. He's ashamed to admit that he forced Taverel—oh, I don't have any sympathy for that murderer. He was probably glad to exchange his birthright for his freedom."

"What's the idea of staying in the Manor tonight?" asked Costigan abruptly.

"Oh, no particular idea. There's nowhere to take hold to work, in this case—if you could call it a case. I've got to do my best for Marjory's sake, but I can't see anything to it. I pity the girl from the bottom of my heart, and more because I can't keep from believing that Sir Haldred must have had reason for running away."

"The villagers say he was snatched away by the ghosts of the long dead Taverels."

"Bosh—there's the shore."

Wild, bare and rugged rose the cliffs, at the foot of which the gray waters tossed endlessly. The droning gray waste spread out before them to vanish in the fog, and the men, struck by a sense of loneliness and futility of human endeavor, were silent. Then Gordon started.

"Look! What's that?"

Through the fog there winked and flickered a faint light far out at sea.

"Look! The flickering is too regular to be by chance! They're signalling somebody ashore!"

"A fellow at the village told me a foreign-looking ship had been hanging off and on for a couple of days," muttered Costigan. "He said he figured she had a passenger to put ashore here and was waiting for favorable weather to work inland. Bad place along this coast for a ship to come inshore. Likely to be thrown on the rocks."

Gordon wheeled with a sudden intuition and looked back the way they had come. In the thick fog the stark bulk of Taverel Manor could be but vaguely seen, but from the highest tower on the castle a pinpoint of light began to wink.

"Something here!" rapped Gordon. "Good thing we decided to stay! Here, let's leg it back to the Manor! Maybe we can catch whoever is signalling!"

They hurried along in silence, the fog growing denser.

"By Jove," said Gordon suddenly as they brushed past a clump of stunted shrubbery, "I wonder—"

At that moment Costigan cried a sharp harsh warning, but it was too late. Beneath the sudden vicious blow of the figure which rose from the shrubbery, Gordon went to his knees. In an instant Costigan was the center of a whirlwind attack; dark figures seemed to materialize from the earth to leap at him.

But in the first instant of attack, the unknown assailants found that they had essayed no easy task. With a snarl of battle fury the powerful American went into swift and deadly action. He met the first attacker with a smashing straight arm blow that dropped him writhing, flung off another who had leaped on his mighty shoulders, and whirling with cat-like speed for all his weight, met the charge of a sinister form who bounded in with a shimmer of cold steel.

Costigan felt a keen edge slice along his upflung arm, then his iron-hard right hand crashed against the attacker's jaw and the other shot backward, to fall in a grotesque heap, ten feet away.

At that moment a pistol cracked and someone yelled and cursed. Gordon was on his knees, firing. Like ghosts the unknown thugs faded away in the fog, leaving behind them only the crumpled form of the last man Costigan had struck.

The American was at his friend's side in an instant.

"Hurt?"

"No, just a trifle dizzy, thanks to this heavy cap. But you're bleeding!"

"Nothing to it," Costigan impatiently put his arm behind him. "Just a scratch. Let's see about the fellow that did it. He's still out."

Gordon bent over the fallen foe, and then with a sharp exclamation, tore a thick strip from his shirt and swiftly bound it about the man's leg, above the knee.

"Tourniquet," he explained hurriedly. "The beggar's bleeding to death; he may die anyway. He's fallen on his own knife and it's apparently severed that great artery behind the knee. Gad, he's lost a raft of blood!"

Costigan was leaning over the unconscious man, frowning.

"That fellow's a Malay!" he said suddenly. "Look at his knife—a crooked bladed kreese—if his face wasn't evidence enough!"

"Thunder!" Gordon ejaculated as the man opened his eyes. "Malay? I should say! And what's more, he's Ali Massar, wanted in both Burma and Siam for a score of crimes! I've seen the rascal before! What are you doing here?"

The Malay was fully conscious now, though the white tinge about his lips showed that he was in a bad way. His evil eyes gleamed with recognition, but he said nothing.

"Talk!" snarled Gordon. "Or we will leave you here to die."

The steady snake-like eyes of the Oriental never wavered.

"No," said the detective calmly, "you won't die; you'll live to expiate your crimes on the gallows."

The Malay's eyes flickered. No true Moslem can face the thought of hanging without flinching.

"You will hang me?" he spoke for the first time; his voice was very weak, almost a whisper.

"If you tell me what you are doing here, and what this mystery means, it may go easier with you."

The Malay's eyes brooded in the faint moonlight which filtered through the fog. Then he moved and his action was unexpected and horrifying. With a fierce wrench he tore loose from Gordon's clutching arms, whirled on his side, and tore the tourniquet from his leg. An incredible burst of blood followed; the body of Ali Massar shuddered once and then lay limply, but the dead eyes stared upward with a seeming malignant triumph.

"Gad!" John Gordon whispered, shaken.

Costigan looked on unmoved; his grim life in the underworld had hardened him more than the average man, even more than Gordon who was used to scenes of violence.

"Scarcely looks possible that a man could bleed to death so quickly from a stab in the leg," said he.

"He'd lost a terrific amount of blood before I bound his leg up," said Gordon. "That artery is a large one and connects directly with the great aorta of the abdomen."

"What are we going to do with the corpse?" asked Costigan, touching the dead man with his foot, as impersonally as if he had been a dead snake.

"Have to leave him here," Gordon decided. "Looks a trifle cold-blooded, but we can't carry him across these moors with the expectation of another attack on us any minute. We will get a cart and come back after the body. Just now we're in a hurry. They're still signalling from the castle, see? But the ship no longer shows a light."

As they hastened toward the Manor, Gordon mused: "Suppose that ship might be waiting to take someone on instead of putting someone off? What if there was someone in the Manor who had been lying low, waiting for a chance to escape without being seen? Someone who'd been hiding there a month or more!"

"You mean Sir Haldred? Do you think Sir Haldred is up there signalling?"

"There's no telling."

After what seemed an endless time, they stood at the door of Taverel Manor and were admitted by Hanson, the man of all work—a stocky, heavily built man with heavy unintelligent features.

"You're hurt, sir; your arm's bloody!"

"Mr. Costigan fell and cut his arm on a sharp rock," Gordon cut in. "Hanson, is your master in bed?"

"Yes, sir."

"Very good. Lead us to the highest tower in this building."

"Very good, sir," the man turned and led the way without question. The detectives followed him up innumerable flights of winding stairs, and through dark corridors, coming at last to the top room in the tower which rose above the west wing. This tower Gordon knew to be the one from which the signal light had flashed. Now it was empty of human occupants; a small barely furnished chamber, the dust and cobwebs bearing out

Hanson's statement that it was never used.

Gordon moved to the window which faced seaward and on an impulse took from Hanson the single candle which formed their only means of illumination. He believed that some other mode must have been used, since it seemed impossible that a mere candlelight could be seen that far through the fog, but on impulse he began to move the flickering candle back and forth in regular motions.

Scarcely had he done so, when Hanson, glancing toward the door into the darkness of the outer corridor, cried out wildly, and springing backward, caromed full into Gordon, knocking the candle from his hand and plunging the room into darkness.

4

On the instant, Gordon wheeled toward the door which he could not see, drawing his pistol. He heard the quick gasping intake of Hanson's breath beside him and Costigan's measured untroubled breathing in the silence that followed.

"Blast it, Hanson," he asked rather irritably, "what's all the bally row?"

"A face, sir," gasped the man, clutching in the darkness for the detective's arm. "A face just outside the doorway! A fearful, yellowish face it was, with loose hanging lips!"

Costigan laughed grimly in the dark. "I'll go out and see if it's still there!"

"Stay where you are!" Gordon ordered sharply. "Hanson, here's a match. Strike it, find the candle and light it while I watch the door."

A flicker of light followed, framing the black opening of the door in momentary radiance, but revealing nothing of what might be lurking just outside.

"Too bad, sir," said Hanson presently. "I don't know what we're going to do, but the candle's gone!"

"Nonsense! It must have dropped close to my feet when you blundered into me."

"You can see for yourself, sir." Hanson held a lighted match close to the floor. Gordon's eyes took in the whole dusty surface.

There was the mark in the dust where the candle had fallen, but of the candle there was no sign.

"Somethin' darted in and snatched it!" babbled Hanson, shaking with apparent fright. "I know it did! Nor it ain't the first time, either. I've warned the master, but he won't heed me! I've told him about the footfalls after night through the empty chambers, and the rustlings of the hangings—aye, and the foul yellow face that peeps through the dark at you! Twice I've seen it!"

"Indeed!" Gordon rapped. "And why have you said nothing about it?"

"The master ordered me to keep shut," the man said sullenly. "Hints I been drinking. It's little I care. I'm leaving this terrible place tomorrow. I wouldn't stay, not for no amount of money."

"Are you going to stay here all night?" Costigan broke in impatiently.

"Come on," Gordon answered shortly, and strode through the door, pistol ready. It was uncanny work, groping their way down those dark stairs, but nothing attacked them. Not a sound disturbed the grisly silence.

Once in the great lower hallway, Gordon said, "Hanson, unless I'm much mistaken there is a man hurt out on the moors. Have you a cart that we can use to get him in?"

Hanson seemed to have recovered from his fright and to have lapsed back into his usual stupidity.

"I have, sir."

"Harness a pony to it and bring it around to the front at once."

"Very good, sir."

The order was obeyed with commendable promptness and as they jogged through the fog which seemed to be growing ever thicker, Costigan said: "Stupid fellow."

"Stupid or unusually shrewd. Do you believe that guff about a yellow face? I scarcely do. What if Hanson didn't want me to be waving a candle in the window where it might be construed as a signal? What if he lurched against me on purpose and pretended the rest? He could easily have secured the candle and put it in his pocket while we were waiting for some hobgoblin to burst through the door on us."

"But if it's Sir Haldred who's hiding in that tower, how is Hanson connected with him? And how could Sir Haldred hide without being found by the police who ransacked the house?"

"I can't say as to Hanson's possible connections with Sir Haldred. From what I can learn, the man came here with Hammerby. As for the vanished nobleman's hiding—most of these old castles are full of secret passages, hidden rooms and such like."

"No one knows of them, then. The police were unable to find any trace of hidden passages."

"They would be cunningly concealed, of course. Here's the place where we left the body—and no body! I half expected as much."

The corpse of the Malay assassin had vanished.

"Friends in the offing!" muttered Gordon, turning the horse about and starting back for the castle. "Looks like we've run into a thicker mystery than we bargained for. I came out to please Marjory Harper who thought I could help her find her vanished lover. We've found no clue of him, but we've seen a mysterious ship signalling to the castle, discovered that a gang of murderous thugs are lurking about for some unknown reason, and—unless we choose to discount Hanson's tale—we've been haunted by a yellow-faced ghost."

"The men who attacked us are connected with the ship out there, some way."

"I believe so. And the ship is connected with someone in the castle—who?"

They drew up at the gate, hitched the horse. No sign of Hanson. They went up the long driveway and knocked at the door. No one answered.

"Shove in, Costigan," said Gordon impatiently. "It's getting along toward morning and Hanson must be asleep. We'll rouse him up and send him out to take care of the horse, and—"

He broke off suddenly. From somewhere inside the unlighted building there came a sudden scream, horrifying in its intensity and volume.

"Help! Help! Oh God, help!"

"Hammerby!" exclaimed Gordon, electrified. "In with you, Costigan. Wait—let me go first!"

The screaming broke off in a sudden hideous gasp and silence fell like a black fog.

5

Harry Harper woke from a sleep full of chaotic and disordered visions. Someone was knocking softly on his door. He sat up in bed and called: "Who is it?" There was no answer, but he heard a stealthy sound outside the door, then the noise of light footfalls retreating. He rose, donned his bathrobe and turned on the light. The white corner of a note protruded under the door, but when he looked out, the corridor was empty.

The note read as follows: "Bring Marjory and Joan and come at once to Taverel Manor. This is imperative. Speak to no one, but come at once." It was signed "John Gordon."

Why the detective should desire their presence at this time of night, Harry could not understand, but he prepared to obey. He crossed the hall to the girls' room, knocked lightly at the door, and soon the three of them were speeding across the moors through the light rain which had begun to fall.

They drove up the shadowed driveway and alighted. The great castle rose above them, dark, gloomy and forbidding. Harry felt the silent fear of the girls and he himself was guilty of a tremor or two. Where were the detectives? He made for the door, his sister and his fiancée clinging close to either arm. He lifted the knocker and the hollow reverberations which echoed through the house in a ghostly, muzzled manner, filled him with a crawling fear. He waited for the door to open, but there was no movement inside. At last he drew forth a flashlight in one hand

and a pistol in the other, and pushed the door open. Utter darkness met his eyes.

The girls, fearful of entering that black building, but more afraid of being left alone, crowded in after him. Harry was cursing under his breath, berating the folly of the men who had caused him to bring two frightened girls into such a place. And where in the name of heaven, were Gordon and Costigan? Where, for that matter, was Hammerby—and Hanson—and Mrs. Drake? A sudden ghastly panic took hold of him. He felt as if they were all in the grip of some inhuman sorcerer of another world. He turned on his flashlight and the white shaft lit up the furnishings, making the rest of the room seem darker by comparison. The circle of light hovered a moment on the dark stain near the stairs, wavered a moment as the wrist that directed it shook slightly, then shot down the hall.

The ghastly face of the idol of the shrine was illumined, the uncertain light adding tenfold to its diabolical appearance. And Joan screamed wildly; Harry, shocked and horrified, fired wildly and without conscious thought. The same motion jerked his thumb off the switch and utter darkness fell over the terrified group. In the darkness there came a stealthy sound at the other end of the hall, but Harry did not find the courage to press the switch and bring that ghastly image into life again. He stood there in the dark, speechless and sweating blood, while Marjory clung to him and Joan, who had fallen at his feet in a near faint, clutched his knees and whimpered wildly.

"Joan!" how husky and unnatural his voice was. "Brace up!"

"Don't turn on the light again, Harry," the girl whimpered. "If I see it again, I'll die! Oh, Harry, Harry, *I saw its eyes blink* !"

"Nonsense," Harry desperately refused to believe what his senses told him and his reason denied—that he had seen the same phenomenon. "It's just the way the light fell on the face. I'm going to turn it on again."

Joan promptly hid her face in his trousers leg and refused to even breathe.

Harry turned a beam of light again down the hall, bracing himself against the shock of bringing that frightful face out of the dark again.

"There, Joan," he said with a gusty sigh of relief, "it's not winking now; it's real—I mean it's stone."

Joan looked fearfully. Marjory begged: "Harry, let's be going. There's no one here; otherwise your shot would have brought them. There must have been a mistake."

"There must have been." Harry lifted Joan to her feet and turned toward the door. He had let the light go out while lifting the frightened girl; now he turned it on once more. Even as he did, both girls screamed terribly. Harry was aware of a dim bulk looming up beside him, of a shadowy arm which shot down with a cold shimmer of steel.

6

"Gordon!" Costigan's low-pitched voice cut the stillness. "The idol's gone!"

The two secret service men stood in the shadowed hallway of the great Taverel mansion. Utter silence reigned, yet the ghastly screams which had but an instant ago reverberated through the house, still seemed to re-echo in their ears.

Gordon's flashlight played down the hall and halted on the shrine. He swore under his breath. The great carven pedestal was bare. All along there had lurked in the detective's brain the feeling that somehow all this mystery centered on that silent grim shrine. The screams which had brought them bursting into the house had seemed to come from the end of the hall. He strode down the hall to the shrine and narrowly examined the pedestal. He had supposed that the idol had been fastened to it in some way, but he now saw the surface was perfectly smooth. He began to tap the wall behind the shrine.

Costigan grunted; a narrow panel had swung inward.

"This was hidden by the idol," whispered Gordon, playing his light into the dark aperture. A narrow passage, walled with stone, was disclosed.

"Stay here," the Englishman ordered. "I'm going to explore this; I think it's the answer to our questions."

"So do I," answered Costigan, "and that's why I'm going with you."

Gordon knew the futility of arguing with his companion. He shrugged his shoulders, climbed over the pedestal and dropped into the passage on the other side. Costigan followed him, leaving the secret door open. A flight of rough stone steps went down and the two men followed them, to come down into another, wider passage. The walls, ceiling and floor were of rough stone, beaded with dank moisture.

"Must be pretty far underground," muttered Gordon. "These were built by Sir Haldred's pirate-baron ancestors, no doubt. Regular catacombs," he added, noting the dark openings on either side, which evidently marked other passages leading away from the main one. The flashlight flung a faint wavering radiance which seemed stifled by the surrounding gloom.

"Listen!"

From one of those dark doorways there sounded the faint clink of chains and a low groan. Gordon snapped off the light and the companions stood in the darkness. The groaning voice became audible and intelligible.

"Gordon! Help! Help! For God's sake! They're torturing me!"

"It's Hammerby!" hissed Gordon, gliding toward the opening from which the racked gasps seemed to emanate. Suddenly he snapped on the light and sprang through the doorway, pistol in his hand and Costigan close beside him. The light, flashing swiftly from corner to corner, revealed only a bare cell-like chamber, with a smaller doorway in the opposite wall. Hammerby was nowhere to be seen and the groaning voice had ceased. Suddenly, Costigan, long blood brother to the underworld rats, with sudden intuition struck the light from Gordon's hand and jerked him to the floor. Even as he did so, a sudden crackle of pistol fire split the darkness and half a dozen bullets sang viciously above the heads of the crouching men. Above all there rang a hideous insane laugh.

A silence painful in its intensity followed the volley. Moving with infinite caution, the two trapped men crawled to opposite sides of the cell, and crouching against the walls, waited, pistols in hand for what might next chance.

"Gordon!" a voice suddenly broke the silence, a voice sardonic, mocking and with a strange foreign inflection. "This is an unexpected pleasure! I had not thought to have you for my guest at this time."

Gordon, crouching in grim silence, made no move to give

away his position to the unseen snipers.

"Is it that I must give you credit for more intelligence than I had thought for?" the mocking, illusive voice went on. "Or is it a mere train of circumstances that led you here? I had thought—ah, well—after tonight, Mr. Gordon, you will no longer interfere in my affairs—"

Gordon's pistol spat viciously as he fired in the direction of the voice; a low mocking laugh answered him and another volley from the outer corridor rattled against the wall above him.

Again the voice spoke, this time from another quarter. "I am sorry I cannot remain to watch your demise, Mr. Gordon, and yours, Mr. Costigan, but time presses and I must leave you to the watchful care of my faithful friends."

Again stillness closed down like a pall. Gordon heard the faint drip of water from the dank walls. Then far back the corridors in the direction from which they had come, there sounded a shot. Instantly the corridors were filled with sound, strident and confused. From both doorways pistols cracked and the cell hummed with the passage of the leaden pellets. Gordon felt his sleeve jerked as if by an invisible hand and something stung his cheek sharply. Above a medley of unknown tongues, a harsh voice was shouting savagely in English, but the detectives could not understand the words.

Gordon fired at the flashes in the doorway through which they had come, and someone or something howled like a stricken wolf. Another storm of lead pelted across the cell, then there sounded a pattering of feet which dwindled away down the corridors. Gordon ventured a low call: "What now, Costigan? Do you think they've gone, or is it a trap?"

"Lie low," growled the American. "Wait—did you recognize that fellow that was talking to us?"

"I think I did," snapped Gordon. "But what—"

A light glimmered outside. People were coming down the corridor.

"Oh, Gordon!"

The detective swore. "It's Harry Harper!" He sprang erect and ran recklessly out into the passageway, stumbling over a form which sprawled there. The light which illumined the place showed him that the man was a Chinaman. Now a strange scene presented itself. Harry Harper was marching down the passage, flashlight in one hand, pistol in the other. Close behind him came Marjory and Joan, clinging together; in front of the boy, hands bound fast behind him, walked a short sullen-faced man.

"Hanson," ejaculated Gordon.

"Gordon!" cried Harry sharply. "Your face is bleeding!"

"Just a slight cut," Gordon passed his hand over his cheek. "A bullet grazed me."

"Thank God you're not hurt!"

"But what are you doing here?"

"Well," said Harry, "when I got your note at the tavern—"

"Note? I never wrote you a note!"

"Well, somebody did, telling me to come here and bring the girls. We got here, but there was no one here. Then in the hall, somebody jumped me with a knife. I knocked him silly with my pistol barrel, and behold, when I turned the light on him, it was this fellow—Hanson.

"He came to in a moment, but not before I'd tied him up well. He seemed pretty desperate and told me he'd spill the whole thing if I'd promise to speak for him later. About that time we heard shots, faintly, and he said it was you and Mr. Costigan, trapped underground somewhere. So—"

"You young imbecile," broke in Gordon, "you mean to say you came barging along through these tunnels with the girls?"

"Well, I couldn't stand by and let you be butchered, you know. As for the girls, I thought they'd be in as much danger in the house as they would with me. And anyway, I made Hanson walk in front. Didn't figure they'd dare shoot at us for fear of hitting him. And he must have thought so, too; he's been shaky no end. He told me to push on the idol, and I did and a door opened. But I guess you know about it—we came through and at the bottom of the stairs I caught a glimpse of something that looked like a big bat. But it was human, because it fired at me and I fired back. A fellow with a curious kind of disguise on, no doubt. I don't think I hit him, but he legged it down the passage as fast as he could go and we followed."

7

John Gordon pounded a beefy fist into the palm of his open hand. "Never mind what I think of that, Harper! Your intentions were surely good, but you don't realize what danger you've placed these two girls in. Let's get them back above while there's still a chance to save them."

He started to lead the girls back to the stairway but Harper stopped him. "What about the man I shot? At least—I think it was a man. We have a chance of catching him and unravelling this mystery right here and now. Surely Joan and Marjory can stay here and watch out for themselves for the little while it will take us to pick up a trail of blood and find that bat-like figure."

"You don't understand the enemy we face," Gordon rejoined. "Ask young Costigan here, if you don't believe me. But not now! For heaven's sake, trust me, and let's move before it's too late! We are in a rattler's lair and at any moment his venomous strike may come."

He hesitated no longer but grasped Harper by one elbow, Costigan by the other, and moved off at a space-devouring trot along the stone-carpeted corridor. Steve Costigan took the lead as they approached the ancient stairway. Harry Harper, after a moment's hesitation and a futile glance into the murk where the bat-figure had disappeared, followed reluctantly, dragging the still struggling Hanson by one arm. The servant's spirit seemed broken, his face ashen even in the dim light of the musty passageway. Marjory and Joan, still clutching each other, followed in their wake.

When they reached the great hall they emerged behind the empty pedestal that had previously housed the enigmatic idol brought from Thibet so many years before by old Captain Hilton Taverel. The idol was not in the room. As the men stood gaping there was a double scream behind them. They whirled to find Marjory and Joan nowhere in sight!

"All right, you!" Stephen Costigan turned blazing eyes upon the trembling Hanson. "You're the only link we've got left with—whatever is going on here. The girls are gone. Sir Haldred Taverel is gone. Thomas Hammerby is gone. Even the yellow idol is missing. We're surrounded by nothing but mystery. We need some answers and you'll give them to us, quick, or I'll—" He raised a calloused fist that had flattened thugs from San Francisco to Soho and back again.

With his other hand Costigan reached forward and grabbed the quivering Englishman by the wrinkled lapels of his woolen jacket. Hanson's eyes grew as wide as hen's eggs as he felt himself lifted bodily from the stone flagging and lifted, slowly, steadily, a foot into the air. Hanson waved his two hands pleadingly as if to ward off the blow he knew he could never prevent.

"I—I don't know nothing, sir! I'm just the man-of-all-work here at Taverel Manor, just a handyman, so to speak! I never did like that heathen yellow idol! I always told Sir Haldred that he ought to ship it back to Thibet where it come from. I told Sir Rupert that too, but nobody'd listen to me!"

Costigan lowered his eyes from Hanson's face, keeping the servant suspended above the heads of the others. The muscles of the American must be incredible; the feat of lifting Hanson, difficult though it might have been, was nothing compared to that of holding him in the air. Costigan looked at John Gordon. The British investigator nodded to him. Costigan looked at Harry Harper.

"Knows nothing, does he?" Harper spat angrily. "Then what about this? What about my arm?" He turned to give the others a clear look at the place where Hanson's knife had come within inches of doing serious, perhaps fatal, injury to him. Harper's soft tweed jacket showed a gash from shoulder to elbow. A red stain was slowly spreading along the edges of the gash.

John Gordon stepped closer to the young man. He peered at the wound. "Incredible luck, Harper. Another inch or two and you'd have been crippled in that wing. Half a foot and he'd have planted his blade squarely between your ribs. As it is, you'll have just a nice little scar there to keep as your souvenir of Taverel Manor."

Costigan turned back to fix Hanson with a glare. "Well, you slimy rat, what have you to say? Know nothing? Do you just attack strangers for the fun of it? You'll talk or—" A strange grin passed across Costigan's face. Somehow, to the servant Hanson, that grin was more terrifying than even the most terrible scowl might have been. The American raised his other hand and held the servant by both lapels, his scuffed shoes still hanging well above the floor.

Hanson felt himself carried across the room as steadily and with as little apparent effort on the American's part as if Hanson had been a newborn babe and Costigan his doting father. The servant glanced fearfully across his shoulder to see where Costigan was carrying him. A suit of medieval armor, trophy of some ancient knightly ancestor of the Taverels, stood mounted before a priceless tapestry against one wall.

Costigan raised the servant another half a foot and speared the collar of his jacket neatly on the sharp-honed point of a halberd. "All right, you traitor," Costigan growled. "You'll hang there like a hunting trophy till you tell us what you know. And if you still think you're going to get away with that know-nothing story, I'll persuade you to change your mind." He stood before the dangling Englishman, measuring with a glinting eye the distance from his own mighty fist to the other's trembling jaw.

"Gawd be my witness, sir, I don't know nothing! *I don't know nothing*!" Hanson's voice rose to a scream as Costigan drew back that fist, ready to deliver a hay-maker to the chin of the servant.

Hanson burst into tears. "I'll tell, I'll tell," he gasped between sobs of sheer terror. "Gawd help me, I'm through now. I'm as good as dead if I breathe a word but you'll kill me here and now if I don't. Oh, Gawd, the Master'll destroy me if I tell, I know he will!"

A look flashed between Costigan and John Gordon, a silent bolt of surprise and recognition. The Master! it seemed to say. Gordon came and stood beside Costigan, peering up into the eyes of the terrified Hanson. "Come on, man," the tall investigator said soothingly. "Your only chance is to play square with us. Costigan here, and I, know all about the Master. We've encountered him before. But—wasn't he destroyed in the terrible blast at Soho 48?"

"The Master can't die," Hanson sobbed hopelessly. "He's a million years old, ten million years old, nobody knows! He ain't even a man, he's a devil or a god or something from out of the sea. And he'll get me now, I know he will." Hanson wrung his hands helplessly, hanging there from the spear-like blade that tipped the ancient halberd. Now that his terror had carried him beyond the silence of desperation he was babbling like a child, jabbering out his fear of the sinister force that had caused him to attack Harry Harper.

"Lo Kung was his man, too," Hanson babbled. "He's dead now, the Master was through with him so he had Mrs. Drake and me finish him off."

"Mrs. Drake?" Harper gasped incredulously. "The house-keeper?"

"Yes, sir," Hanson sobbed. "Me and Mrs. Drake was in his power for years. We got rid of old Sir Rupert Taverel when the Master told us to. We didn't want to—we're not murderers."

"I'm afraid that's for others to decide," John Gordon interrupted. "His Majesty's courts will make that determination, and I think you may be disappointed in the verdict that they render, my good man."

Hanson's eyes popped wider even than they had been. "But we couldn't help ourselves! You claim you know the Master," he pleaded, "then you know nobody can resist his will. He promised that when the old empire came back he'd make me Lord of Taverel Manor. Me! Just old Hanson the man-of-all-work, Lord of the Manor! I'd have servants of my own, I would! And sleep in the splendid big bed upstairs and not in my old cottage on the moor. But if I failed him—if I failed him—*aauagh!*"

With a final moan the servant slumped forward, his jaw slack, his head hanging onto his chest. Harry Harper started forward to examine the man.

"Don't touch him!" John Gordon snapped at the younger man.

"But—but I think he's dead."

"That he most surely is."

"But then—he must have died of heart failure, frightened to death of that Master person he mentioned. In simple decency we should at least take him down from there, and—"

"And die into the bargain, I shouldn't be surprised." John Gordon took Harper by the wrist and led him to a place beside the suit of armor. "Don't touch anything that I don't tell you to," Gordon warned. "At the risk of your life. Costigan, you'll probably want to have a look at this too."

"If Hanson's Master is the Master we know, Gordon, and I see every sign to indicate that he is, then I think I can guess what you're about to find. Still, all right." Costigan joined the others.

"You see that wire leading from the pedestal and running behind the old tapestry?" John Gordon asked Harper. The younger man nodded that he did. "Then suppose you pull back the tapestry and tell me what you find," the investigator continued. "Just lift it by one corner. Be careful not to touch the armor or anything else of metal."

The younger man rose and did as he had been told. "Why— why it's an alcove of some sort. Something like the passageway we found behind the yellow idol, or rather the pedestal where the idol had stood. Only—this opening behind the tapestry is filled with an elaborate electrical apparatus of some sort. It's hooked up to a whole bank of storage batteries, and there's a control panel here at the end."

He stood, blinking for a moment, gaping at the bizarre installation. "This means that—Hanson didn't die of heart failure at all, did he?"

As if they were one man, John Gordon and Stephen Costigan shook their heads. "No, Harper," Costigan said bitterly. "He was electrocuted. In America we electrocute our killers *after* they're tried and convicted. But apparently the Master doesn't feel the need for such formalities."

He walked over to the young Englishman and stood beside him, glaring into the darkness behind the electrical gear. "The only question is, why did the Master wait so long before disposing of Hanson? Why didn't he—or his operative—shoot poor Hanson the juice as soon as I hung him on the armor?"

John Gordon reached into his pocket and extracted a blackened bulldog pipe. He clenched it angrily between his teeth and paced back and forth. "Probably just a trifle slow on the uptake, Costigan. That would be my guess, anyway. And lucky for you that he—or she—was a trifle slow. My guess is that the Master hoped that you would stay beside poor Hanson, maybe even place your hand on the metal of the armor to steady yourself. He must have underestimated your strength, and that little mistake saved your life! Finally the Master gave up on waiting for you to lay your hand on the armor, and decided that he'd better dispose of his servant before too much information was divulged."

"Precious little that he told us," Costigan grunted. "But we know this much—the Master is alive and at large again! The world stands at peril!"

8

A brilliant flash illuminated the old room, casting livid shadows on the stone walls and turning the faces of the three living men and the one dead into chiaroscuro masks of heightened emotion. The dead servant Hanson's mouth was drawn back in the rictus of his convulsive death. Harry Harper's expression mirrored the anxiety and fear that he felt not only for himself but for his sister Marjory and his fiancée Joan La Tour. Joan was an American girl of Eurasian ancestry. A one-time denizen of the half-world of opium dens and tong wars, she had broken with the gangsters and vice lords of America's Asiatic enclaves and fled to England where she had built for herself a new life and won the love of this youth.

Now Joan, along with Marjory Harper and Marjory's fiance', Sir Haldred Taverel, was gone—in the clutches of the Master whom Stephen Costigan and John Gordon had thought dead, blasted to hades along with his festering minions.

When the lightning ceased it was followed by a titanic boom of bass, rumbling thunder. The thunder rolled away, fading into the blackness of the northern English night, only to be followed in turn by a shrieking, gale-like wind and the patter of heavy black drops against the leaded glass windows of Taverel Manor.

The almost hypnotic spell of the moment was shattered.

John Gordon bent to the control panel of the electrical apparatus concealed in the alcove behind the tapestry. In a few

221

moments he emerged, lowering the tapestry once again into place.

"That's done," he announced in a businesslike voice. "The infernal device is disconnected. We can take poor Hanson down now in safety."

At the tall investigator's signal Stephen Costigan advanced and they began to lower the servant's corpse from its place atop the antique halberd. Only Harry Harper stood his ground, holding back from the task.

"What's the matter, Harper?" Stephen Costigan glanced over his muscular shoulder. "That little slash bothering you?"

The young Englishman shook his head. "It isn't that, Costigan. I'm just afraid that I cannot lend my endorsement to any act of kindness directed to—" He shrugged and nodded toward the corpse, now laid in more usual fashion on the cold flagging of the manor's floor.

"Well, what?"

"Great blazes, man, need you ask? Never mind that the blackguard tried to kill me and very nearly succeeded. But he and his partner have conspired with the Master to abduct everyone I hold dear in this world. Hanson dead? I shall dance on his grave! Hanson, damn his black soul! Hanson and Mrs. Drake—Mrs. Drake!"

He broke off his outburst and charged across the room, plunging behind the tapestry that concealed the electrical rig and disappearing as the old weaving flapped down into place once again.

John Gordon shouted after him. "Come back here, you fool! It's a regular rabbit-warren down there! You'll never find Mrs. Drake and you expose yourself to mortal danger!"

But only the rapidly fading sound of Harper's footsteps answered the investigator. A pained expression entered Gordon's eyes as he said to Costigan, "I wish him well, my friend. The poor chap! One can hardly blame him for feeling as he does, but I fear for the boy. I fear for him with a cold and shadowing fear."

"No point in trying to follow him," Costigan replied. "We were lucky to find our way back from the hidden passage behind the yellow idol. This maze looks even more difficult. We'd be playing into the Master's hands to even attempt it."

John Gordon's face betrayed the firmness of purpose that had marked his long career as a roving crime-fighter from

Burma to the Ivory Coast of Africa. He had close ties with Scotland Yard, but was not himself an official of that organization. Rather, he held a roving commission from the highest levels of the British government, with authority to go anywhere and do anything he deemed necessary to his mission.

With a brusque heave of his shoulders the investigator turned toward the entryway of the manor.

"Come along, Costigan. Let's head for the village. We can telephone to London from there and get a squad of expert men up here. Trained scientists who can apply forensic techniques. I'm convinced that the clues to the disappearances lie in this old building, and that those clues will lead us straight to the Master. I'm convinced also that this matter is tied up somehow with the opium ring we've been pursuing. Taverel Manor is connected with Asia. You saw that yellow idol before it disappeared, you heard that Captain Hilton Taverel brought it from Thibet.

"Somehow—I don't know how, but by Jove I'm going to find out—somehow this all ties together."

He started once more toward the entryway but Stephen Costigan stopped him with a strong grip on one elbow. "I'm not going, Gordon," the American rasped. "There's too much mysterious happening at this house, and I don't intend to leave it tonight. You go ahead and summon help if you want to. I won't accuse you of cowardice, my friend. I know you too well even to think such a thing of you. I know you're going out there to summon specialists who can check for fingerprints and perform chemical analyses and things like that. But I'm going to stay!"

He shook his head to show his determination.

"I'm going to stay here and take this place apart until not one stone stands upon another, until I find some kind of clue that leads me to the Master. The last time we met, you and I barely escaped with our lives—and we thought that the Master had been blown to smithereens. This time there will be no miraculous escapes. The Master will be blown back to the slimy pit from which he sprang, or I will give my life in the attempt!"

"Well said, Costigan," John Gordon barked. "I shouldn't want to leave you alone if I could persuade you otherwise, but I know that iron will of yours. I know there's no making you leave if you want to remain here. But I'll get down to the village and summon the forensics squad as quickly as I can, then I'll return at once."

He jammed a formless hat over his graying thatch, wrapped a

woolen muffler around himself against the chill of the northern night and shrugged into a great mackintosh coat to keep the rain out. The two men shook hands briefly and Costigan saw the Britisher to the door. He watched Gordon push manfully through the pitch blackness and the driving rain, his inverted pipe glowing briefly every now and then as Gordon strove to keep its flame alight.

Once again there was a blinding flash of lightning and Costigan saw his friend throw his arms skyward as a blaze of bluish-yellow glare surrounded him, silhouetting the tall, spare Englishman against the blackness of distant woods and the stygian murk of the storm-swept northern sky. As the lightning played around the form of the investigator a piercing shriek rose across the moor and the crash of nearby thunder drowned out the end of the Britisher's cry.

Costigan bolted from the stone archway that marked the entrance of Taverel Manor. Bareheaded and wearing only his lightweight jacket he raced across the grassy moor, heedless of the tearing wind that flung his hair into an unruly nimbus and pulled his necktie from his coat so it streamed backward over his shoulder as he ran. Heedless, too, of the pelting rain whose massive black drops smashed onto his battle-scarred face and bull-like shoulders.

Costigan ran with a speed astonishing for so massive and muscular a physique, powerful strides covering rods of distance in mere seconds of time. He reached the side of John Gordon and threw himself to his knees, seized the motionless form and turned it over so the face was exposed to the wind and rain of the raving storm.

Gordon was dead. Somehow, Costigan had known that he would be dead, had known it from the moment of the fatal lightning bolt, and that knowledge had sparked a raging, roaring crimson flame within his breast. But the rictus that drew John Gordon's lips back into the hideous caricature of a grin was too much even for Stephen Costigan's iron self-control. That expression, that horrible expression that marred the final moment of John Gordon's life, was identical to the expression on the face of traitorous man-of-all-work Hanson at the moment of his death by electrocution.

Costigan threw back his head to the storm. His knees planted firmly in the icy British mud, the corpse of his friend John Gordon clasped in his mighty arms, the wind shrieking in his ears and the black, massive raindrops smashing into his face, Stephen Costigan shouted his black hatred and red defiance into the night.

"Damn you, Master! Damn you to the nethermost hells but I know you for who you are! Skull-Face, Kathulos of Egypt, I know you! You mummified revenant of Atlantis, I know you! If I have to follow you through the very pits of hades I will find you and with these two hands, with my two bare hands I'll wring your chicken-neck till your eyes pop and your tongue protrudes in death! I'll get you, Kathulos, you million-year-old fiend, if it takes me another million years!"

Again there was a searing flash of lightning, a crackling, quivering bolt of force that smashed into the trunk of a nearby tree splitting it as a woodsman's axe splits a log into kindling, and in an instant the tree flared into great, crackling flames that danced and shook, fighting fiercely against the roaring downpour. And somehow, in the dancing flame that surmounted the tree, Stephen Costigan saw the huge, leering features of a hideous yellow face, a face that grinned and taunted and mocked until the American could all but weep with the shame and frustration of his own impotence.

He rose to his feet bearing the corpse of his friend as lightly as he would have carried a straw dummy. He bent and picked something from the grass where it had fallen in the terrible moment of the Britisher's death. "Don't forget your pipe, Gordon," Stephen Costigan muttered in a surprisingly soft, almost conversational tone of voice. "Sometimes a man's pipe is his truest friend, sometimes his only friend."

Carelessly carrying the one hundred sixty pounds of the slim, rangy Britisher in one hand, Stephen Costigan walked distractedly back across the moor, his path lighted by the weird, flickering light of the flaring tree. In his other hand Costigan carried Gordon's pipe. "A bulldog, eh?" Costigan asked his dead friend. "Nice burl. Has a nice feel to the hand. I'd guess it draws nicely too, eh, Gordon? Nothing like a good pipe for comfort on a storm-ridden night like this, eh?"

He trudged through the archway and into the great hall of Taverel Manor, heedless of the rainwater that dripped off his nose and chin, his clothing and his hands, heedless of the foul yellow mud that he tracked with each step of his heavy, sturdy boots. "Here, you're all in, Gordon," he said. He laid his friend's body beside that of the servant Hanson. "Have a good rest near the fire, Gordon," Costigan muttered conversationally.

He straightened and gazed at the tall window nearest the fatal suit of armor. Stephen Costigan blinked, snapping out of his fugue and returning to the full horror and hatred of the moment. There outside the window, seemingly suspended in the rain and the mist, hovered the same hideous, yellow face!

9

From the far side of the room a voice echoed eerily.

Stephen Costigan spun from his place before the window. In an instant he was ready to face any peril. His feet were planted well apart, his weight held on the balls of his feet so he could shift or spring in any direction. Those two mighty fists were clenched and raised, prepared equally to ward off any foe or to deal a smashing blow that would stop a charging longhorn dead in its tracks. Costigan had done exactly that, once, to the astonishment of a braggart Texan who had offered a poke of assay-pure gold dust against Costigan's slim purse, thinking he had a safe bet and a good laugh in store for him. The Texan had expected Costigan to funk out of the challenge before the steer ever saw him, but Costigan had stood his ground and delivered a wallop to the charging longhorn that had laid it out unconscious for most of an hour.

"Steephen," the voice floated eerily from behind a tapestry. "Steephen, are you there? Can you hear me, darling?"

This time it was Costigan who stood dumbfounded, swaying like a pole-axed ox. There was a ringing in his ears and he all but heard his own heart pounding in his chest at the sound of that voice. If he had heard the cold, remorseless tones of Kathulos he would have been able to deal with the voice, but this was—was—

"Zuleika!" Costigan managed to gasp.

"Yes, Steephen, it is I, Zuleika! Steephen, you must stop your pursuit of the Master! Please, Steephen, have you not seen enough of his power, of what he can do? For your life, Steephen, stop what you are doing. The Master will destroy you as he destroyed John Gordon, as he destroys all his enemies!"

"He destroyed Gordon? Does Kathulos control the very lightnings, then?" Even as Costigan spoke he was advancing slowly, stealthily across the cold stones, approaching the tapestry from behind which the voice of Zuleika drifted.

"Kathulos is all-powerful, Steephen," Zuleika's voice came eerily. "There is no escape from the Master and there is no fleeing from the Master's vengeance. Hanson turned against the Master and he paid with his life. John Gordon opposed the Master and he met a like fate to Hanson's.

"Even I sought to escape from the Master, once—"

"Well I know of that," Costigan cut her off. He was within yards of the tapestry now, keeping his voice to a low growl as he advanced.

"Yes, but the Master had put his mark upon me, Steephen, even as he put his mark upon you, so long ago in the Temple of Dreams in Limehouse. Go away, drop your attempts to oppose the Master, or you will pay a terrible price."

Costigan's mighty arm shot out, the bunched muscles straining the thin cloth almost to the breaking point. He snatched away the tapestry, caring nothing for the age or the value of the woven art object. Jerking the tapestry from its place he confronted—only the electrical apparatus that had been responsible for Hanson's death on the halberd and suit of armor. A tiny red light glowed atop the apparatus, seeming almost to bore into the American like a malevolent eye.

The beautiful, silken voice of the woman Zuleika burst into shrill, mocking laughter. "Oh, Steephen, Steephen, if you could only see yourself as I see you now!"

"How can you see me?" Costigan demanded. "Where are you, Zuleika, and what has that fiend Kathulos done to you to force you back into his vicious service?"

Again the shrill laughter echoed mockingly from the high ceiling and stone walls of Taverel Manor. "As for where I am, Steephen—if you do not turn your path away from the trail of the Master and return to your homeland, you will find out. You will find out all too soon, but perhaps you will not be so happy when you do.

"As for why I serve the Master—Ah, Steephen, Steephen. He is the lord of pleasure, Steephen. He is the emperor of pain. I will say no more of this." For an instant, for just an instant, it seemed that the silken-smooth voice that had earlier been raised in mocking laughter was lowered to a sob.

"All right," Costigan growled. "So you're talking to me by some kind of radio hook-up. I suppose it's connected to that same infernal machine that killed Hanson. But how can you see me, Zuleika?"

"Steephen," the smooth voice purred, once more fully under control. "There is a tiny camera on top of the radio. There are others placed throughout Taverel Manor. The Master has them in the armored suits, he had them installed in the yellow idol, he has them everywhere. There is no escaping the eyes of the Master."

Costigan hurled himself into the alcove where the voice came from, eager to find the wire that carried the pictures of himself to Kathulos, but he found nothing.

"There is no wire, Steephen," Zuleika's voice purred. "But since I see that you are determined to make a nuisance of yourself, I will save you the trouble of tracing the Master all the way from Taverel Manor to—the place where he now makes his headquarters."

Costigan stopped in his tracks, ears cocked to catch every syllable that Zuleika might speak. If he could find Kathulos's home base he could also find Sir Haldred Taverel and Marjory Harper, her brother Harry and his fiancée Joan La Tour. And he could find Zuleika!

He could find Zuleika!

How many nights had he dreamed of that pale, langourous face, those strange, misty eyes, the long, midnight hair of Zuleika! Since the explosion that had destroyed a tenth of the world's greatest city Costigan had grieved for Zuleika—and now to discover that the beautiful Circassian girl was alive after all, but once more in the foul clutches of the detestable Kathulos, was almost more than his reeling brain could absorb!

"Tell me, then!" Costigan shouted at the electrical machine that carried Zuleika's voice to him and his own to the girl. "Tell me and I'll come there if I have to crawl through jungles or swim oceans! I'll get you away from him again, Zuleika, and I swear by all that's holy I'll throttle that fiend with my two hands!"

The silken voice turned to shrill laughter once more. "Very

good, Steephen! I shall enjoy to see your face once again before
the Master passes judgment on you. He may have mercy,
Steephen, and let you off with an easy sentence of death, like
Hanson and John Gordon. Or—he may be cruel, and sentence
you to something far worse than merely the end of your earthly
career.

"Now!" she snapped. "Proceed directly to the village. You
will hire a car there and drive directly to London. Leave the car
and board the boat train for Dover. Take the last steamer
tomorrow for Calais. That and no other. You *must* be on board
that steamer."

She paused as if gathering her breath—or listening to
instructions from someone Stephen Costigan could not hear.
Finally Zuleika's voice could be heard saying, "Yes. I will tell
him. Yes." And then, "Steephen! When you reach Calais, the
Master will have a car waiting for you. You will identify yourself
to the driver and he will do the same. You will exchange the
following passwords with him.

"The driver will approach you first. He will ask, 'Do you
know a certain Mr. Ho?'

"You will reply, 'Do you mean Mr. Ho the brilliant law
student?'

"The driver will say, 'Oh, no, I was referring to Mr. Ho the
dishwasher.'

"If anyone approaches you and does not have the passwords,
do not go with him, even though he knows who you are and
claims to be from the Master. That is all that you have to do. Do
you understand your instructions?"

Costigan nodded unconsciously, then said aloud, "Yes. I will
be on the last steamer tomorrow."

Stephen Costigan stood at the bow railing of the little
channel steamer as it pulled out of Dover harbor, nosing into the
rough, icy waters of the English Channel. The night was filled
with darkness and mist, while a northerly gale swept the salty
spray of the channel's choppy water across the little steamer's
decks, brushing the face of the solitary American with ten
thousand tiny fingers.

Costigan's mind was awhirl with the wild tumble of thoughts.
He had obeyed the orders of the Master of Death, hearing that
cold, emotionless voice behind every word of Zuleika's silken
direction. What Kathulos had done to bring the beautiful

Circassian girl back into his thrall, Costigan couldn't even guess, but the American was determined to rescue the white-skinned, raven-haired beauty from her enslavement. If for no other reason than to free Zuleika, he was on his way to Calais!

A distant light gleamed across the black water, and the mournful call of a foghorn resounded like the moan of a tormented soul lost forever and doomed to wander the unmarked lanes of the stygian night.

Costigan had not even stopped at London to notify Scotland Yard of the death of John Gordon at Taverel Manor, nor to seek assistance through the British authorities, of the French Sûreté. He patted the heavy service revolver that he carried fully loaded and firmly stowed in his shoulder holster. That was Costigan's assistance—although, if the facts were known, the American relied far more often on his two calloused fists than he did on any man-made weapon.

France lay ahead—the first time Costigan had set foot on French soil in the dozen years since the terrible battle of the Argonne. He had been shot in that battle and bayonetted to shreds, left lying on the field of slaughter in the middle of his own red gore. Days later they had come to carry away and bury the dead, and Costigan had moaned and startled the quartermaster by crying out for help.

Followed months of hospitalization, repeated surgery and crisis after crisis that would have carried off a man of any lesser constitution than the iron American. Costigan had fought his way back to physical health, but the drugs they had used to ease his agony in the hospitals, and the tormenting memories of the awful sights he had seen in the War left him less than a man— they had left him a dope fiend!

It was Costigan's unending search for relief from those awful memories that had led him to Yun Shatu's Temple of Dreams in London's fog-shrouded Limehouse, and only when the American was hopelessly enslaved to the hashish provided by the beautiful Circassian girl Zuleika did the Master of Death show his hand. Then had Costigan been enlisted into the enslaved army of the Master, and then had he fought free, bringing Zuleika with him and destroying the Master as well— or so he had thought!

Now the glimmering lights of Calais penetrated the fog-curtained night. Costigan peered ahead, then around himself. He felt the indescribable sensation of eyes all around him, the prickle of the small hairs at the back of the neck that tell a man when he is being watched.

Well, of course—the Master had soldiers everywhere. Probably, Costigan thought, he had been watched every mile of the way from Taverel Manor. If he'd stopped to do so much as make a telephone call he would have been slain on the spot. As it was he was marching, friendless and alone, straight into the arms of his most implacable enemy—and probably the most dangerous man on the face of the earth—Kathulos of Egypt!

He strode down the gangplank of the steamer, pipe clenched in his teeth, the glow of its circular bowl warming and lighting his face against the chilly night. His two fists were clenched in his coat pockets, ready to emerge like a pair of raging beasts and attack any enemy who revealed himself.

At the foot of the gangplank a liveried chauffeur stepped forward. He was a diminutive man, almost wispy. When he tilted his neck to look up into Costigan's face the American detected the skin coloration and eyes of an Asiatic. They stood there for tense seconds, the burly, muscular American and the diminutive Asiatic. Finally the chauffeur broke the silence.

"Do you know a certain Mr. Ho?" he asked.

10

Costigan stood in midst of a splendid, yet decadent, luxury. Thick Persian carpets covered the floor. Giant silken-covered pillows were strewn about, and satin-lined divans stood against drapery-covered walls. Artificial palm trees leaned against an imaginary breeze lending a strange sense of outdoors to the large room. This sense was further accentuated by the clouds of weird, yellowish smoke that drifted up, obscuring the atmosphere of the place, shifting and swirling so that every feature was alternately hidden and revealed with each current of air.

Costigan faced a tall, cadaverous figure seated on a high and ornate throne. The figure was draped in flowing robes of shimmering satin, their color the deepest imaginable sea-green, trimmed with frogging of pure gold and of some reddish metal Costigan did not recognize. A cap of oriental design surmounted the great skull of the figure, but somehow the total effect was not wholly oriental. There was a suggestion of the Egypt of the greatest dynasties, and there was a suggestion, also, of some civilization not known in the modern world, even to archaeologists or historians. A civilization perhaps not entirely human.

The man seated on the throne regarded Stephen Costigan through heavily lidded eyes that peered with an ice-like glitter from deep within the skull, and the yellow skin of the face was drawn tight over the prominent bones giving the appearance of some great mummified pharaoh rather than that of a living man.

Slowly the faintest suggestion of a malevolent smile stole across the mummy-like features. Through the drifting clouds of yellow smoke the figure spoke.

"Welcome to the Temple of Silence, Mr. Costigan. I had feared for a time that I was never to enjoy the pleasure of your company again. But of course, the strongest of men still has his weak point if one but knows how to locate it. Don't you agree?" Without waiting for Costigan's answer the figure inclined its head ever so slightly to one side.

Stephen Costigan followed the motion. Seated upon a silken pillow, the expression on her beautiful, milk-white face one of total inscrutability, he beheld the Circassian girl.

"Zuleika!" Costigan exclaimed. He started across the room to her side, legs driving his mighty body forward like pistons driving a dynamic machine. But Costigan was brought up short in his tracks, just paces from the girl! It was like running into a barrier of some sort. Not like a wall of glass—it was far more transparent than glass, and somehow soft and yielding—to a point. Costigan raged and hammered against the unseen obstacle, his tremendous muscles bunched and straining, but the harder his efforts to pierce the unseen wall the more firmly it resisted.

Finally he stopped, panting, and cried again, "Zuleika! Zuleika! Answer me! How can I get to you?"

There was no response from the Circassian girl. She merely sat watching the byplay that took place mere yards from her. Then she gestured peremptorily and a yellow-skinned servant scurried forward from some place of concealment among the draperies of the room. He carried a tray of hammered brass and inlaid enamel, itself doubtless worth a fortune to some illicit collector of art objects.

Zuleika reached for the tray and lifted from it a long-stemmed brass pipe with a tiny bowl. The servant rolled a little ball of some black gummy substance and warmed it over a dish of glowing coals, then placed it carefully in the bowl of the brass pipe. Zuleika waved him away and reclined on her cushion, drawing clouds of grayish-blue fumes from the pipe and calmly regarding Costigan.

"Opium! More drugs!" the American raged. He whirled and made as if to charge at Kathulos but the latter halted him with a single peremptory gesture.

"That would serve no purpose, Mr. Costigan. I have sealed

the lips of my servant Zuleika and will unseal them again only when it is my pleasure to do so. And as for your unfortunately primitive impulses, Mr. Costigan, should you attempt to reach my throne you would find that the same barrier which kept you from Zuleika would halt you with equal effectiveness before you approached my person."

"You swine," Costigan gritted. "It's the same thing all over again, isn't it? The Temple of Silence and the palms, the dope and your slaves doing your bidding. But we almost had you last time, Scorpion, and I swear that this time you'll feel my fingers on your scrawny neck!"

The subtle, mocking smile that had marked the mummy-like face of the Master disap;;eared and was replaced by a taunting leer. The great, domed head turned slowly on its thin support as Kathulos looked to one side, then to the other. The thin, parchment-like lips opened.

"Suppose we put your boastfulness to a test, Mr. Costigan. At an earlier time I might have been pleased to accept your challenge, to meet you in a personal contest of prowess—although, in truth, I have always been rather, as you would perhaps say, the cerebral type." The yellow grin flickered in and out of being as the Master paused. "But I am sure that you possess that foolish characteristic which is so common to you Americans and your British friends, that thing which you call a sense of fair play.

"I will call upon this and ask to be excused from personal combat on the grounds of my somewhat advanced age." Kathulos leaned back in his throne and raised his face to some unseen vision that hovered over his head. His wild, mocking laughter filled the room, echoing inside Stephen Costigan's head like the laughter of some maniacal demon.

"Instead," Kathulos ground mockingly, "I will call upon another old custom of your soft so-called civilization, the practice of trial by champion. You will, I assume, be willing to serve as champion for your onetime paramour Zuleika." Again the mighty skull inclined slightly, suggestively. "She stands accused of treason to the Son of the Sea. The mildest penalty for such a crime is death. The most severe—ah, that, Mr. Costigan, I will not defile with mere description. It must be witnessed to be appreciated."

Suddenly the figure of Skull-Face rose to its full, majestic height, a height of nearly seven feet from slipper-clad feet to

Asiatic-capped skull. A long arm surmounted by an incredibly long, bony hand was pointed at the Circassian. "I stand as her accuser," Kathulos gritted menacingly, "and as my champion I nominate—"

The great head rolled briefly as if in careless laughter.

"Well, I shall think of someone, Mr. Costigan. Mortal combat, yourself against my champion, a trial by the combat of champions in the case of the Society of the Scorpion versus the accused Zuleika. If you win the challenge, the accused is found innocent. Do you accept, Mr. Costigan?"

The American shook his fist impotently at the tall figure, then, gaining control of himself, Costigan gave his consent.

The Master clapped his hands once, and the draperies surrounding the room near Costigan opened. A servant in black pajama-like garments advanced silently and bowed before the American. He looked up, saw Costigan about to speak to him and halted him with a look and a gesture toward his own open, vacant mouth. He was one of Kathulos's mutes.

The mute turned away, gesturing, and moved toward the opening from which he had emerged. With a backward glance at the still standing Skull-Face and another at the silent, beautiful Zuleika, Costigan followed the servant from the room. The servant led him down a silent, vacant corridor to a luxurious dressing-chamber. A bath had been drawn and Costigan followed the silent instructions of the servant, disrobing and sliding luxuriantly into the steaming, marble tub. He had not realized how fatigued his body had become, between the exertion of his activities at Taverel Manor and the tension of his trip from the north of England to London, Dover, Calais, and finally to the Temple of Silence here in Paris.

Each sinew seemed to unclench in grateful relaxation as the hot water laved Costigan's body. After he had lolled in the tub for a time he emerged and climbed onto a prepared table where he lay nude as silent servants prodded and kneaded his flesh, anointing it with liniments and anodynes. At last he arose, refreshed. He stood, naked, flexing his muscles, stretching tendons that held the power to snap an opponent's neck like a twig when the heavy fists pounded jawbones like a drummer beating out the rhythm of a march.

He stood motionless while black-clad servants wrapped a scarlet breechclout around his loins, then followed them along silent corridors until he found himself in an arena-like room where a single private viewing-box held the cadaverous Master and the beautiful Zuleika. The Circassian girl sat passively at the side of Kathulos, the fatally portentous brass pipe resting in her hands.

Costigan stood before the box, hurling silent defiance upward at his enemy. Skull-Face smiled down at the American, then applauded mockingly with his parchment-covered hands.

"You are a splendid champion, Mr. Costigan. Or at least you appear to be. Don't you think so, Zuleika?" He extended one slipper-covered toe and nudged the silent Circassian. She looked up at him for a moment, then turned her eyes dully away. Costigan felt the crimson rage rising in his craw once again.

"Bring on your damned champion, Kathulos, and have done with it!" he snarled.

11

The Scorpion Kathulos of Egypt gestured peremptorily and Costigan set himself at once on guard. But instead of an opponent entering the arena-like room, a series of tiny doors, each no more than a few inches in measure, slid back around the base of the wall, and a powerful gush of water spurted from each. Almost at once Costigan was standing ankle-deep in brine which rose steadily toward his shins.

He looked angrily up at Kathulos.

"Skull-Face!" Costigan shouted. "What is this? Where is your champion? Surely you don't think you're just going to drown me here, like a rat in a barrel!"

"No, no, Mr. Costigan," the yellow-skinned Scorpion replied. "I suppose I should have mentioned this before. My champion is not a native of France. Of course, you knew already that I myself did not come here from any land with which you are familiar."

"I know where you come from, Kathulos! Poor old Von Lorfmon and Fairlan Morley found that out, and paid for the knowledge with their lives! The Egyptologist Ezra Schuyler learned the truth and was driven mad by it! He knew that you were found floating far at sea in a sealed, lacquered coffin! He deduced that you are no less than a survivor of the sinking of Atlantis!"

The yellow face moved down, up again, in a contemplative nod. "There are those who believe that, yes. And it may be true—or it may not. At any rate, Mr. Costigan, I do feel a certain affinity for the sea, and for the children of the sea."

Costigan looked at the briny water, now well above his knees and lapping greedily at the lower edges of his breechclout.

"You expect me to fight your champion in a swimming pool? You're mad yourself, Kathulos! But I'll do it! I'd fight your champion in the flames of hades itself if I had to, to free Zuleika from the slavery you've caught her in—and to get my hands on you!"

The Scorpion merely smiled.

The water had reached Costigan's muscular shoulders and its flow was slowing, slowing. Finally it reached the level of his forehead. He could tread water easily enough, or touch down on the hard, sandy bottom of the arena when he wished, for as long as the period of a breath.

"Very good, Mr. Costigan," the Master rasped drily. "Now I will keep you waiting no longer." He looked aside, gestured to some unseen servitor.

In the water-filled arena, Costigan could see a larger door slide open near the bottom of the newly created pool. The opening was square, two feet high, perhaps, and equally as wide. When it slid back into the wall only blackness was revealed, and then a something, a something began to slither into the arena.

From the viewing-box above even the opium-sodden Circassian girl Zuleika gasped in horror at what her eyes perceived, and Stephen Costigan's glance flew upward for a split second, long enough to see Kathulos lean down and guide the brass opium pipe back to the subsiding lips of the helpless addict.

Costigan turned back to see what it was that had made Zuleika gasp.

A long, sinuous shape was still gliding silently, with a kind of sinister grace that embodied more evil than the most violent of poisonous reptiles or arachnidae. It was a glistening, purplish black. At its nether end rows and clusters of tentacles streamed backward, flicking left and right to guide the movement of the horrendous creature. It had a head with a circular mouth totally ringed with razor-sharp, triangular teeth. The mouth was surrounded by a circle of suction cups. The monster turned its

head from side to side in a constant seeking, searching motion.
Costigan realized with a chill that the creature was blind.

Not blinded. It had not lost its eyes in any combat. Rather, it
was completely eyeless. It had evolved in some dark world where
day and night were meaningless, where the rays of the sun never
penetrated and the creatures found one another by some other
sense than sight. By touch or odor or by some strange, subtle
sense that men knew nothing of.

Costigan backed away from the monster, treading water,
feeling the smooth, curving wall of the arena against his muscled
back, occasionally dipping one foot to the sandy bottom of the
arena to gain leverage and steady himself. The door in the arena
wall was closed now, the monster entirely through it. It was fully
thirty feet long, from the horrid ring of triangular teeth to the
tips of its black, slimy tentacles.

"What do you think of my little pet, Mr. Costigan?"
Kathulos's cold, dry voice echoed across the water-filled arena.
"Few men have ever encountered its like, and lived to tell the
tale, I can assure you."

A red sheet of hatred filmed Costigan's blazing eyes. He
wished that he had a weapon—any weapon—in his hands. A
spear, a sabre, a machete, even a Malayan *kreese*. He longed to
lunge at the writhing monstrosity and plunge a blade into its
slimy, pulpy body, to rip and slice until the thing flopped and
thrashed and then fell away from him inert in the water.

"A fair fight, Mr. Costigan," Kathulos's voice came again.
"Neither my pet nor you has any artificial aid. Each will use
those tools and weapons provided by Mother Nature. Do you
recognize your opponent? Half giant lamprey, half marine
squid. They live only in the deepest reaches of the ocean. There is
no way to raise them, living, to the surface. The difference in
pressure is fatal. I have tried—and the poor creatures simply
explode!"

Somehow the Master found that humorous, and interrupted
his own speech with a burst of chilling, rasping laughter.

"But I did so miss the companionship of these lovely
creatures that I managed to obtain a clutch of their eggs, and I
hatched and raised this little fellow from the size of my little
finger. Oh—but I see he's noticed you. Well, enough of my silly
chatter, Mr. Costigan. You'll have to forgive a garrulous old
man. Now I shall watch quietly while you and my pet get to
know each other better!"

Costigan had ignored the Master's final sentences. He had turned his attention fully to the monster that twisted and sought for him in the water. Costigan could tell that the monster was fully aware of him now. It lay almost still in the water, its nethermost tentacles waving sinuously.

With a single warning thrash of its tentacles the monster vaulted forward, triangular teeth clashing.

Costigan let himself drop the few inches needed to plant his toes in the sand, then sprang aside and delivered a rabbit punch to the monster. The horrid face that was all mouth and suction cups smashed against the arena wall at the same moment that Costigan landed his rabbit punch. That blow would have cracked the spine of any man or beast, but the monster seemed unfazed by it. With a sinuous motion of its tentacles the huge creature backed away a few feet. Its head began that awful searching motion again.

Stephen Costigan looked around for any handhold or object that he could use against the monster. But all that he could see was the smooth-walled arena, the viewing-box above with the gloating Kathulos and the drug-sodden Zuleika in it, the monster slithering toward him once more.

Again the monster shot forward through the water and again Costigan made to dodge its advance, but this time his feet failed to gain full purchase on the sandy floor of the arena and his sideways move was a split-moment too slow. The monster did not strike him full on, but managed a glancing blow with the side of its head. There was a bony ridge behind that row of suckers, as the monster glanced aside Costigan felt a searing pain in his side. He looked down and realized that even the glancing blow of the monster had bruised his ribs, possibly even cracked one. And the suction cup that had failed to clamp onto his flesh still left an ugly oval discoloration.

The monster was circling for another charge but Costigan swam rapidly forward and to one side, grasping the monster by a handful of its writhing tentacles. It struggled and writhed and tried to get its murderous head turned toward Costigan, but however the monster thrashed Costigan stayed behind it, clinging desperately to the slimy, whip-like extensions.

Costigan tried to work his way up through the tentacles to the body of the monster, but it writhed and twisted, bucked like a furious bronco pony. Costigan clung desperately but he was thrown off at last. He backed against the arena wall, watching warily for the next move of the monster—but it, too, had backed away, halfway to the opposite side of the arena. A smile crept around the corners of Stephen Costigan's mouth. Somehow, he realized, somewhere in the simple brain of that primitive, ferocious monstrosity, he had awakened some feeling of fear.

The fight was far from over, but Costigan knew that he had won a round. He gave himself the luxury of glancing up at the viewing-box. Kathulos was caught in rapt attention to the fight. Costigan looked back at his opponent. The monster was gathering itself for another rush, but Costigan had long since learned that the way to victory was not to wait for the opponent's attack but to launch a crushing, roaring attack of his own.

He drew his legs up tight against his body, braced his bare feet against the wall of the arena and launched himself forward, all but flying across the surface of the pool. The monster was rushing forward toward Costigan. The last thing it expected was to have its prey charge forward. Puzzled and frightened, the monster swerved aside, missing its intended victim entirely, but as the creature swept past him Stephen Costigan landed another rabbit punch, finding this time the place where the monster's bony head joined its softer, pulpy body.

The creature seemed to collapse under Costigan's blow, then swam away through the water as rapidly as its tentacles could propel it. Behind it a trail of some purple-black inky stuff stained the water.

Costigan grinned wolfishly.

He swam slowly after the lamprey-squid, gathering oxygen in a series of deep breaths. When he was a few yards from the creature he sucked in a final deep lungful of oxygen and dropped beneath the top of the water in a surface dive. The monster was weaving back and forth, trying to zero in on Costigan. It seemed confused now, as well as frightened. Costigan decided that he had damaged it with his last rabbit punch.

He found himself creeping across the pale, sandy bottom of the arena. The monster was above him, apparently totally unaware of where he had gone. As if a long-dormant mechanism had gone into effect, the monster suddenly jetted out great clouds of purple-black opacity. In an instant Costigan was blinded as totally and as effectively as was the monster—but he lacked its mysterious sense of locating prey without eyes.

But Costigan had already planted his feet on the sandy bottom of the arena and launched himself upward with all his strength against his enemy. He breathed a silent, momentary prayer to God or Lucifer or any other principle or being who would listen, and offer the single flash of help that Costigan needed.

In pitch blackness he knifed upward through the water and felt his hands close in the slimy, noisome flesh of his opponent. With one mighty hand he dug into the soft, pulpy body of the monster. With the other he reached forward and closed his fingers around the edge of the monster's carapace. He shoved forward against the bone with all his might in one arm, and with the other tugged, tugged, tugged backwards.

The monster threshed and beat against him with its tentacles in its mortal agony, thrashing with its yards and yards of ropy extensions, but now there was no escaping the raging, muscular American.

Costigan pulled, the monster struggled and thrashed, and then with a final horrible scream—the only sound that the monster had made in the entire course of its struggles—the soft, pulpy body came away from the bony head. A great flood of the obnoxious dark fluid poured into the arena. The monster threshed once more, then lay still.

His breath spent, Costigan barely managed to get his face above the surface of the now-inky water and draw in a welcome lungful of oxygen. He squeezed the inky water out of his eyes and looked up at Skull-Face. An expression of ineffable rage marked the features of the ancient being.

Dragging the monster behind him by its pulpy body, Costigan swam laboriously toward a place just beneath the viewing-box. He looked up and saw Skull-Face glaring down at him, rage and frustration writ clearly on the ancient parchment-like features. Costigan drew back his two mightily muscled arms, still holding the slimy remnant of his opponent, and with a great heave, hurled the body of the monster forward and into the air.

Trailing its limp tentacles behind it, the dead monster sailed upward, struck the top wall of the arena with a wet thud, then tumbled over the edge and lodged heavily in the box at Kathulos's feet.

Stephen Costigan seized the nearest handful of slimy tentacles and drew himself to the edge of the arena. Planting his bare feet to either side of the hanging tentacles, grasping hands full of the noisome, ropy extensions, he began climbing hand over hand up the sheer wall of the arena!

12

Costigan heaved himself over the edge of the box, ready to face anything—Skull-Face himself, a ring of knife-wielding thugs, a nest of snakes, a vat of flesh-searing acid. Any of these would have been in character for the Scorpion. Instead, Costigan found—

Nothing!

The box was empty. The Master was gone, and with him the beautiful Circassian opium-slave Zuleika. Where they had gone there was no way of telling, but how they had made their exit was amply clear. A ceiling-high velvet drapery flanked by two of Kathulos's trademark palm trees still swayed. Costigan hurled the cloth aside, faced a heavily carved oaken door, and burst through it with a single heave of his muscular shoulder.

The corridor behind was deserted but a trail of footprints marked the path of the Master and his slave. Of course—the noisome inky excretion of the monster that Costigan had hurled into the box. The horrible stuff had flooded the box and both the Scorpion and Zuleika had been forced to wade through it as they made their way out.

Costigan hurled his body forward at a rate amazing for so massive a figure. The footprints ran straight to the end of the corridor, then seemed to disappear at a blank wall. Costigan searched frantically for a crack or opening that must indicate a secret doorway. Even his keen eye failed to detect a line—or rather, he detected far too many lines! The wall was a virtual maze of interlocking stones and decorative tiles, enamelled bricks and carven inlays. The picture that it made was one of oriental splendour overlying a marine motif that suggested the ancient sea home of Kathulos.

Finally Costigan decided to risk one attempt. He searched the wall for some representation of the monster he had conquered, the being half lamprey and half squid. He found it, grasped it by the horrible head, shuddering inwardly at the thought of its living counterpart that he had so recently conquered. He twisted at the monstrosity, and—

The entire section of wall gave way before him. Heedless of any deadfall trap that might have been laid in his path, Costigan charged into the room beyond. It was the throne-room of the Master, and the American beheld Skull-Face ensconced once more on his ornately graven seat, Zuleika sprawled luxuriously on a silken cushion at his feet.

Ranged beyond these two, Costigan beheld an appalling sight!

Dressed in the black, pajama-like costumes of the zombie-like minions of the Son of the Sea, their faces blank, their eyes glazed and vacant with hypnosis or drugs, stood ranged the four hostages of the scorpion: Sir Haldred Taverel and his fiancée Marjory Harper, Marjory's brother Harry Harper, and Harper's American-born, Eurasian sweetheart, the beautiful Joan La Tour.

The Master signalled to his zombies with one hand and they turned slowly, mechanically in their tracks, and began with relentless determination to advance upon Costigan.

A film of searing red flames seemed to rise before the eyes of Stephen Costigan. Like a fullback charging through a line of enemy tacklers, Costigan straight-armed Harry Harper. Harper tumbled sideways, tumbling over Joan and Marjory like the headpin in a bowling-alley knocking down the three and five pins on a too-high hit.

Only Sir Haldred Taverel stood now, between Costigan and Kathulos. The nobleman reached inside his black garments and withdrew his hand clutching the hilt of a wavy-bladed Malayan *kreese*. He raised it to strike down at Costigan but the American landed a single pile-driver uppercut that sent Taverel flying through the air, lifted completely off his feet. The *kreese* sailed across the room, struck hilt-first against the trunk of one of the

Scorpion's palm trees and clattered down its trunk to land on a Persian rug beneath.

Taverel himself crashed into the silken-robed Master, knocking him backward so he collapsed with a startlingly heavy thud into his throne. Sir Haldred tumbled to the floor where he landed beside the others in a tangle of black-garmented limbs.

Costigan didn't waste any time now with palaver. He launched himself through the air like a flying tackler heading off an opposing ball-carrier. He landed with his iron fingers wrapped irremovably around the thin, bony throat of his enemy.

He was not satisfied to throttle the Scorpion, but lifted him bodily from his throne, twisting and wrenching at the neck of the other as Kathulos struggled futilely, thrashing about with his lengthy arms and legs. There was a crackling sound, a final marrow-freezing snap and the great head toppled aside, hung limp upon the brocaded shoulder of the Master.

Costigan hurled the body aside as a terrier would discard the corpse of a filthy rat whose neck it had snapped. He turned to confront the others who sprawled dazedly before the throne. Their faces were beginning to clear as they looked at Costigan and at one another.

"Listen to me," Costigan commanded. Still half under the spell of Kathulos's hypnotism, the four black-clad figures stood dully awaiting the other's command. "We have to get out of here. The Scorpion's men will be on us at any second!"

Costigan bent and lifted the somnolent Zuleika in his powerful arms. He commanded Taverel and Harper, Marjory and Joan to follow him closely. Still clad only in breechclout, his body smeared with the purple-black ink of the monster, Costigan led the party through the corridors of the Temple of Silence, expecting at any moment to encounter *kreese*-wielding minions of the Scorpion Society. But none were seen!

An hour later, clad in clothing borrowed from sympathetic officials of the British and American consulates, Costigan and the others sat in a comfortable office of the Paris Sûreté. An inspector of the Sûreté had taken their reports of the incidents at the Temple of Silence. The two couples had recovered from their hypnosis within minutes of the snapping of Kathulos's neck. Zuleika was another matter; her enthrallment had not been entrusted to simple hypnosis this time. Rather, Kathulos had deliberately enslaved her to the dream-drug opium, and the

Circassian girl had been taken to a sanitorium where, it was hoped, patient and sympathetic care might eventually wean her of the fatal craving.

A uniformed *gendarme* of the Paris constabulary entered the door and saluted smartly before the inspector's desk. The conversation took place in French, but thanks to his service in the AEF, Costigan was able to follow its content.

"Did you bring in the body of the fiend Skull-Face, sergeant?" the inspector asked.

The uniformed officer, ashen-faced, shook his head. "There was no corpse, *mon capitain*. We searched the premises of the temple from top to bottom. We found terrible things, horrendous things. The monster that Monsieur Costigan killed, that we found, still hanging from the wall of the arena. The room of the palms, yes, and drugs! Opium, kif, hashish, enough to enslave a battalion! But not a soul, neither living nor dead."

The inspector turned toward Costigan. He spread his hands in a typical Gallic expression of resignation. "The little fish, they have all slipped through the net, monsieur. And it seems that they carried away with them, the body of the big fish. But the ring is broken up. France owes you a debt of gratitude, Monsieur Costigan. The whole world owes you a debt of gratitude."

Costigan ground his teeth together in frustration.

"I'll settle for carfare back to Taverel Manor, Inspector. My friends here are planning a double wedding as soon as they recover more fully."

Harry Harper chimed in. "And we'd all be honored if you would serve as best man for both couples, Costigan."

Almost in unison, Joan La Tour and Marjory Harper expressed the wish that Zuleika serve as their maid of honor. "As soon as she gets out of the hospital, of course. It may be difficult, but we'll wait."

They shook hands all around and rose to leave the headquarters of the Sûreté. As they started through the great doorway letting onto the Champs Elysée, Sir Haldred Taverel stopped suddenly. He smote himself on the forehead with the heel of his hand.

"We've all left somebody out of this!" he exclaimed. "What about Mr. Hammerby?"

There was a moment of consternation, then Costigan said, with a grin, "I expect we'll find poor Mr. Hammerby manacled somewhere in the catacombs beneath Taverel Manor. We've only been gone—all of us except yourself, Sir Haldred—for a little over forty-eight hours, hard as that is to believe. Mr. Hammerby will be chilly, hungry, and for certain frightened out of his wits by now. But he'll be safe enough."

"And he'll be happy to give up his pretensions to a manor and a title that are not his by rights," Sir Haldred added. "But—"

The Britisher halted in his tracks as if stunned by a blow—or a thought. "What if he isn't alone at Taverel Manor? Poor Hammerby may be a bit of a prig and a *poseur*, but he's not really a guilty party. And—we've left him with Mrs. Drake. The way Kathulos infiltrated Taverel Manor with his hirelings—Lo Kung, Hanson—I expect that Mrs. Drake was in his employ as well. As far as we know, she simply disappeared when all of this began to break out. She's probably still at Taverel, or else has carried poor Hammerby off to Skull-Face's hideaway, wherever that may next be."

Stephen Costigan shook his head ruefully. "You're right on every count save one, Sir Haldred. Mrs. Drake *was* an agent of the Scorpion. If only I'd realized it in time! As you know, Kathulos and his agents are all masters of impersonation and disguise. Mrs. Drake was no simple housekeeper, Sir Haldred."

The noble, baffled, asked simply, "Then who was she, Costigan?"

Bleakly, the American gritted, "She was Zuleika. We were in the same house—in the very *room*—and I never recognized her! The torment I could have saved that poor girl, had I but penetrated her disguise!"

"She'll recover," Sir Haldred Taverel muttered encouragingly. He clapped Costigan heartily on the shoulder. "She has the pluck, and she has a reason for recovering, if you take my meaning. She'll make it!"

Briskly the five of them stepped out into the sunlight of a sparkling Parisian afternoon.